"What we do after ho

Duncan said, slipping his fingers beneath the hem of her shorts.

His lazy smile widened when he ran his finger along the inside of her thigh. Sunny shifted, easing her legs slightly apart. He took her hands and placed them behind her, narrowing the space between them. Holding her immobile, he dipped his head and kissed her.

This was what she would be giving up, and she wasn't sure she had the strength. Was she really willing to risk everything she'd worked for just for a few nights of what promised to be unbelievably memorable sex?

She tore her mouth from his. "Duncan, what if we get caught?"

He lifted his head to look at her. Desire burned in his gray eyes. Oh hell, the way he was looking at her, she decided she didn't care about tomorrow. No way was she letting this man out of her sight until they finished what he'd started.

"Forget I said anything...."

Dear Reader,

When FBI agent Sunny MacGregor first appeared in my RITA®
Award-nominated Blaze novel, *Seduced by the Enemy*
(#41, June 2002), I was unprepared for the impact she
would have on my life. Not only did she demand her own
story, she also made it clear from the beginning nothing less
than perfection would do for her hero. Despite all who'd
applied, in the end only one proved himself worthy of
Sunny—Duncan Chamberlain, a hotshot insurance recovery
expert who knows the meaning of absolute pleasure.

The writing of *Absolute Pleasure* was a nonstop thrill ride
for me, but not without a few bumps in the road. If a writer is
lucky, she'll have a few special people in her corner to help
navigate the roadblocks. Thankfully, I am extremely fortunate in
that regard. Not only did my very wise husband keep a steady
supply of dark chocolate on hand, but without the constant
encouragement and unwavering support of my editor, I never
would have had the courage to write this very special story.

I hope you enjoy Sunny and Duncan's romance, and I'd love to
hear your thoughts. Please write to me at P.O. Box 224, Mohall,
ND 58761, or via e-mail at jamie@jamiedenton.net, or visit my
Web site at www.jamiedenton.net.

As ever,

Jamie Denton

Books by Jamie Denton

HARLEQUIN BLAZE

10—SLEEPING WITH THE ENEMY
41—SEDUCED BY THE ENEMY
114—"IMPULSIVE" STROKE OF MIDNIGHT

ABSOLUTE PLEASURE

Jamie Denton

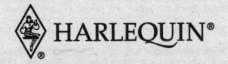

HARLEQUIN®

TORONTO • NEW YORK • LONDON
AMSTERDAM • PARIS • SYDNEY • HAMBURG
STOCKHOLM • ATHENS • TOKYO • MILAN • MADRID
PRAGUE • WARSAW • BUDAPEST • AUCKLAND

This book can only
be dedicated to Phyllis,
for reasons she will understand.

ISBN 0-373-79145-3

ABSOLUTE PLEASURE

Copyright © 2004 by Jamie Ann Denton.

This edition published by arrangement with Harlequin Books S.A.

® and TM are trademarks of the publisher. Trademarks indicated with ® are registered in the United States Patent and Trademark Office, the Canadian Trade Marks Office and in other countries.

www.eHarlequin.com

Printed in U.S.A.

1

"HEY, MAC!" Agent Caruso called from the back of the white surveillance van. "I gotta know, exactly how hard-up does a woman have to be to pay a half-a-mil to get laid?"

Special Agent Sunny MacGregor surprised herself by seriously considering Agent Jack Caruso's question as she left her car and walked toward the pair of agents assigned to the Seducer's last known crime scene. Although she wouldn't exactly place herself in the same category as the victim she'd come to interview, she had been stretching the limit on abstinence since she couldn't immediately recall the last time she'd invited some guy to join her under the covers. Still, that didn't mean she'd ever be desperate enough to actually *pay* someone to have sex with her. At least she hoped not.

"I'm here to work the case," she told Caruso when she reached the open doors at the back of the van. "Not judge the victim." She did have an opinion on the subject, but one best not divulged to a pair of field agents assigned watch-dog duty outside the arched wrought-iron gates of the Wilder estate.

Caruso's rookie-agent partner, Walt Weidman, climbed out of the van. "I need to see your ID, Mac."

"For the love of Pete, Weidman," Caruso complained. "This is her freakin' crime scene."

Weidman ignored Caruso. "Sorry, Mac," he said apologetically. "Rules, you know."

She slipped the black leather ID holder from the pocket of her navy linen blazer and handed it to Weidman. "Don't let Jack get to you," she told the rookie. "He's always a pain in the ass until he's downed a couple of thermoses full of that ink he calls coffee."

"Yeah, and then he's just a wired pain in the ass."

She hid a smile and glanced around the well-kept grounds before turning her attention to Caruso. He sat on a padded bench in the van before an instrument control panel monitoring the immediate vicinity and keeping in contact with another van with two more agents at the rear of the estate. "See or hear anything unusual?"

Caruso reached for the pack of cigarettes on the seat beside him. "I've been in cemeteries at 3:00 a.m. with more action," he complained. "The lab techs left about an hour ago. They didn't tell us dick, either."

Sunny bit back the reminder hovering on her lips that smoking was strictly prohibited inside a government vehicle. Surveillance could be dull as dirt under the best of circumstances. Watchdogging a nonviolent crime scene was dead work, occasionally handed out as punishment for agents on the shit-list of someone higher up the Bureau food chain. Since she'd worked with Caruso in the past during her own days as a field agent in the D.C. office, she figured he, rather than Weidman had ticked off her old boss, Gib Russell, big time.

Caruso flicked the lighter. Weidman handed Sunny her ID and shot the older, seasoned agent a disapproving glance. "Do you have to do that in there?"

Caruso blew a plume of blue smoke in Weidman's direction as he climbed out of the van. "Go read a manual or something," Jack groused. To Sunny he said, "You want to talk pain in the ass, spend an hour with Whiny Wally. Makes me look like Sister Mary Sunshine."

Caruso shielded his eyes from the harsh glare of July midmorning sunshine and squinted in Sunny's general direction. "And who did you piss off to get stuck with this piece of crap case, Mac?"

Sunny slipped a recently permed curl behind her ear before straightening her shoulders. "I requested the assignment."

Caruso drew deeply on his cigarette, then shook his head and emitted a raspy chuckle. "You still a glutton for punishment? They have therapy for that sort of thing, you know."

SEDSCAM, Bureau-speak for the Seduction Scam Investigation, remained an unsolved nonviolent crime under the Criminal Investigation Division's jurisdiction. So far, a grand total of seven thefts had occurred nationwide. Just because Sunny had asked to run the investigation didn't necessarily mean she suffered from masochistic tendencies. What she really wanted was to garner the attention of the head of the Investigative Support Unit.

The crunch and spray of gravel from the tires of a big black SUV moving too fast down the graded driveway kept her from putting Jack in his place. The vehicle slowed, then stopped as Caruso approached, exchanging a few words she couldn't discern with the driver.

"Probably a reporter," Weidman said with distaste from inside the van. He pulled a pristine white handkerchief from his pocket and mopped his sweaty forehead. "We've been waiting for them to start sniffing around all morning."

"A rich heiress bilked by a smooth-talking con artist to the tune of half a million dollars in cash and property and the FBI is suddenly involved? You bet the newshounds will be here." Not that she had any concerns on that score. She had experience with the press and wasn't above using the media to her advantage if necessary.

Sunny glanced toward the driver when he got out of his vehicle and joined Caruso. One look at the guy and she had him pegged him as a reporter. He had the whole I'm-your-new-best-friend thing going for him, which gave good journalists an edge over the competition. And this guy definitely had an edge, she thought, but it had zero to do with instilling confidence in a would-be source and everything to do with heightening her curiosity.

He walked with Caruso across the drive in her direction. As he neared, Sunny stared in utter and complete fascination. Generally she preferred brains and substance over beauty and brawn, but in this instance, she'd seriously consider making an exception.

Not that she was hard up or anything.

The crisp white shirt with fine gray pinstripes he wore enhanced a wide set of shoulders that tapered down to a lean waist, slim hips and long, powerful legs emphasized quite nicely in a pair of neatly pressed gray khakis. She enjoyed the rebounding view, as well, noting the casual way he rolled back the sleeves of the shirt to reveal tanned and powerful-looking forearms. A tie, one of those Wall-Street-power types, was knotted loosely at his throat, where he'd left the top button of his shirt undone. He came off looking crisp and rumpled all at the same time, in a way no woman with a pulse could ignore.

Continuing the mesmerizing journey into beauty and brawn, she wondered exactly when she'd become so shallow as to fall for a pretty face and a hot body. Probably the moment she realized she'd gone without a man in her bed for more than just a few months.

The bright morning sunshine made his slightly wavy, blacker-than-midnight hair gleam. Oh, she really needed to get a grip, here. Except that deeply tanned face with all those sharp lines and angles did nothing to aid her recovery from a lust-induced stupor. The directness of his brilliant, bluish-gray eyes when he removed his sunglasses didn't help much, either.

The barest promise of a breathtaking smile touched his lips as he tucked the pair of Maui Jim's inside the breast pocket of his shirt. "Duncan Chamberlain," he said in a voice so deep and rich a skitter of pleasure skimmed across the surface of her skin. Or were those delightful tingles the result of the warm clasp of his hand enveloping hers?

The answer evaded her, but she decided it made no difference. Not long after she'd joined the Bureau she'd come to the depressing conclusion her job intimidated a good percentage of the male population. The meager remaining percentage operated under the misguided assumption she lacked the double X chromosomes that made her very much a woman in every sense of the word. Just once she'd like a man to look beyond the 9mm Glock she carried and see the woman beneath the shoulder holster.

Of course, finding a man to hold her interest for more than two minutes would be a helpful improvement. She suspected that wouldn't be much of an issue with a major hottie like Duncan Chamberlain. The man had managed to snag her attention and then some.

Sixty seconds and counting.

"Sunny MacGregor." She pulled her hand from his and resisted the urge to dig her fingernails into her palm to quell the sharp tingling making her hand itch. "You've already met Agent Caruso," she said with an inclination of her head toward the older agent. "And this is Agent Weidman," she indicated his partner, who must have exited the vehicle when she'd been entranced by Duncan's worship-worthy shoulders and all that mouthwatering sex appeal.

Duncan's lips twitched again, as if he found something amusing, but she'd noticed the barely perceptible movement. How could she not? She'd been staring at his full bottom lip wondering if he tasted anywhere near as scrumptious as he looked.

Ninety-three seconds. Things were looking up for a change.

"*You're* Agent MacGregor?" Duncan asked, looking to Caruso for confirmation. "She's Mac?"

Caruso chuckled. "She's the one."

She didn't much appreciate the note of amusement in either man's voice, even if she had grown accustomed to similar responses in the six years she'd been an agent. The Bureau didn't exactly employ a platoon of five foot, three inch female agents.

"Special Agent MacGregor," she corrected. A relatively new title bestowed upon her, and one she'd worked damned hard to earn. The move from the Washington D.C. field office to the criminal investigation division's nonviolent crime unit two years ago had come her way after she'd gained a blip of recognition for her contribution on another difficult-to-solve case. Since her transfer, she'd garnered an even greater reputation for solving the unsolvable, which made her a natural for some of the more complex investigations the nonviolent crime unit offered. As far as Sunny was concerned, the promotion put her one step closer to what she really wanted—to become a member of the elite team of FBI profilers in the Investigative Support Unit.

"What business do you have here, Mr. Chamberlain?" she asked.

He reached into his hip pocket and withdrew a brown leather billfold, extracting a business card. "Chamberlain Recovery and Investigations. My firm's been hired by Ms. Wilder's insurance company."

He handed her the card along with another jolt to her feminine senses with the return of his killer smile. Needing a moment to recover her common sense, she concentrated on the card. Plain, simple, without frills.

"And the name's Duncan," he added.

Her West Virginia roots perked up at the slight trace of a southern accent. Texas or Oklahoma she guessed by his somewhat lazy drawl.

Weidman peered over her shoulder to read the card. "Hired to do what, exactly?" he asked.

"Recover the personal property stolen from Ms. Wilder last week." Duncan turned all that charm in her direction. "Agent Caruso here said I need permission from the agent in charge to enter the estate. Mind if I poke around a bit?"

Despite that sexy-as-hell grin, Sunny instantly became suspicious. In her experience, recovery firms and the people that ran them were a microstep above repossession agents on the humanity food chain. All too often they had a reputation for unorthodox, or even unethical, means of recovering stolen merchandise. The last thing she needed was some self-proclaimed hot shot recovery expert screwing with her investigation, especially one attempting to charm his way onto her crime scene.

"I'm here to conduct an interview with the victim," she said. "Considering the sensitive nature of this case, I'm not sure Ms. Wilder would appreciate an audience." In all honesty, *she* didn't feel comfortable conducting the interview in *his* presence. "A *male* audience, in particular."

The wind stirred, rustling the leaves of the trees but

doing little to cool the air so heavy with summer humidity. A lock of wavy hair fell across Duncan's forehead.

"I would think it'd be easier on the vic the less she has to relive the humiliation." He shoved the hair back in place, then leaned slightly toward her, his gaze intent. "Come on, Mac. You're not going to make me beg, are you?"

She seriously doubted any guy as tempting as Duncan Chamberlain ever had to resort to begging, especially from a woman. Interagency cooperation was hardly unusual, though, and they were supposedly on the same side. Did it matter if that wasn't the only reason she considered allowing him to sit in on her interview?

"All right," she agreed. "In the spirit of cooperation, I'll permit it, provided the victim has no objections." She did her best interpretation of hard-ass agent and gave him an appropriately matching stare. "But *I'm* conducting this interview. Forget that, and I'll have you banned from the premises."

Despite the threat, his smile deepened. She struggled to remain standing and not have herself a good old-fashioned Victorian swoon.

"You won't even know I'm there," he promised.

She had her doubts. Based on her reaction to the sensuous tilt of his mouth and those get-lost-in-me eyes, if he was in the vicinity she'd know it—with every last, rudely awakened, nerve ending in her body. Okay, so maybe he *had* managed to capture the attention of her neglected libido, but that didn't mean she was willing to dive headfirst into the steamy waters of sexual attraction. Or was she? The idea sure held a wealth of intriguing possibilities she found hard to ignore.

"I'll need to see some ID," Weidman said.

While Weidman entered Duncan's information in his

neatly kept log, she issued reminders to Caruso about keeping quiet should the press show up again. Five days after the incident, Margo Wilder was officially old news, but Sunny expected more attention once word leaked to the press the FBI was conducting an investigation into the theft. Her only hope was that the nonviolent nature of the crime would hold little interest to reporters.

Weidman returned Duncan's ID, and she took off on foot for the main gate. Duncan fell in step beside her and her libido instantly zinged back to life. She had a job to do, but professional or not, she really wanted to take a flying leap off the high dive and go for a nice long swim in those steaming waters.

DUNCAN TRAILED Sunny and the uniformed butler who led them away from the foyer with an elaborate, curving, gilt staircase, down a long rosewood-paneled corridor. While Sunny was busy taking in the opulent surroundings, Duncan enjoyed the view of her curvy backside swaying enticingly beneath her navy slacks.

He'd spent eight years in Dallas as an agent for the FBI, the last three working deep-cover assignments. In all that time, he'd never seen anything on the Bureau's payroll as remotely sexy as the perky little superagent that had managed to spark his interest in something other than his work.

Too bad she was off limits.

He gauged her age to be in the vicinity of thirty. She was young to have attained the status of a special agent, which told him she was being fast-tracked by someone high up in the Bureau. An agent on the rise wouldn't be caught dead fraternizing with someone drummed out for gross misconduct. Still, what she didn't know couldn't hurt his chances of their becoming better acquainted…at least until she discovered he was ex-Fibbie and dropped him faster than a fence with a cache of hot gems.

They were shown into an elaborate sitting room that smelled of fine whiskey with a faint trace of expensive cigars still clinging to the furnishings, heavy velvet draperies and plush Persian rug. Real estate mogul Jerome Wilder had been dead three months, yet the room still held his essence. Duncan couldn't help wondering what the old man would have to say about his niece and sole heir losing a half a million bucks worth of personal property and cash to a con artist.

Not that it mattered, he reminded himself. Whether the client had more money than God or was some poor schmuck who'd lost his last dime, Duncan's goal never changed. It wasn't supposed to matter if the loss wouldn't put so much as a dent in the claimant's holdings.

Except lately, it had started to matter. A lot.

"Ms. Wilder has been detained and has asked me to convey her apologies. She will be with you shortly," the butler informed them. "May I offer you some refreshment while you wait?"

Sunny set her briefcase on the rug next to a tapestried love seat and sat. "No, thank you. We're fine."

Duncan took the heavy leather chair across from her. Leaning forward, he braced his elbows on his knees. "So you wanna tell me why CID is involved in this case?" he asked her once the butler disappeared. "An isolated incident of grand theft doesn't exactly fall under federal jurisdiction."

She looked at him from beneath a crown of chin-length, burnished-gold waves, her soft green eyes full of cautious suspicion. "Why Mr. Chamberlain, surely you're not asking me to divulge facts from an ongoing FBI investigation?"

The corner of his mouth tipped upward at her feigned innocence routine. *Never con a con, babe.* Still, she was damned cute and sassy, which equaled one lethal, hard-to-resist combination.

"Yes ma'am," he said in a congenial tone intended to chase the doubt she attempted to hide from her gaze. First rule: gain the trust of the mark. "I believe that's exactly what I am asking."

The innocent facade faded, and she leveled him with a direct stare full of determination. "Don't try to play me, Duncan, and I won't attempt to bullshit you."

She inflected enough of a warning in her tone to let him know she was no easy pushover. Too bad. He'd like to push her right into the closest bed.

"Fair enough," he conceded with a brisk nod. "But I'd still like to know what the feds are doing here."

Her golden eyebrows slanted downward into a frown. "I fail to see how the Bureau's interest is relevant to your investigation."

He recognized a tap dance when he saw one, having performed enough of them himself during his stint with the FBI. Unfortunately, he'd made a drastic error in judgment and had danced across the line one time too many.

"I know I'm here only as a matter of professional courtesy, but I believe your involvement *is* relevant." The last of his smile faded and he returned her direct stare with one of his own. "My firm is currently investigating two other similar cases of women recently coming into substantial sums of money and basically handing over the keys to their newly acquired kingdoms. Unless the Supreme Court issued a surprise ruling this morning that I haven't heard about, then the rules of federal jurisdiction remain unchanged. My guess is Wilder isn't the only vic on the Bureau's radar screen."

Sunny would have information at her fingertips that he was no longer privy to, and in his opinion, that made her a valuable asset. One he needed to carefully cultivate.

She glanced away for a split second. To consider her answer, he wondered, or to fabricate one.

"I'm lacking solid evidence to link the cases," he admitted, baiting the proverbial hook. "The M.O. is nearly identical, even if all the information I have is circumstantial at this point."

Like a hungry trout, she nibbled the bait he dangled in front of her. Curiosity filled her eyes. "Exactly what do you know?"

"Three very wealthy women and what appears on the surface to be three individual perps. If CID is involved, then I'm thinking it's because you have physical evidence to connect the cases." He paused and waited for his hungry little trout to swallow the bait.

"Go on."

"And that you're looking for *one* unknown subject." He set the hook with practiced skill. "I just might have what you need to bring the bastard down."

"I may be willing to share *some* information with you," she emphasized, albeit with a modicum of caution lining her voice. "Provided you allow me complete access to your investigative files."

She'd taken the bait he offered so easily, he almost felt a slight sting of guilt. "I'll show you mine if you show me yours." Almost, but not quite.

Her green eyes darkened considerably and his gut tightened in response. A quick sweep of his gaze down the length of her revealed a tantalizing glimpse of her nipples beading against her white linen blouse. A whole host of show-and-tell scenarios charged through his mind, and not a single one of them had to do with evidence or criminal investigations.

She smiled. A slow, sexy, thoroughly distracting curve of her lips that fired his imagination. If that wasn't enough to redline his libido, she had the gall to call in backup when a hint of mischief filled her eyes.

"Only if you promise to show me yours first," she said in a husky voice laced with pure sin.

For the first time in his life, Duncan forgot how to breathe.

2

NO ONE HAD ever accused Sunny of shyness. Backing away from whatever she might want, at least insofar as her career was concerned, rarely occurred to her. Currently, she had two wants—access to information in Duncan's possession that could prove useful to her investigation, and the man himself. The sooner, the better. On both counts.

Her conscience gave her a hard shove. The man was trouble with a capital *T*—tempting…tantalizing. *Trouble*.

Perhaps she should consider the potential conflict of interest, but so long as any involvement with Duncan didn't interfere with her ability to perform her duties, she failed to see a problem. An attractive man had finally managed to hold her interest for a whole lot longer than two minutes. If the hungry look in his eyes was any indication, apparently he had no difficulty whatsoever seeing the woman beneath the shoulder holster. She wondered if he even realized she carried a gun.

Before she could issue the all-important, albeit clichéd, your-place-or-mine line, Margo Wilder swept into the room with all the regality of a queen. Only they weren't loyal subjects eager for a scrap of Her Majesty's attention. Sunny had come to interview a material witness, while Duncan was along for the ride hoping for clues to lead him to the recovery of her stolen property.

Sunny and Duncan stood as Margo approached.

"I'm very sorry to have kept you waiting." Margo extended her manicured hand to Sunny for a limp handshake. "A minor crisis with the planning committee for a charity auction the Wilder Foundation is sponsoring." She shook Duncan's hand before graciously inviting them both to sit again.

She summed up Margo Wilder as a somewhat attractive woman in her late forties with ash-blond hair. The youthful gleam may have faded, but still showed no signs of gray. Appropriately coiffed for someone of her social standing, she wore ivory silk slacks with an ice-blue silk shell. The ivory cashmere cardigan draped casually over her slim, erect shoulders easily cost more than Sunny made in a month. A few too many country club lunches had probably added the ten or so extra pounds Margo carried on an otherwise slender frame. What Mother Nature hadn't provided, a skilled plastic surgeon had compensated for or enhanced.

"Ms. Wilder," Sunny began once they were all seated, "I realize you've already been interviewed by the local authorities, but I'm here because the FBI would like me to clear up a few matters for their investigation." She spoke softly, keeping her tone neutral in an effort to elicit confidence and gain the trust of the witness. In reality, she'd come to ask the hard questions, ones that would become extremely personal.

"Mr. Chamberlain is here to observe on behalf of your insurance carrier," Sunny continued with a brief inclination of her head in Duncan's direction. "I hope that doesn't make you uncomfortable, but any information you provide could aid him in locating your stolen property."

Considering the interview could become quite personal, his presence made Sunny about as comfortable as a perp in handcuffs locked in a room full of rubber hoses and bright lights. No less than she probably deserved for having a serious case of lust for the guy, but she wisely kept that thought to herself.

"I understand," Margo said with a regal nod.

Sunny slipped a small tape recorder from her briefcase and leaned forward to set it in the center of the round rosewood coffee table. "Do you mind if I record this session?" she asked, struggling to maintain focus on the interview and not the intoxicating whiff she'd just caught of Duncan's spice-scented aftershave.

Margo shook her head. "Not at all."

Sunny made note of the date, time, location, the purpose of the interview and indicated the parties present. She retrieved her notepad from her briefcase and flipped to the list of questions she'd jotted down while reviewing the case file last night. In the privacy of her newly purchased condo, she'd slipped into her favorite pair of cotton pj's, turned on the television to the cable news network and tried to crawl inside the twisted mind of a con artist preying on vulnerable, unsuspecting women.

The reminder pricked her anger, renewing her tenacity to put an end to the Seducer's lucrative criminal activities. With any luck, she'd nail his ass before he could pluck his next pigeon.

Including Wilder, the Bureau had a total of seven cases stretching from Seattle all the way to the D.C. area, that made up the SEDSCAM investigation. When the different state authorities had independently requested assistance from the Bureau's lab hoping to nail the unknown subject's identity with DNA found at the crime scenes, someone in the lab had been paying attention, bringing the incidents to the attention of the nonviolent crime unit's chief. The reports had all been same, *DNA nonidentifiable,* but all that meant was the UNSUB had never been imprisoned, else his DNA would've been in the FBI's DNA database. In Sunny's opinion, that made her UNSUB either one clever crook or a lucky SOB. Maybe both considering his ten-month crime spree.

Forcing a serene expression, she smiled at Margo. "Let's begin with the day you first met the man you knew as Justin Abbott. In the initial report you gave to the police the morning you discovered the theft, you indicated that following a meeting with your attorneys, you went to the Georgetown Café for lunch?" At least Margo had immediately notified the authorities, something not all of the vics had done. For reasons beyond her comprehension, Sunny had one case where the vic had waited close to two weeks before filing a police report.

Margo's golden-brown eyes brightened and her collagen-smooth lips lifted into a wistful smile. "Yes," she answered, her voice softening considerably. "The café was horribly crowded and Justin offered to share his table with me."

Sunny tucked a loose curl behind her ear again. "Do you recall ever seeing Abbott before that day in the café?"

"No."

"You're certain?"

"Absolutely."

"There was nothing familiar about him?" Sunny pressed. "Perhaps he'd been to your home disguised as a repairman, or had attended a social function where you may have seen him prior to that day in the café?" None of the other victims she'd interviewed reported ever seeing the Seducer on a previous occasion, either. Circumstance had little to do with initial contact between UNSUB and vic, but so far Sunny had been unable to confirm her suspicions.

"Ms. MacGregor," Margo said patiently, "it simply is not possible. I assure you, I would have remembered if I'd met Justin previously."

"Why is that?" Sunny asked in a milder tone than her curiosity demanded.

"Presence," the older woman told her. "Justin has a presence that is not easily forgotten."

Now there was an explanation Sunny easily understood, courtesy of the man seated across from her. She glanced at him and their gazes met, held, and the air sizzled around them. On cue, her heart rate accelerated, and she felt another sharp tug in her tummy.

Ducking her head, she pretended to consult the list of questions she'd prepared. She needed her mind on the job, not in places she had no business venturing—at the moment.

Sunny cleared her throat. "How long after your initial meeting with Abbott did you see him again?"

"That same evening," Margo answered. "He asked me to accompany him to the symphony. He had a private box."

From the file Sunny had read, she knew Margo had lived a sheltered, privileged life in the ivory tower her rich uncle had built, but Margo wasn't a naive kid fresh off the farm. The woman might be low-mileage, but she didn't strike Sunny as the type to fall for a slick pickup line, either.

So what was it about this particular UNSUB that made his victims fall for an obvious con like naive little fools? As much as she wanted—no, *needed*—to understand, she simply could not wrap her mind around the concept of being some guy's patsy.

Duncan shifted slightly in his chair, instantly drawing her attention. She might be entertaining the possibility of exploring the physical attraction between them, but she possessed enough intelligence to know when he was feeding her a line. Sure, she'd flirted with him, but she was also well aware of the fact he wanted something from her, just as she wanted a look at his files. And whatever else he might be willing to show her.

Looking back to Margo, Sunny asked, "Did anyone else accompany you to the symphony? Did Mr. Abbott have a driver?"

"He drove himself." A slight blush colored the other woman's unnaturally smooth cheeks. "We were…alone."

Why did normally reasonable women lose all common sense when it came to the opposite sex? Sunny never would be so stupid as to invite a guy she didn't know into her home. Didn't Margo read the newspapers? The world was filled with lunatics and psychos.

She was a fine one to talk. Hadn't she been on the verge of inviting Duncan to her place? And what did she really know about him? Not much, other than the possibility that for the first time in months she could be changing the sheets on her bed for something other than laundry day.

"And after the symphony?" Sunny asked.

"He brought me home." A deeper blush this time. "We had a glass of sherry and then he left after we made plans for the following evening to attend the art gallery."

Sunny frowned and consulted her notes again. Not a single reference existed in the case file about Margo accompanying the UNSUB to an art gallery. "Did you provide the investigating officer with the name of the gallery?" she asked.

"He never asked. But it was the Fifth Street Art Center."

"Were you aware it hasn't been open in six months?" Duncan asked suddenly.

"Yes, I was," Margo answered. "Justin had arranged for a private showing."

"He may have arranged a private showing, Ms. Wilder," Duncan said, his gaze intent as he studied the witness closely, "but not with the property owner's permission. The Fifth Street Art Center went out of business."

Margo frowned, a barely perceptible action courtesy of regular Botox injections. "That's impossible. I was there. I even purchased one of the paintings on display."

This was all news to Sunny and it irritated her that the local authorities hadn't been more diligent in their investigation. "Do you have the painting?" she asked, but she already suspected the answer.

The older woman's frown deepened by the slightest degree. "No, not as yet."

And she never would, Sunny thought, struggling to remain calm. Never one to suffer fools lightly, herself included, she had little patience for stupidity. At this rate, by the time she solved SEDSCAM, her usual lack of empathy would be finely tuned.

She couldn't help wondering if any of the women victimized had an inkling how fortunate they were to have lost only their material possessions and not their lives? So far the UNSUB's twisted fantasy thankfully didn't include physically harming his victims. Hopefully that wouldn't change.

"Are you sure there were no other individuals present at the gallery that night?" she asked.

Margo shook her head. "No. No one."

"Then how were you able to make a purchase?" For a painting, Sunny had a feeling, that was a fake.

"I made the check out to Justin. He is a substantial patron so I just assumed…"

Exactly what he'd wanted her to assume. He'd conned her into believing he was such a wealthy supporter he'd practically been given his own key to the place.

Regardless, Sunny finally had a fresh piece of information. In order to pull off such an elaborate scheme as detailed as an operational art gallery, the UNSUB couldn't possibly be flying solo. Although she'd never personally been involved, she'd heard the stories of the networks of traveling grifters. They moved around the country duping the elderly, ripping off department stores by returning stolen merchandise for cash refunds and running the classic carnie cons. With the exception of big real estate rip-offs and boiler room scams, cons generally ran penny-ante operations nowhere near as sophisticated as the UNSUB's game.

She jotted down a reminder to have the art gallery searched by the Bureau's crime lab technicians, then added another note to have the theater checked out, as well. Private boxes hardly came cheap. No doubt the UNSUB had "borrowed" the box for the night—without the box holder's blessing.

Sunny continued to question Margo, gathering specific details of the woman's "dates" with the UNSUB not included in the initial investigation reports. The only date that had been public was the night of the symphony, and for the ten days that followed, the Seducer kept his liaisons private, just as he'd done with his previous victims. In addition to the art gallery scam, there'd been a midnight picnic in the park, a couple of moonlit drives and a few romantic dinners for two at the Wilder estate, with the staff dismissed, at Abbott's request, of course.

Having taken part in several of the ISU's specialized training courses in criminal investigation, Sunny understood the best profilers possessed a talent for climbing inside the heads of victim and perpetrator. But what about *her* victims? How was she supposed to walk in their ridiculously expensive designer shoes when she lacked a basic understanding of how any reasonably intelligent woman could be duped by a con with romance as an M.O.?

Setting her notepad beside her, Sunny looked at Margo, determined to imagine herself as this victim. "You do realize that Abbott intentionally seduced you to gain access to the items he's stolen from you."

"Yes," the older woman agreed, her expression sheepish. "I, too, have come to the same conclusion."

Sunny let out a pent-up breath. "Ms. Wilder. Margo." She struggled for compassion when all she could muster was an overwhelming sense of self-directed frustration. "I need you to help me understand how this is possible."

Duncan cleared his throat, but Sunny chose to ignore him for the moment. Despite what she'd told Caruso upon arriving at the estate, she realized she secretly agreed with his hard-up assessment. But if she wanted to solve the case, then she also understood she had to set her judgments aside. Otherwise she'd never learn what made Tansey Middleton, Maddie Bryson, Joy Tweed, Bettina Manchester, Celine Garfield, Katrina Pescadero, and now Margo Wilder the Seducer's perfect victims.

Margo's puffed-up lips twisted into a smile. "Have you ever been swept off your feet?" she asked Sunny. "Or been so completely caught up in a storm of passion all that matters is physical pleasure?"

In a word, no. Rhetorical or not, Sunny wasn't about to divulge the truth about her own lacking sex life with a material witness. Not after she'd spent the better part of the morning openly flirting with the man seated less than three feet away from her, giving signals to the contrary. In truth, today went on record as a first for her. She'd never considered surrendering to rampant hormones, but the idea held more than a few interesting possibilities.

A few weeks shy of her thirtieth birthday, she'd had exactly three relationships of any great significance in her lifetime. The sex had always been good and she never considered it an issue, but she'd never experienced the kind of passion Margo described.

"Ms. Wilder," Duncan interrupted, saving Sunny from having to formulate an intelligent response. "We're going to need every detail of your association with Abbott."

Sunny turned to stare at him, certain she'd just entered her own personal *Twilight Zone*—in *Sex and the City*-esque style. *We? What's this* we *business?*

He must have sensed her apprehension because he turned that lethal gaze in her direction. "If we're going to catch the UNSUB," he said, "then we need to know his habits. His quirks. From the way he combs his hair down to the shape of his scars and what he eats for breakfast. The smallest detail, no matter how insignificant it might seem, could be the break we need."

We. There was that word again. Sunny tried to push aside the warm fuzzy feeling the concept of "we" gave her, and failed. Instead, she concentrated on Margo. But Duncan did have a point—dammit.

"If you would prefer Mr. Chamberlain leave us at this juncture, I'm sure he wouldn't object." Sunny prayed the woman would take her up on her offer. Regardless of how immature or hypocritical, the idea of dissecting the intimate details of Margo's liaison with the UNSUB in Duncan Chamberlain's presence made her want to squirm.

Upon joining the Bureau, her first assignment had been conducting in-depth background investigations. She'd interviewed countless witnesses and delved into various backgrounds, from the lowest government employee all the way up the ladder to some of the country's top political officials. As a result, she'd uncovered odd quirks, stranger-than-fiction habits and more than a few bizarre sexual appetites. At first she'd been shocked by the information she'd uncovered, but since she was determined to become a player on the FBI's team of profilers, she'd conditioned herself to take it all in stride. Violent crime and sexual homicide were hardly a job for the squeamish.

So where the hell had the cool professionalism, the detachment, the composure she'd consciously developed, gone when she needed it most?

"I was his canvas," Margo blurted.

Sunny's eyebrows shot upward. "Excuse me?" Certainly, she misunderstood the implication. As much as it pained her to do so in front of Duncan, she asked, "Could you be more specific?"

Margo's expression remained composed, as if she were about to discuss the last social event she'd attended rather than her sexual exploits with a con man. "I was his canvas," she repeated. "He liked to paint me with scented oil."

At a loss for words, Sunny started at the woman. No. She absolutely had *not* heard what she thought she'd heard. Maybe Margo was making some obscure reference to the night Abbott had taken her to the fake gallery. Yes, that was it, a reference to the art gallery. She hoped.

"I'm sorry, but I don't understand," Sunny said. "He put scented oil on one of the paintings?"

"He didn't paint on a traditional canvas," Margo clarified. "He asked *me* to be his canvas. At first I was nervous—what he was asking was so…unorthodox—but I must admit, I've never experienced anything so completely erotic in my life."

An image flashed in Sunny's mind. Marble floors, bronze sculptures, paintings by masters she couldn't name hanging on unobtrusive-colored walls. And Duncan. His heat, his body surrounding her, pressing her up against the smooth, cool plaster, his hands slowly caressing her breasts…his mouth hot, demanding…

Sunny grew more uncomfortable by the second. *Find a way into her head,* she reminded herself. *Become the victim.*

"Was this…technique something he did each time you made love?" she forced herself to ask. "Did he often use…props?"

Margo nodded. Another wistful smile slowly tilted her lips. "Justin was an incredible master at foreplay."

Against her will, Sunny's gaze slid to Duncan. Her breath caught at the intensity shining in his brilliant blue-gray eyes as he returned her stare. Was he a master at foreplay, she wondered?

Please, please, please.

Sunny bit her bottom lip to squelch the moan bubbling up inside her. She couldn't very well close her eyes in the middle of an interview, so instead she remained entranced by the blatant heat in Duncan's gaze.

Losing herself in the fantasy, she listened to Margo's words, mentally placing herself in the role of willing victim. No faceless UNSUB twirled a painter's whiskered brush over her nipples. In her mind she saw the handsomely chiseled features of the man across from her, felt the strength of his hands on her body.

Her breathing turned shallow as pure hunger filled his gaze. Was he transported by the same wild fantasy?

"He'd start by using a variety of brushes, each one tipped in oil, warmed precisely to 98.6 degrees," Margo explained. "And then he'd stroke them over my nude body."

Sunny could have sworn Duncan physically stroked her just as seductively when his gaze traveled the length of her. Oh, this was not good.

Margo continued to speak of the intimacy and sensuality Abbott had demanded of her. Sunny envisioned Duncan's mouth covering hers, kissing her deeply while he painted her flesh at his leisure. The slick, moist oil against her skin, his hands pressing her thighs open, exploring, painting, touching…kissing her intimately.

There was nothing imaginary about the pressure between her legs, only the reality of the insistent need clawing at her, reminding her it'd been months since her last sexual encounter. The incredible sensitivity of her breasts as they swelled and tightened inside the cups of her sensible cotton bra served as another reminder that reality had indeed intruded upon fantasy.

A serene expression encompassed Margo's face and her gaze slipped to somewhere over Sunny's shoulder. "Justin was slow, very deliberate in my pleasure," she said. "He exposed me so completely, his exploration erotic and incredibly thorough. I never realized the depths of sensuality until I met Justin, or understand how many places on our bodies were capable of providing fulfillment. He even asked me to touch myself in front of him, to make believe my hands were his hands stroking me. I was so completely entranced by the hypnotic sound of his voice as he described various acts of making love and the depths of pleasure he promised me, I never felt an ounce of embarrassment the first time I came that way in front of him.

"With Justin I became a greedy, decadent lover," Margo continued in that same faraway voice. "Becoming aroused and bringing about my own fulfillment for the pleasure of a man was unlike anything I'd ever known. Not once did I contemplate holding back. I willingly gave him everything he wanted from me."

Sunny remained fully conscious of the reality of Duncan's presence. Not only physically, but prominently in her mind where she pleasured herself for him. The fantasy was wild, uninhibited and erotic on a level she'd never dreamed possible.

She'd gone too far. Climbing inside the victim's head was one thing. It was quite another for her to become so thoroughly aroused by the mere image of making love to Duncan that she couldn't do her job.

The need to escape overwhelmed her. She had to leave. Now. Right now, before she went up in flames.

But departure was not an option. Dammit, she was supposed to be a professional. If it killed her, she'd get through this interview. She forced her gaze away from Duncan to concentrate on the witness. Thank heavens she'd had the foresight to record the session, although replaying Margo's erotic recounting of events did fill her with a modicum of dread.

For the next thirty minutes she continued to question Margo, obtaining details of the property stolen from her, the type of car the Seducer drove and the like, until she'd miraculously made it through all the questions on her list. Her body still hummed with awareness, but if she refused to so much as glance in Duncan's direction, she remained hopeful of bringing the interview to a conclusion without going up in flames.

Her hand shook as she reached for the tape recorder. After fumbling with the switch, she dropped it into her briefcase along with her notepad. "I need…" *A cold shower. Preferably with ice water.* "I'll need to schedule another appointment," she said, not the least bit surprised her voice trembled. Her nerve endings were still vibrantly alive with sexual awareness. "I'd like to bring in a sketch artist for a composite."

Still ignoring Duncan, she stood and faced Margo, extending her hand for another polite, limp handshake. "I'll be in touch."

"I'll wait for your call," Margo said graciously.

She made the mistake of glancing in Duncan's direction. A smooth, lazy smile canted his mouth. The look in his eyes nearly did send her up in flames.

"I can see myself out," she said, anxious to put a whole lot of distance between herself and Duncan's knowing, I-want-you eyes.

Offering only a weak, apologetic semblance of a smile, she bolted from the room and hurried down the paneled corridor toward safety…er, the exit. She had a single moment's hesitation about leaving Duncan alone with the witness, but she was too close to freedom now to turn back. Besides, he did have a right to be there since he'd been hired by Wilder's insurance carrier to recover her stolen property.

She let herself out, shaken by the knowledge that not all lessons were easily learned. Still, she finally had firsthand knowledge of what Margo had meant by being so completely caught up in a storm of passion that nothing else mattered…except absolute pleasure.

3

SUNNY PROPPED HER bottom on the edge of her desk and faced the U.S. map pinned to the wall of her closetlike, windowless office. Tapping her index finger against her lips, she studied the neon-orange pinheads. Seattle, Napa Valley, St. Louis, Atlanta, Miami, Philadelphia and Baltimore. "Random choices?" she mused aloud. "Or preselected for reasons we still haven't determined?"

Georgia Tremont, a tall, willowy redhead fresh from Quantico consulted the computer printout in her lap. "The computer wasn't able to establish a pattern to the UNSUB's choice of locations," she reminded Sunny. As one of a handful of analysts employed by the unit, Georgia's job was to dissect evidence and other pertinent data provided by the senior agents in charge of investigations. "I say random."

"Possibly," Sunny said slowly. Her instincts told her otherwise. And she always trusted her instincts.

"Computers aren't infallible," Ned Ball added. "I don't trust them."

"Oh, that's rich," Georgia laughed. "For a guy who investigates Internet fraud."

"Among other things." Ned pushed his glasses back in place. "But that's my point. Computers make it easier for the criminals. The Net is a hotbed of illegal activity."

Georgia rolled her big blue eyes. "It's not the computers, or the Internet, Ned, but the people using them."

Sunny pushed off the desk. "Play nice now, kiddies," she
teased the rookie agents. "We're supposed to be brain-
storming here, not debating the alleged evils of the information superhighway."

For a guy who claimed he didn't trust computers, Ned
Ball was the CID's answer to Bill Gates and Steve Jobs
all rolled into one pocket-protector-sporting computer
nerd. The guy was golden when it came to ferreting out
glitches, back doors and security hazards. His first week
in the unit, he'd single-handedly tracked down the devel-
oper of a nasty e-mail worm responsible for temporarily
shutting down the computer system of several of the na-
tion's banks.

Sunny dropped into the chair behind her desk. "Georgia, any word on those search warrants yet?"

"Sorry, Mac. We're still waiting. I put another call in to
the clerk half an hour ago, and she said the judge was still
on the bench in closed session."

Frustration bit into Sunny hard. Upon returning from the
Wilder estate, she'd obtained authorization from the unit
chief to have the crime lab search the art gallery and theater. She'd had the paperwork prepared and sent to the
judge for signature within the hour. Three hours later and
still no warrants. "Can't you find another federal magis-
trate in this town? We need those warrants signed so the
lab can get moving on this."

Ned dropped a sheaf of papers on the edge of Sunny's
desk and frowned. "If this was a violent crime, the scenes
would've been searched already," he complained.

"True," Georgia commiserated. "But we should be
thankful these aren't violent crimes." She looked back at

Sunny. "Do you really expect the lab to find anything after all this time?"

"Maybe. If we're lucky, they'll give us something new to go on," Sunny said, but she wasn't about to pin her hopes on the lab turning up viable evidence. For one, it'd been over two weeks since Wilder accompanied the UNSUB to the theater. Countless individuals had no doubt contaminated the private box, from patrons to theater staff and cleaning crews. With any luck at all, they might turn up physical evidence from the art gallery since the place was closed, but even she had to admit it was unlikely. They already had the guy's DNA from four of the known crime scenes, but no identifying factors to provide them with a name. All she could realistically hope for would be a match confirming Abbott was their UNSUB.

Georgia offered her a sympathetic smile. "The clerk did promise to call as soon as the warrants were signed."

Sunny frowned at the silent phone, wishing Duncan would return her call. Whether or not he could give her the information necessary to form that pattern she suspected existed, she could only guess. She wanted to know more about those two cases he'd mentioned he was investigating in addition to Wilder. Were the claimants on her existing list of victims? If not, that would bring the total number of victims to nine nationwide. And if there *were* more victims, why hadn't local authorities advised her office when she'd published an alert weeks ago?

Because SEDSCAM was a nonviolent crime, she reminded herself, making it a low priority for local jurisdictions. If rich, affluent, campaign-dollar-contributing women were being raped, murdered and dumped along the roadside for Joe Citizen to discover on his morning jog, she'd have the high-ranking officials from those cities storming her office demanding action.

By sheer accident they'd discovered the connection to Wilder, albeit five days after the fact. The credit belonged solely to Georgia for bringing an article in the newspaper about the theft to Sunny's attention. If the incident hadn't occurred in their own backyard, or if the Wilder name hadn't attracted press coverage, weeks may have passed before they'd been notified, if at all. She'd acted quickly and rather than dealing with the usual pissing contest over jurisdiction, the local authorities had been happy to hand the investigation off to her.

The time factor was short in relation to the other cases, not that it had garnered her much headway with regard to solid leads thus far. They still had no idea where the UNSUB might strike next, where he went after pulling a job or what he did with the millions in cash and property he'd lifted from the vics.

Sunny let out a frustrated sigh. "I need to get a visual on this case." She dragged a yellow legal pad in front of her and drew two lines down the page. "What do we know? What do we suspect? What can we prove?" Once she had a list, the entries would go onto three-by-five index cards which she'd be able to move around on a chart, like a giant jigsaw puzzle.

"We know there are seven vics in seven different states and no confirmed pattern," Ned started. "We also know one man is responsible for at least four of the crimes based on DNA evidence collected."

Georgia flipped through her printouts. "DNA was collected from hair samples in Philly and St. Louis. Miami from a cigar stub…" Confusion filled her blue eyes when she looked up at Sunny and Ned. "A sweatband from the Atlanta location?"

Sunny shrugged and entered the names of the victims

and their geographic locations in the first column, followed by the DNA links. "We suspect he's responsible for all seven crimes." She looked up at the two rookie agents. "There's a possibility we could have nine victims. A recovery expert hired by Wilder's insurance carrier was at the estate this morning. In addition to Wilder, he claims his office is handling two additional cases with similar M.O.'s."

"Did you get the names?" Georgia asked. "Do you know which locations?"

"Not yet," Sunny answered. She wasn't proud of the fact she'd been so thoroughly distracted by the awareness sizzling between her and Duncan that she'd failed to ask him even a few pertinent questions regarding his investigations. "I've left a message for him."

Georgia moved the printouts and other documents from her lap to the floor, then reached across Sunny's desk for the file containing the six composite sketches of the UNSUB they'd obtained from the victims. "Which of these four guys match our DNA evidence?" she asked.

"Ian Banyon, Burke Conners, Scott Kauffman." Sunny consulted her notes. "And Adam Hunt."

Georgia separated the four composites, helped herself to the plastic box of pushpins from Sunny's drawer, then hung the four sketches on the wall near the map. "Okay, now give me the order?"

"Conners first in St. Louis, Atlanta was Hunt," Sunny told her. "Miami is Banyon, and put Kauffman last for Philly."

Georgia pulled the neon-orange pins from the map, exchanging them for bright yellow, then arranged the composites in corresponding order. She stood back and examined the map, then looked over her shoulder to Sunny and Ned with a satisfied smile. "Do you see it?"

Sunny pushed out of her chair and moved in to get a closer look at the map.

"He's getting sloppy," Ned suggested from behind her. He indicated the first two locations with the tip of a pen. "Seattle and Napa produced no DNA evidence. The UNSUB was careful, cautious. By the time he got here," he said, pointing to the yellow pinhead marking the St. Louis crime scene, "his confidence was up, so he relaxed and got careless."

"I don't think so," Sunny said. "He's not careless, he's very thorough and methodical. I'd suggest arrogance, but you don't get cocky from only two successful jobs. Plus, it was a hair sample found in the drain pipe of the victim's shower in St. Louis, so that could be a fluke. By the time he hit Miami, it may have been intentional if he's playing with us, but our involvement isn't public yet. If there's any meat to Ned's theory, though, then we have more crimes to worry about."

She looked over at Georgia. "Can you pull all the data reported from crimes in the last two years that match our UNSUB's M.O.?"

"I can try," she said, but didn't look too hopeful. "If the stats aren't entered into the national database, there's not much I can do."

"They usually don't bother," Ned added, "unless it involves a violent crime. On the surface these have the characteristics of theft. That's not something anyone would commonly associate with a serial-type offender."

Sunny turned her attention back to the composite sketches. "See what you can find anyway," she said to Georgia. "I know it's a long shot, but we could find gold."

"The lab could come up with more DNA from Wilder's place," Georgia suggested. "How long before you'll hear something?"

"Could be days." Sunny moved closer to the map, meticulously studying each sketch for what had to be the six hundredth time. She was missing something…but what?

Ned adjusted his glasses and peered at the sketches of Burke Connors and Ian Banyon. "How does he do it?" he asked. "How does he manage to completely alter his appearance? I see basic similarities, but it just doesn't look like the same guy. You know, I could style my hair differently, wear contacts, but I'd still look like me."

"I know what you mean," Georgia agreed. "I could go brunette or blond but I'd still be me. If it wasn't for the evidence, I'd swear we should be looking for four different men. Nothing suggests this is the same person. It's spooky."

"Oh my God," Sunny blurted. "That's it!" She turned to look at the two agents and grinned. "These are *not* sketches of the same person."

Georgia took a step back and looked down at Sunny as if she'd lost her mind. "Come on, Mac. You're reaching. The evidence indicates otherwise."

"I'm not refuting the evidence," Sunny explained. "Stay with me a minute." She went to her desk for the remaining two composites, then pinned them to the wall above the other four drawings.

"Marcus Wood." She pointed to the first sketch. "Tansey Middleton's favorite cause is animal rights. She writes big checks to support no-kill shelters and foots the bill for an adopt-a-pet event twice a year. Wood comes along posing as a dog-loving, animal-rights activist."

Ned folded his arms and rocked back on the heels of his polished wingtips. "Yeah, so?"

"Maddie Bryson takes over the operation of the family vineyard when her brother loses a lengthy battle with cancer. To recoup their losses, Maddie explores the possibility of exporting their award-winning Napa Valley grapes to several French winemakers. Travis Reisner shows up claiming to be a buyer for a French winemaker."

Georgia's eyes filled with understanding. "Joy Tweed is a professional college student," she said. "Some guys don't change their socks as often as Joy changes majors. She's what they used to call an M.R.S. degree candidate way back when. Burke Connors *is* a Ph.D. candidate, another professional student, in Joy Tweed's eyes."

"Exactly," Sunny agreed. "Bettina Manchester falls for the supposed owner of a chain of sporting goods stores. Celine Garfield is conned by a guy posing as an importer of Egyptian artifacts. Scott Kaufman is a rich playboy for a socialite, and Justin Abbott is a patron of the arts to an art connoisseur."

Ned pushed his glasses up the slope of his nose again and studied each of the composites more closely. He looked over his shoulder at Sunny, his pale blond brows knit in confusion. "Sorry, Mac. I'm not following you."

Sunny tapped her finger on the first drawing. "Doesn't Marcus Wood *look* like one of those lunatics that would run through a dog show opening cages, freeing the dogs in the name of animal rights? And Conners here has egghead professor written all over him." Next she indicated the composite drawing of Adam Hunt. "This guy looks like a jock, just the kind of guy you'd expect would own a chain of sporting goods stores."

Ned scratched the back of his head. "I still don't see what you're saying."

"Each of these drawings appear to be a completely different guy, right?" She waited for Ned and Georgia's acknowledgment before continuing. "That's because the vics aren't remembering the *way* the UNSUB actually looks, but how they *saw* him. The composites aren't going to give us an accurate physical description because they aren't of the actual man, but of the image he portrayed to his victims."

"It is an interesting theory," Georgia said. "Didn't Celine Garfield say that Banyon spoke with some sort of British, or maybe a South African, accent?"

"She did," Sunny confirmed. "And when Wilder sits down with the sketch artist tomorrow, if the composite of Justin Abbott isn't a perfect example of a patron-of-the-arts type, lunch is on me."

Ned still didn't look as convinced as Georgia. "The UNSUB's ability to transform himself may very well be his recipe for success," he eventually conceded, "but how is your theory going to lead us to him?"

Undaunted by Ned's lack of vision, Sunny's smile widened. "We might be able to narrow down possible locations since we know what attracts him."

"Money," Georgia added. "A whole lot of money."

"You're talking haystacks and needles, Mac," Ned argued. "You know how many people in this country come into big bucks every day? How many of them are women? A new millionaire comes along every couple of weeks if all the state lottery stats are accurate."

"But we're only interested in the perpetually single and recently unattached," Georgia added helpfully. "That should narrow the field considerably."

"Divorcées, widows," Sunny told the analyst. "Any woman between the ages of twenty and fifty-five that fits the profile."

"I'll play with some data, see what comes up."

"Great." She'd been on the SEDSCAM case for almost four weeks and finally felt as if they were making progress. "Ned, what about the bank in Atlanta? Any luck?"

"None yet," he said. He propped his shoulder against the wall. "We do know the UNSUB didn't clear out Manchester's accounts with a stolen check the way he did with Bryson. If there's a hole in the bank's software, give me enough time and I'll have it for you."

"What about an Internet transfer?" Georgia suggested, gathering up her printouts and reports.

"First place I looked," Ned told her. "Neither Manchester's personal nor business accounts were set up for Internet banking. Doesn't eliminate a hack job, but banks are required to report security breaches so don't hold your breath."

"Did you tell Mac about the check?" Georgia asked Ned, lifting the stack of papers to the chair.

Ned stuffed his hands into the pockets of his dark trousers. "Bryson's bank finally released the original check the UNSUB forged to clear out her account."

Sunny glanced down at the still quiet phone. "That's progress."

"You were unavailable for consultation." Ned cleared his throat before continuing. "I hope it's okay, but I went ahead and asked Milken over in check fraud to give us his opinion on the Bryson check."

"No, that's good," Sunny told him, hiding a smile when Ned stood just a tad straighter under her praise. "Don't be afraid to ask the other divisions for assistance when you need it."

"Ah, here it is," Georgia said suddenly. She stood, a sheaf of papers clutched in her hand.

"How would you like to get out of the office tomorrow?" Sunny asked her.

"I'd love a change of scenery. What do you need?"

"Accompany the sketch artist to Wilder's tomorrow.

Take notes of anything else she might recall," Sunny instructed. "If those warrants come through, Ned and I will
be hanging out with the techno jocks at the gallery and theater."

Georgia's smile turned sly as she handed a set of documents to Sunny and Ned. "This caused production to
grind to a halt in word processing."

A warming blush heated Sunny's cheeks as she scanned
the cover sheet of Margo Wilder's recorded statement. "No
doubt," she muttered, grateful she'd used a tape recorder
rather than a video camera. "This was quick."

"It's the weekly supply of Krispy Kremes she feeds
them," Ned said with a quiet laugh, flipping through the
statement.

"Works like a charm," Georgia agreed good-naturedly.

"Good God," Ned blurted. He pushed off the wall he'd
been leaning against and gave the knot of his tie a tug.
"People actually do this kind of thing?"

Georgia burst out laughing. "If you have to ask, then
you're spending way too much time with computers."

"Okay, that's enough," Sunny warned gently. "Georgia,
why don't you try the clerk's office again."

"Will do. But first tell me who is the hunk?"

Sunny frowned. "Hunk?" she hedged.

"Chamberlain," Georgia clarified. "The man has a voice
that could melt granite. That spells hunk in my fantasies,
not short, fat and bald."

"I'm gone," Ned announced and quickly gathered up the
notes and files he'd brought with him. "Maybe Milken has
something for us." He practically jogged for the door.

Sunny waited until she and Georgia were alone. "How'd
you hear his voice?" she asked in a hushed tone.

She hadn't dared replay the session herself, afraid of

what she might hear—like her own heavy breathing. When she'd arrived at the office, she'd turned the tape over to word processing as a rush job. Not that she was eager to relive the fantasy she'd conjured during the interview, but she did need to thoroughly dissect Wilder's statement for clues.

Georgia sat on the edge of the chair and leaned forward, resting her arms on Sunny's desk. "My cubicle's next to word processing," she said, keeping her voice low. "When all the gasping and giggling started, I got curious."

"Oh God." Sunny closed her eyes and groaned. "They were playing the tape aloud?"

Georgia's grin widened. "There wasn't a headset in use. So? Is he as good-looking as he sounds?"

Sunny bit her bottom lip, then shook her head. "We're federal agents, Georgia."

"Statistics show that more and more couples are meeting on the job. We're agents, Mac, and women. With the hours we put in, where else are we going to find a man?"

Georgia did have a point. Hadn't Sunny just been bemoaning how long it'd been since she'd found a guy who could hold her interest? Duncan certainly had done that…and more.

"So?" Georgia prompted when Sunny remained silent. "Is he or isn't he?"

Sunny looked toward the door to make certain they wouldn't be overheard. "That voice," she whispered, looking back at Georgia, "isn't all that could melt granite."

They giggled. Like women, not agents.

"He has these bluish-gray eyes, and they are so intense," Sunny said once they stopped laughing. "When he looks at you, it's like he really sees you."

"Unlike cleavage crawlers," Georgia said with distaste.

"You know the type. They never look you in the eye because they're too busy staring at your chest."

Sunny wrinkled her nose. "How would they feel if we stared at their crotches?"

"Like we're speaking their language. So, is he tall? Short, what?"

"A little over six foot."

"Hair?"

"Wavy. Black."

"Ass?"

Sunny grinned. "The nicest I've seen in a while."

"Oh, it's not fair." Georgia let out a sigh. "Such luck. Beauty and brains, too."

Sunny pushed out of her chair and walked to the filing cabinet. "How does a nice ass equal brains?" She pulled open the top drawer for the bottled water she kept on hand.

"Well, he's not stupid. He made an interesting point when he said if we're going to nail the UNSUB, we need—" The phone on Sunny's rang and Georgia automatically reached for it. "It's probably the clerk's office."

Sunny handed Georgia a bottle before she twisted the cap off her own and took a drink. "Need to know his habits," she said quietly, recalling Duncan's words during the interview. "His quirks."

"Special Agent MacGregor's office," Georgia said into the receiver.

UNSUB. CID.

How many more terms did he use that she couldn't immediately recall? And was Duncan's use of Bureau slang nothing more than a coincidence? He could've picked up the terminology from hanging around law-enforcement personnel. Except when he spoke, it'd been…unconscious. Natural.

"Yes, she's here." Georgia shook her head, signaling the call wasn't from the clerk's office.

Sunny had one of the most powerful databases at her disposal. In a few keystrokes, she could easily satisfy her curiosity. Was it an invasion of privacy if the party wasn't aware they'd been invaded? she wondered.

"One moment, Agent Caruso."

Sunny frowned and took the handset from Georgia. "Mac, here." The only reason any of the agents assigned surveillance of the Wilder estate would call is if something had happened at the scene. The UNSUB was no doubt long gone, so the call probably was nothing more urgent than an eager reporter caught trying to sneak onto the estate or claiming she'd given him permission.

"You gotta see what Quantico is teaching these new kids to do with a laptop and a cell phone. This Eggbert stuff ain't half bad."

"Is there a point to this call, Jack?"

"Not really, Mac. Just called to see how it's hanging." His gravelly voice was drenched in sarcasm. "You know, in between pissing in the bushes and sweating like a friggin' pig out here on the hottest day of the year. Hell yes, I have a point. Weidman pulled up something on your boy and I thought you should know about it."

She wasn't sure she appreciated Agent Weidman's checking up on her UNSUB or his aggressiveness. A lead was still a lead, and considering her current level of progress, she'd withhold judgment for the time being. "My apologies, Jack. What'd he find?"

"The kid ran a basic background check. Chamberlain has an impressive résumé with a ton of high-end experience as an investigator."

"Chamberlain?" As in Duncan Chamberlain, the hottie

capable of melting granite and a whole lot more. *Not* the UNSUB as she'd mistakenly assumed.

Dread crept up her spine and settled in her shoulders. A knot of tension formed at the base of her skull and began to throb in a slow, steady rhythm.

"You wanna take a shot at where he got his training?"

Sunny briefly closed her eyes. "Where?" she asked, even though she had a good idea of the answer.

"Quantico, Virginia, Mac." Jack's tone sobered. "The son of a bitch is FBI."

4

SUNNY APPROACHED THE young, pretty brunette seated at the reception desk of Chamberlain Recovery and Investigations and flashed her ID. "Special Agent MacGregor," she said, her tone brusque. "FBI. Is Mr. Chamberlain in?"

The receptionist's wide-set brown eyes filled with caution. "I'll see if he's available."

Sunny tucked her ID back inside the pocket of her linen blazer. "You do that," she said. "And tell Mr. Chamberlain he'd be smart to *make* himself available."

The girl deserted her post and took off around the corner, leaving Sunny alone. She walked toward a pair of navy padded chairs, but she was too restless to sit. What she really wanted to do was kick something. Hard. She considered the brass planter with a thick potted palm in the corner as a possible target, then decided she'd rather unleash her anger on a certain some*one,* with seductive eyes and a kiss-me smile who'd made her look like an incompetent moron in front Caruso and Weidman.

The minute she'd hung up the phone with Jack, she'd accessed the Bureau's personnel directory. The slow simmer of anger had silenced her disbelief the moment Duncan's image had loaded on the screen of her monitor. Her temper still hadn't cooled, even on the drive across town to his office.

The personnel file hadn't provided her with a scrap of useful data other than to confirm Weidman's findings and Duncan's dates of service with the Bureau. No reference whatsoever to the reason behind his termination. A resignation? Perhaps, but to her "relieved of duty" sounded as if he'd been canned. Without the appropriate clearance level, though, she had no hope of verifying her suspicions, leaving her with no choice but to go directly to the source and demand answers.

Any number of reasons could result in a security classification of an agent's service record. The need for clearance didn't necessarily mean Duncan's personnel file contained information on sensitive national security issues or even the whereabouts of a material witness to a crime. The medical findings of his last physical could've easily garnered the tag.

She blew out a stream of breath. Irritation made a fine companion to anger. She wanted answers, and was determined to have them, one way or another, along with whatever other information he may be keeping from her. He'd ignored her warning not to try to play her once. If he refused to take her seriously, then she'd simply confiscate his files related to SEDSCAM and ban him from the Wilder estate until the conclusion of her investigation.

The receptionist returned with a pleasant smile and an armload of files, which she placed on the center of her desk. "Mr. Chamberlain can see you now," she said amiably.

Guilt nipped Sunny's conscience for coming off as a hard-ass with the girl. Before she could formulate an appropriate apology, they'd reached the end of the short corridor and the receptionist ushered Sunny into Duncan's office, closing the door quietly as she left.

He stood behind his desk, a cordless phone edged between his shoulder and ear as he flipped through a binder lying open on the desk. His tie was gone, and the khakis were not pressed so neatly now as they'd been that morning. All that thick, black hair was tousled, as if he'd been ramming his fingers through the wavy mass. Rumpled and sexy, she thought again. And still a damn fine specimen of massive sex appeal, no matter how much he'd ticked her off.

He glanced up and their eyes met. As if he were happy to see her, those incredible lips tipped upward in a smile, making her heart beat in an erratic rhythm. Did his office qualify as his place?

Only on a technicality, she decided. Not that it made a difference. She'd come for answers, not a little afternoon delight.

He motioned for her to sit while he finished his phone call, indicating the navy armchair across from his desk. The chaotic atmosphere was so arbitrary to her impression of Duncan. But what did she know? She hadn't exactly been a shining example of sound judgment on that subject considering the enlightening phone call from Caruso. She never should've allowed him onto the estate without having him checked out first. She didn't know what she'd been thinking, but a plea of lust-on-the brain made for a pathetically thin defense.

Ignoring the offer to sit, she clasped her hands behind her back and took in his surroundings. The cool blues, deep wines and creamy whites of the color scheme would have been more soothing if nearly every available surface of the heavy furnishings weren't a cautionary tale in the hazards of disorganization. Several stacks of files threatened to topple from the edge of the monstrous oak desk. The matching credenza parked beneath the window was no improvement, nor were the trio of lateral oak file cabinets along the wall. She caught sight of a pair of silver picture frames on the center file cabinet, but the photographs were obscured by a landscape of documents bound together with thick rubber bands.

She strolled over to an imposing armoire pulling double duty as a bookcase. In reality, the piece acted as a catch-all for more files and banded documents. A row of bulky binders were crammed to overflowing with papers, while the shelf directly above held a line of books, oddly arranged by height in a neat, organized row, ranging in topic from the federal penal code to rules of evidence along with several investigation trade manuals and journals. Taped to the interior of the open doors of the armoire, in no observable cohesive order she could determine, were brightly colored squares of paper with varying handwriting.

"I'll get back to you once I review the police reports," Duncan said to his caller. "Monday at the latest." He paused. "I'll talk to you then."

She turned to face him as he set the phone on the desk. He wrote something down on another square of paper, then taped it to the armoire with the others. His to-do list? she wondered.

He set the tape dispenser on a tower of files. "To what do I owe the pleasure?" he asked. The files threatened to spill, but he caught them before they toppled to the floor, shoving them back in place. The chaotic disorder didn't seem to faze him. She, on the other hand, was overcome with an urge to organize.

She reminded herself not to fall for his charm again. Or that impossible-to-resist tilt of his mouth. The pure male interest simmering in his eyes as he swept his gaze down her length didn't affect her in the least. She just wished her nipples hadn't tightened. Or her tummy hadn't flipped.

Straightening her shoulders, she attempted a hard glare. Somewhere between the reception area and his office, her anger had cooled, so she settled for one filled with minor annoyance instead.

"I'm not here for pleasure."

His expression turned downright wicked. "Too bad."

Maybe his charm wasn't her problem, but those recurring fantasies that kept playing hell with her resolve not to let him get to her. "You lied to me," she accused, pretending to ignore the images of tangled sheets and entwined limbs taunting her.

A single dark eyebrow winged upward. "I did?"

She moved to the chair and braced her hands over the back. "I warned you not to play me. You should have told me you were with the Bureau."

"I'm not *with* the Bureau," he said with calm emphasis. "Past tense."

She narrowed her eyes at that innocent-of-all-charges expression on his too-handsome face. The guy was cool, she'd give him that much. Her reprimand elicited no remorse from him. "I don't appreciate being lied to. Even by omission."

He tucked his hands in the front pockets of trousers. "I never lied to you, Sunny."

She let out a sigh. "Then why not tell me about it?" she asked, wanting to believe him.

"It's no big deal. Besides, the subject of my past employment never came up."

"It *is* a big deal," she argued. "You're a former agent, connected to a case under the Bureau's jurisdiction. You of all people should know procedure. How am I supposed to know you're not hoping for an opportunity to sabotage the investigation?"

His expression became tolerant. "Oh, come on," he said with a wry chuckle. "That's a stretch."

Maybe she was overstating, but he should've told her. Because it could have an effect on her investigation? Or because if he was terminated for cause, she could kiss any hope of turning that tangled-sheet fantasy into reality goodbye?

He shook his head and moved to the desk. "I've done nothing to interfere with your investigation. I even offered to give you copies of my files. That should tell you there are no ulterior motives at work here."

She wasn't quite ready to agree with him, even if she did believe he was telling her the truth. "Were you fired?" she asked.

His gaze remained steady. "I was no longer employable."

Which was not an answer and only heightened her curiosity. "Will you tell me why?" she asked. Agents were relieved of duty for any number of reasons, from failure to pass a psych exam to illegal activities. He didn't look like a crazy or a crook. But then, neither had Ted Bundy.

Duncan looked away and pushed the stack of case files from the edge of the desk, considering how much, or how little, to reveal to Sunny. He'd had no illusions that he'd be able to keep his former association with the Bureau a complete secret from her, he just wished he'd been able to milk information from her before the door to opportunity was slammed in his face. Three cases with hefty recovery fees that would go a long way to keeping his business solvent were on the line.

Perched on the edge of the desk, he shifted his attention back to Sunny and her caution-lined gaze. "I bombed my annual firearms recertification," he stated honestly. Since she'd come asking questions, he was banking that she'd been unable to access his full service record. "But why ask me? You must've looked me up on the system before coming here."

She glanced away. "So why couldn't you pass?"

Bingo. She didn't know squat, which was fine by him.

"An undercover assignment went bad," he told her, again truthfully. "I caught a bullet in the shoulder and ended up with a torn rotator cuff and a lot of nerve damage." He leaned forward and brought his left hand down hard on the edge of the desk a couple of times.

She winced. "You have no feeling at all?"

"Almost none. What isn't numb, hurts like the devil when the mercury dips too low." And served as a daily reminder of choices he'd made, resulting in the end of his career.

He squelched the resentment before it had a chance to surface. "The nerve damage was too extensive," he added. "Managing a firearm was enough of a challenge, let alone taking aim on a moving target."

She circled the chair and perched on the padded arm. "I'm sorry," she said quietly.

The sincerity in her voice made him uncomfortable. Arrogance deserved no sympathy. Wasn't that what he'd been told?

"Old news," he said, anxious to change the subject. "Any other questions?"

She held up her index finger. "One more."

The smallest trace of a smile touched her lips, and he started to relax. For now, at least, his secrets remained safe.

"Were you really an undercover op, and where?"

"You sound surprised," he said, tactically avoiding the second half of her question. The Bureau's computer system might keep his past hidden, but he couldn't say the same for the men he'd put in danger.

"A little." Her smile widened a degree. "No, I take that back. You have the same…intensity as a guy I know who used to work undercover out of D.C. As if you've seen more, done more than the rest of us mere mortals."

A few images from his time as an undercover operative haunted him some nights, making sleep all but impossible. He'd crossed the line, a fact he wasn't particularly proud of, but her assessment still made him smile at the reminder of better memories.

"A false sense of superiority comes with the territory," he admitted. "Eventually someone reminds us superhuman capabilities only exist in sci-fi flicks."

Her green eyes sparkled with amusement. "Even Achilles had a weakness."

That smile of hers was easily becoming *his* Achilles' heel. She'd looked damned cute, too, when she'd first shown up with her superagent feathers all ruffled. "So this guy," he said, watching her closely. "Exactly how involved are you?"

"Not *that* involved," she said, her voice laced with more humor. "He's very happily married with a baby on the way."

"Good." He couldn't help himself. His grin widened. "Then it's safe to ask you to dinner without trespassing?"

Her frown would've been effective if it hadn't been for the brief flash of pleasure in her eyes. "Why would I want to have dinner with you?"

Slowly, he came off the desk and walked toward her. "Because you think I'm irresistible." Arrogance did have a certain usefulness.

"What I *think* is that you're awfully sure of yourself." Nervousness coated her gentle laughter, taking the sting out of the insult.

Nervous was good, when it translated to interest. "So,

how 'bout that dinner?" he pressed, narrowing the remaining distance between them.

She caught the edge of her bottom lip between her teeth. Weighing her options? He hoped the scale tipped in his favor. Just thinking about kissing her was making him hard. A romantic entanglement with a federal agent probably wouldn't be his wisest move, but he had nothing against playing out a fantasy or two. Besides, he was only offering dinner, he reasoned. For now.

She tilted her head back to look up at him. Uncertainty mingled with longing in her eyes. "We probably shouldn't." Her voice lacked the conviction necessary to dissuade him, courtesy of her soft, husky tone.

"Why not?" He took one last step, his thigh brushing against her knee. Heat shot to his groin. "Let's take all this chemistry out for a ride and see where it leads." He knew exactly where he wanted it to lead…right to the nearest bed.

"I…"

"You what?" He bent toward her. Her breath fanned his lips. "Want me to kiss you?"

"Yes," she whispered.

Not about to give her an opportunity to change her mind, he cupped the back of her head with his good hand and brought his mouth down softly over hers. Apparently gentle wasn't her thing, nor was she shy about upping the ante. Her slender arms wound around his neck, bringing their bodies together, but not close enough to suit him.

The silken glide of her tongue taunted him, teased him, dared him to deepen the kiss. He willingly obliged, slanting his mouth over hers and stealing inside to take all she offered. She tasted sweeter than he'd imagined. And minty, he thought. Like fresh peppermint taffy.

Moving his hands to the swell of her hips, he urged her

off the chair and into his arms. She pressed against him, her beaded nipples brushing temptingly against his chest through the thin material of her blouse. He skimmed his hand up her side and along her rib cage to cup the side of her breast with his palm. She issued a soft moan and pulled her arms from around his neck. For a brief instant he thought he'd taken things too far—until the coolness of her fingers interlaced with his and she guided his hand over her breast.

His dick swelled to the point of pain and throbbed. Need ripped through him. He didn't give a damn if she was appointed the next director of the Bureau, he wanted her, preferably naked and beneath him with her legs wrapped tight around his waist.

He dragged his thumb over her nipple, and slid his other hand over her bottom. She moaned into his mouth and her fingers flexed over his. Maybe she liked it on top where she called the shots and set the pace. He imagined her above him, the enticing sway of her breasts as she rode him. Slow. Easy, taking him deep inside her tight, hot sheath until the pressure built and her body demanded more. Harder. Faster, driving toward fulfillment with each thrust of their bodies until they came together in an explosion of heat.

She guided his hand from her breast, over her flat stomach and lower, sighing into his mouth when he cupped her sex. She tested his control when she rocked against his hand.

A loud rap on the door sent them scurrying in opposite directions. Duncan dragged his hand through his hair and watched Sunny walk unsteadily to the far side of his office. Her shoulders rose and fell as she drew in a deep breath then let it out slowly. When she slipped a bouncy curl behind her ears her hand trembled.

He took comfort in the fact she was obviously as rattled as he by the unexpected passion of that kiss. The past few months he'd been too swamped with work to pay much attention to anything not related to business. The explosion of heat between them reminded him that he hadn't gotten laid in weeks, nothing more.

Another loud knock saved him from having to think too much on the subject. He went to the door and opened it to find Lucy Barstow, the agency's office manager, giving him one of her cast-iron glares over the rim of her bifocals.

He blocked the door, but that didn't stop her from craning her neck to get a better look. "Yeah?" Somehow he managed to maintain a civil tone. "What is it?"

"We have a situation." Lucy handed him a neon-yellow sticky note. "Abe from Able Pawn just called. He acquired a sizeable diamond engagement ring last week that showed up on the regional hot sheet that went out today. He's giving you twenty minutes to see if it's one of ours before he has to call it in to the Baltimore P.D."

Despite the interruption, a slow smile spread across his face. Hot merchandise often showed up in pawn shops. By law, the owners were supposed to notify the cops when they inadvertently received stolen goods, which the cops would then confiscate. Since the brokers would be out the cash they'd paid for the pawn, as a result, they were only too happy to line their pockets with the finder's fee Duncan paid them if the property turned out to be an item he'd been hired to recover.

In Duncan's opinion, it was a win-win situation. The client paid a recovery fee, not a full-loss claim and the claimant's property was returned. The brokers were happy because they recouped a fraction of an otherwise total loss. The system wasn't perfect and pushed the spirit of the law, but when all concerned were pleased with the final outcome, he didn't see a problem.

Duncan checked his watch. "Call Abe back and tell him I'll be there within the hour. And have Marisa track down the Burbank and Ricci files."

"What about Locke?" she asked, jotting down his instructions. "It's a three-carat rock, and Abe did say he had a big one."

"Pull the file," he said. "I'll just be a minute."

Lucy rose up on her toes, trying to get a peek inside his office. "Anything else you need? Bail money? A lawyer?" She lowered her bifocals. "A cold shower?"

Lucy had been in his employ from day one and knew as much, if not more, than he did about the agency, the cases they handled, the people he employed and even himself. He couldn't begin to imagine how the agency would ever get along without her. At the moment, however, the concept suddenly had merit.

"Just get me those files," he told her. "I can handle the rest."

She made a "harumph" sound, clearly indicating her opinion on the subject. With one last glance, she strode down the hall calling for Marisa, his administrative assistant.

Duncan closed the door and turned back to Sunny. "Sorry about that," he said.

Uncertainty clouded her eyes when she faced him. "I better go." She made no move to leave.

He snagged the tie he'd removed earlier from the hook on the back of the door. "How's seven sound for dinner?"

She glanced nervously around the office. "Good," she said, not looking at him. She cleared her throat. "Uh, where should I meet you?"

He would've preferred to pick her up himself, but he understood and respected her caution. Despite the hot kiss that still had his blood simmering, she knew very little about him. But that didn't mean she couldn't follow him back to his place after dinner, he thought hopefully.

Finished with his tie, he jotted the name of a casual restaurant close to his apartment on a piece of paper and handed it to her. "See you at seven." He considered the wisdom of one last kiss. One final taste of sweet peppermint and hot passion.

She folded the note and slipped it inside her pocket. "I'll see you then."

He circled the desk. The door swung open and Lucy stormed in with one of the files he'd requested. "Here," she said, thrusting the file in his direction. "The rest is somewhere in this mess."

"I'll find my way out," Sunny said, then disappeared down the hall.

He turned to glare at Lucy. "Whatever happened to knocking?" Duncan complained. Her interruption— again—annoyed the hell out of him. So much for testing the wisdom of one last kiss.

Lucy planted her thick hands on her wide hips and scowled at him. "Whatever happened to discretion? Playing footsie in the office? With a Fibbie?"

He didn't question how Lucy knew what he and Sunny had been up to behind closed doors. Nothing ever went on within the walls of the tenth-floor office suite that she didn't know about—his personal life included. "Not that it's any of your concern, but what's the big deal?"

"If it concerns this office, it concerns me." She looked pointedly at the mountain of work scattered around his office. "What you need to be playing with, are these open cases."

He let out a sigh. "Point taken." He joined her in the search for the files he needed for his meeting, but his thoughts remained centered on sweet peppermint and hot, wet kisses.

5

LUCK. DUNCAN NEVER put much stock in the concept. He didn't buy into misfortune or the half-baked theory of an all-powerful, mystical puppet master pulling the imaginary strings of humanity to satisfy its whims. Hard work met with reward, and ensuring that reward entailed paying close attention to detail, occasionally tweaking a rule or two when necessary and having the ability to persuade others to see his way was the *only* way.

Contrarily, if a man was ill-prepared or ill-equipped in the determination department, opportunities were often missed. He wasn't so arrogant to believe he held absolute control over every aspect of his universe, although he did his best to disprove the theory whenever possible. If he made an error in judgment, then he promptly set out to rectify the problem by compensating for his gaffe and acting accordingly to bring about the positive outcome he sought.

When it came to mistakes, he'd made plenty. Odds were he'd make a few more, too. He was wise enough to appreciate the value of hindsight in providing him with the vision to dissect a problem. Most were traced back to poor judgment on his part, which in his opinion, stemmed from plain lack of preparation.

Regardless of his beliefs, the occasional opportunity still managed to land in his lap through little or no extra effort on his part. While he'd been focusing his attention on cultivating his "in" with the Bureau, which could result in some highly impressive recovery fees, he'd unexpectedly recovered a three-point-four-carat diamond engagement ring. The payout itself wouldn't set any agency records, but with almost zero effort and a nominal reimbursement paid to one of his contacts in the pawn industry, he'd managed to impress a new client. The rep had been so pleased he'd promised to courier over three new assignments next week—along with a check for locating the missing rock.

All in all, not a bad day's work. He'd asked the pawn dealer to keep his antennae raised for rumors about a fresh cache of hot gems. Not that Duncan seriously expected the jewelry collection stolen from Margo Wilder to show up locally, but in his experience, someone always knew someone who had heard that someone else had seen….

A lead, no matter how obscure, was still a lead in his business. Since he'd offered a minute percentage of the take he'd collect on Wilder, he hoped to have a viable tip to chase down within the next forty-eight to seventy-two hours minimum.

A movement near the door caught his attention. Marisa poked her head into his office. "You wanted to see me?"

He waved her inside. "How are those files coming along?" Before leaving for Able Pawn, he'd asked Marisa to locate and copy the Dearborn and Garfield files for Sunny. He'd debated the wisdom of presenting them to her at dinner tonight, and had concluded it'd be best not to mix business with what he hoped would be a very pleasurable experience.

"The property photos are scanned and printed, but I'll have to send out for the copying of the case files." She smoothed her hand down her summery dress and gave him an apologetic smile. "The copier crapped out again. For good this time."

Duncan's grin faded. "Are you sure?" Considering most of the equipment in the office had been used or reconditioned, he'd known the need for replacements was imminent, but the copier was the third mechanical disaster this month. One Lucy would no doubt tell him they couldn't afford to replace.

Marisa nodded. "Sparks. Black smoke. A fatality. It needs an undertaker, not a tech."

He let out a sigh. "I'll have Lucy order a new one."

"If you don't need anything else," Marisa said, "I'm outtie."

"Outtie? Been hanging out at the mall on your lunch hour again, haven't you?" he teased her. She'd probably been holed up in the conference room with a tuna sandwich and a textbook, as had been her habit for as long she'd worked for him.

She laughed. "Not quite." Her wide smile reminded him suddenly of Sunny. Bright, cheerful, sans the accompanying caution usually lining Sunny's gaze.

"You should get out more," he said, but his mind was already focusing on the possibilities of his dinner date with Sunny. The *after*-dinner possibilities specifically.

"I plan to," Marisa said, reaching for the overflowing stack of files threatening to fall off his desk and pushed them back in place. "I'm finished with class until fall, so I promised my girls we'd do more together this summer. It's movie night."

According to Lucy, who made it her business to know every intimate detail of the lives of the people he employed, Marisa's existence revolved around her two young daughters. No husband, though, if he remembered correctly. The bum had skipped out during Marisa's second pregnancy, leaving her to raise her kids alone.

"Go. Get out of here," he told her. "If anything comes up in the next twenty minutes, I'll bully Lucy into handling it."

"Yeah, right. Good luck," she said with a chuckle, and walked to the door.

"Marisa," he called before she disappeared. "Any word from Colin?" Last week he'd spoken to his little brother about slowing down on generating new business until Duncan wrestled his current workload into submission. No one had seen or heard from Colin since. Duncan had thought about calling his mom, but if Colin had returned to his old habits, he didn't want to upset her.

This wasn't Colin's first disappearing act, but it was the first since they'd gone into business together, and Duncan worried. From the day Duncan had approached his brother with the idea of being partners, the kid had miraculously cleaned up and had stayed that way. Working with Colin had been a gamble with high stakes, and Duncan had known going in his plan could fail. His hope had been if his brother had a purpose, then maybe he'd steer clear of the booze, drugs, gambling or some other new vice or obsession.

Thankfully, the gamble had paid off. Colin's handling of what he'd jokingly referred to as the corporate ass-kissing end of the business had been flawless, to the point where Duncan had accumulated more work than he could possibly handle alone. Rick Yeager, a college student who worked for them part-time, pretty much single-handedly covered the jobs for their law firm clients and had mentioned to Duncan recently even he had more work than his scheduled allowed. Asking Colin to cut back until Duncan could get through some of their present cases had been a necessity, but may have been one more error in judgment. He hadn't anticipated the lack of activity would make Colin slip off the deep end again after all this time.

"No," Marisa told him. "I haven't. Not since he took off around noon last Friday. There's a new business proposal presentation day after tomorrow on his calendar, too. Do you want me to reschedule, or will you cover it?"

He looked at Marisa and an idea took hold. According to the balance sheets the past couple of months, he couldn't afford to hire another recovery expert. If Colin had indeed gone off on another bender, someone had to take care of the clients. "Why don't you handle it?"

Her eyes widened in surprise. "Me? Are you serious?"

"Why not?" The hopeful note in her voice made him smile. "No reason why you shouldn't start putting that education to use."

Marisa had been taking night courses while working full-time for him as a glorified secretary and raising her two young daughters on her own. She'd already been over-qualified when he'd hired her, but now more than halfway into earning her business degree, he figured if he didn't eventually offer her a more challenging position she'd be moving on to a bigger and better paying job. With Colin M.I.A. five days already, he couldn't help but fear the worst. Covering his bases was the best option.

"Besides," he added, "you know the drill. Probably better than I do." She should, since she prepped the presentations in the first place and had assumed the responsibility of writing the quarterly status reports on open files to their insurance-carrier clients since he'd fallen so far behind.

"All right," she said carefully, slowly nodding her head in agreement. "If Colin is a no show, I'll do it."

"No," he said, his tone firm. "You take the meeting." He

didn't bother to explain his faith in her far exceeded what he held at the moment for his brother. "Whether Colin's here or not, this one is yours."

"You won't be sorry."

"I know I won't," he told her. "Now get out of here. Go have fun for a change."

Once alone, he picked up the phone and dialed his brother's apartment. The answering machine picked up on the fourth ring, and Duncan left another message. He tried Colin's cell next, only to be informed by an annoying computerized voice the mailbox was full before disconnecting him.

Irritation mingled with his concern for his brother's welfare. He'd just have to stop by Colin's apartment before meeting Sunny for dinner. Depending on what he found at Colin's, he may end up having to cancel.

His mood dramatically soured at the prospect, he left his office and took off down the corridor to speak to Lucy about the demise and replacement of another expensive piece of equipment. Not even the thought of Sunny and the memory of her lust-filled green eyes, an image that would remain embedded in his mind for a good long while, improved his mood.

What good was all that chemistry if he had to cancel a date at the last minute? The sparks they'd been setting off at the Wilder estate hadn't been a fluke and, dammit, he wanted to see her again—even if his motives were marginally questionable.

During his tenure with the Bureau he'd tweaked, twisted and ignored more than a few rules and regulations, but until today, he'd never consciously compromised another agent's integrity. The partial truth of his answers had apparently satisfied her, at least temporarily. If he didn't raise suspicion, then she'd have no reason to doubt he'd been anything but completely honest with her, and he planned to keep it that way. She had access to information which could lead him to the property stolen from Wilder, Garfield and Dearborn. If the Bureau put its hands on the stolen merchandise before he did, it could take months before he'd see the recovery fees. And if she learned his service with the Bureau had ended for failure to follow a direct order that had nearly cost another agent his life, he could kiss her cooperation, along with any hope of taking all that chemistry between them out for a spin, goodbye.

He rapped on the side of Lucy's cubicle so as not to startle her. "Marisa tells me the copier's as good as dead."

Lucy glanced up from her computer monitor to look up at him. "I'm not surprised. That monster has been a swift kick away from the junkyard for months." She reached for a silver travel mug that never left her side and took a drink of the contents. "If you took the time to read my memos, you'd have known it's been dying a slow, painful death for a while now."

He ignored the reminder. Lucy always told him the information contained in her daily memos anyway; the woman had an affinity for paper trails. "And you didn't call for repair because…?"

"Because we couldn't afford the luxury of renewing the service agreement." She gave him one of her hard stares over the gold rim of her bifocals. "If you don't close some of the files we have open around here, paychecks will soon be a luxury."

He walked into her cubicle and sat on the edge of the lateral file cabinet she used as a credenza. "Monument Insurance is sending over a check just as soon as I drop off the ring I picked up from Abe today," he told her. "With three new cases."

"Like we need more work." She made a sniffing noise. "And that scrawny fee won't even cover last month's electric bill."

"What about Ellington Casualty?" he asked, but he had a good idea of the answer. "I recovered property for two of their claimants last month."

"Slow. Could be at least another five to six weeks before we see a check." She clasped the silver mug between her stubby fingers. "If we're lucky."

"Call their accounts payable people and lean on them," he told her.

She made a note on the legal pad at her elbow.

"What about District Insurance?" He'd personally located the antique coin collection with an insured value of a few hundred grand that had been ripped off by the claimant's own grandson. The weasel had stupidly bartered the collection for a lousy kilo of pot. Their standard fee of twenty percent of the insured value should've generated some decent revenue. "Or the Langley and Joel files? Those claims alone should've covered operating expenses for the next ninety days or more."

Lucy took another drink before answering. "More like the *last* ninety days. Those funds were spent long before the money even made it into the bank."

He knew the balance sheets had been pathetically thin the past couple of months, but he hadn't realized exactly how thin. "That bad?"

Her hazel eyes filled with worry, and she nodded. "As of this afternoon, we have a grand total of two hundred and seventy-three unresolved recoveries. I know it's none of my business—"

"As if that makes a difference."

"As I was saying…couldn't Colin handle the smaller

cases? Rick has hinted he's capable of more, but he's spending every minute he's on the clock out serving subpoenas." She let out a gusty sigh. "Duncan, this is serious. You have to do something. If we don't start generating more revenue, you'll have to lay off support staff. Selfish or not, I'm in no mood to look for another job at my age."

Duncan frowned. The thought of pink slipping any of the staff had him helping himself to the jar of antacids on Lucy's desk.

Her expression remained grim, telling him all he needed to know. In the three years since they'd started the agency after being booted out of the Bureau, he'd weathered a few financial pitfalls, but never to the point where layoffs were a likelihood. "Lucy?" he prompted.

Her reply was a long, slow release of breath along with a skeptical lift of her peppered eyebrows. They were in it deep this time. He owned the burden. People depended on him and he'd do whatever was necessary to take care of business. Wasn't that what he always did?

He scrubbed his hand over his face and let out a sigh. "How much do you need to cover payroll and expenses for the next two months?"

Lucy's eyebrows rose another notch. "What are you going to do? Write a check?"

"Do you have a better suggestion?"

"Hire someone to help out, even if it's on a temporary basis."

"And what do we pay him with? IOUs? How much do you need to get us through the next two months?" he asked her again.

She shut down her computer, then pushed her chair back to drag a big canvas bag from beneath her desk. She dropped it on the laminated oak top with a loud thud. "Give me a couple of days to crunch numbers. I'll have something on your desk by Friday."

He nodded, then left Lucy to stroll through the office, checking to make sure all the equipment was shut down for the night. When he returned to the outer office area, Lucy was waiting for him. She swung her bag over her shoulder, the contents rattling and slamming around inside.

She waited while he locked up the office, then they walked together toward the elevators that would take them to the parking garage. "Do you want me to get the copier fixed?" she asked, punching the button to the call the elevator car.

"Order a new one. And whatever else is about to take a dump around here. We can't afford to lose a minute of production time."

"And how do you think we're going to pay for these new toys?"

He gave her one of his most charming smiles. She frowned.

"Don't worry about it," he told her. He'd cover the additional expense himself.

"You pay me to worry," she reminded him for the second time that day and stepped into the elevator. "So you wanna tell me what an FBI agent was doing snooping around the office today?"

"Not especially." He thought about what he and Sunny had been doing in his office earlier that afternoon and grinned.

She gave him a pointed glance. "Exactly what is going on, Duncan? I thought those FBI types gave you hives."

"You're exaggerating," he said. His only itch at the moment was one he had for Sunny.

They reached the fourth floor of the parking garage

and he followed Lucy out of the elevator. "Well?" she prompted.

"The Bureau has jurisdiction on Wilder."

Her gaze held genuine interest. "This sounds interesting." Code for *tell me more.*

"Dearborn and Garfield could be connected to Wilder, but that hasn't been confirmed." Maybe if he hadn't been tempted beyond belief to kiss Sunny he would've remembered to ask her about the case. "CID is involved, though."

Lucy remained thoughtful for a moment then shrugged her bulky shoulders. "BFD. NYP."

He stopped and looked down at her. "What the hell are you talking about?"

"Lost your decoder ring again, didn't you?" She chuckled. "Big freakin' deal," she explained. "Not your problem."

"It is if I can put a stop to this bastard."

"Since when is that *your* problem?" she asked, her tone stern. "You find stolen goods insured for large sums of money. Period. *That's* your job. Not taking down bad guys. Not anymore."

Irritation climbed up his spine and settled in his neck, making the muscles tighten with tension. He rubbed at the spot, but the pressure refused to ebb. She was right, but what bothered him more was that he hadn't even realized what he'd said until she'd pointed out his mistake.

"Don't you have small children to torture?" he groused.

"Not at the moment, no. Don't you lose sight of what's important. We could operate for a good twelve to eighteen months easy on the recovery fees from Garfield, Dearborn and Wilder alone. I'm not the expert here, but I do know you've never had to track down any individual first before you locate the stolen property."

"Maybe," he conceded reluctantly, although he refused to state with any degree of certainty that he agreed with Lucy in this instance. So far he hadn't managed to cull a single lead on Garfield or Dearborn. Only one person knew the whereabouts of the stolen goods, and that was Sunny's UNSUB. "Or maybe not."

She opened the car door and swung her purse onto the seat. "If the Feds are involved, don't think they'll be welcoming you with open arms," She reminded him. "You aren't exactly on their Christmas card list."

"What they don't know—"

"They'll eventually find out."

Her habit of shooting straight from the hip with brutal honesty was starting to really irritate him. Just once he wished she'd keep her opinions to herself. Especially since they conflicted with his.

Lucy climbed into her car and started the engine. "That little girl agent you were tickling tonsils with today might be blond, but she didn't look like a dumb blonde to me. What's she going to say when she finds out?"

"She already knows." *Sort of.*

He shrugged off Lucy's concerns with a dismissing wave as she drove off, but not before she cast one last skeptical glance in his direction. What could the Bureau do to him anyway? He'd already paid their asking price for failing to follow a direct order when they'd stripped him of his credentials, not to mention the bum shoulder and left hand that both ached like hell in damp weather. He had nothing to lose as far as the Bureau was concerned.

Except maybe the chance to have Sunny MacGregor in his bed.

6

SUNNY SMOOTHED a wrinkle from the satin jacquard comforter. A few more fluffs to the matching shams and one final adjustment to the array of lace and satin accent pillows she'd found on sale, and she was finished. Taking several steps backward, she attempted to view the new, less-feminine look of her bed with a man's perspective in mind. "What do you think? Too froufrou for a guy?"

Georgia folded the large plastic storage bag the comforter set had come in and set it on the padded chintz bench at the foot of the queen-size bed. "This is why you sent me to the courthouse for the SEDSCAM search warrants? So you could sneak off to purchase masculine-sensitive bedding?"

"The cabbage roses were too girly," Sunny argued. "I couldn't picture him in all that pink."

"When exactly were you fantasizing about this guy all tangled up in turquoise satin? Was it before you banned him from the Wilder estate, or did you wait until after you confiscated his files? That part is still a little fuzzy."

Sunny gave Georgia a wry glance. "Very funny. And the color is muted teal."

She'd missed lunch, so after leaving Duncan's office, she'd made a quick stop for a bite to eat at one of her favorite delis and had spied the discount linen store across the street. While she'd been cruising the aisles, she'd received a call from Georgia on her cell phone. The warrants were signed but the clerk was leaving early. Unless they wanted to wait until noon the following day, they'd have to be picked up immediately. Sunny knew she'd never make it across town in time, so Georgia had offered to handle it and bring the warrants by Sunny's place.

She still couldn't believe she'd allowed herself to get so completely distracted that she hadn't obtained a single scrap of information from Duncan. Once the issue of his termination from the Bureau had been resolved, she should've questioned him about the additional files he'd mentioned, asked him the names of the claimants or, at a minimum, the locations which might help establish a pattern to the UNSUB's path of seduction. Apparently, the only seduction she'd been interested in involved Duncan.

Georgia sat on the bench and crossed her long legs. "If you're meeting Duncan at the restaurant, then why go to all this trouble?" she asked, indicating the bed behind her with a hitch of her thumb. "It's not like he's going to be seeing the inside of your bedroom anytime soon."

Sunny tightened the sash of her robe. "I could invite him here afterward," she said a tad too defensively.

"You?" Georgia shook her head and chuckled softly. "I don't think so." Her eyes filled with a wealth of understanding. "When it comes to men, you play it safe."

Although they'd only been friends for a few short months, Georgia did know her well. As a rule, Sunny *did* proceed with an abundance of caution when it came to the opposite sex. No wonder her affairs were so few and far between—she practically demanded security clearance.

Except there'd been nothing "safe" about the way she'd kissed Duncan. She'd left little room for doubt in his mind exactly how much she'd wanted him. Short of tearing off his clothes right then and there, she didn't think she could've been more daring.

Or foolish.

She knew what could happen to a woman if she failed to take precautions in regard to her own safety. The consequences could be deadly. Because of their total disregard for their own safety, she also understood she may never be able to relate to The Seducer's victims.

Just because she never rode in a vehicle with someone she didn't know didn't mean she was mistrustful, only sensible. So what if she kept her phone number unlisted and her monthly bills came addressed to S. R. MacGregor? She was careful, not fearful.

When she'd purchased her condo six months ago in the newly built, ten-story complex, she'd chosen a unit on the fourth floor rather than one on the first as a deterrent to would-be intruders. Instead of hiring a locksmith, she'd asked her dad to install extra security locks to her windows and the sliding glass door leading to her balcony. She'd insisted the building manager replace the single lock on the front door with two heavy duty deadbolts and a security bar. Because she wrote a check each month for the additional protection of a home security system which alerted the authorities in the event of an emergency situation didn't mean she was paranoid, only prudent.

"You wouldn't know it by my behavior this afternoon," she admitted to Georgia. "I was a regular shameless hussy."

"Oh, please," Georgia laughed. "Hussies went out of fashion two centuries ago. If you're attracted to a man, there isn't a damn thing wrong in letting him know it."

"I'm sure I left no room for doubt in his mind," she said and walked to the closet. Maybe accepting a date with Duncan pushed the limits of professionalism, but she couldn't ignore the attraction between them, either. "Help me find something to wear that'll bring him to his knees. Just to alleviate any lingering confusion he might have."

Sunny threw open the double doors and stared in dismay at her pathetically dull wardrobe consisting of tan, navy or black skirt and pantsuits in seasonal-friendly fabrics. Wools and heavy polyester blends for fall and winter, cotton and linen for spring and summer. Her selection of tops, blouses and sweaters were equally innocuous. White, ivory, navy and black in either silk, cotton or linen.

Georgia appeared beside her. "Good grief," she said scanning the contents. "Talk about Bureau Drab."

Sunny let out a sigh. Not a knee-driving garment to be had. "This is bad, isn't it?"

"Color," Georgia said slowly. "Repeat after me. Color."

"And when was the last time you wore a red suit to work?"

Georgia ignored the rhetorical question and stepped into the walk-in closet. "Your wardrobe is in serious crisis." She fingered several blouses hanging from the top wardrobe bar. "Next week we're going shopping, and don't even think to argue with me. At the very least we'll pick out a couple of things that aren't so painfully..."

"Conservative?" Sunny offered hopefully.

"Boring."

Sunny wrinkled her nose. "I hate shopping."

"So I gathered," Georgia said dryly. "All right." She rubbed her hands together. "Where are you meeting him?"

"Toucan Sam's in Georgetown. Do you know it?"

Georgia nodded. "Good food. And lucky for you, a casual atmosphere."

"Thank God for small favors," Sunny muttered as Georgia started plucking hangers from the wardrobe bar and handing them to Sunny.

Taking her minimal wardrobe choices into account, thirty minutes later Sunny admitted to being pleasantly surprised with the final outcome. Denim was always her favorite choice, and the button-fly carpenter jeans were not only comfortable, but flattering. Georgia had unearthed a sleeveless cream-colored silk shell with a deep scoop neckline that still had the store tags attached, and a wide, black vintage leather belt Sunny had forgotten she'd even owned.

She'd followed her stylist's instructions on drying her permed hair for maximum volume, and with style-savvy Georgia's assistance, the tight, springy curls were swept away from her face in soft, gentle waves of artful disarray. In addition to her standard, conservative berry lipstick, she'd added a layer of shimmering gloss, then selected gold chandelier earrings for an even bolder look.

Tossing the tube of lengthening mascara into her makeup drawer, she looked in the mirror and hardly recognized herself. She looked like…a woman who didn't know the meaning of caution.

Georgia emerged from the closet as Sunny walked back into the bedroom. "These," Georgia said, holding up a pair of black leather sandals for Sunny's inspection, "say comfortable, easy to be with, good for a few laughs. Coy, but promising." She dumped the sandals on the floor and held up a pair of black four-inch heels that had been sitting in the closet for months. "These say sex. Red would scream multiple orgasm, but we don't have a lot to work with here. Definitely more blatant than subtle, so there's hope."

Sunny didn't hesitate. "We're way beyond coy," she said, snatching the pumps from Georgia. She'd initially regretted giving in to the impulse to buy the shoes. They'd been an impractical extravagance, but now she was grateful she had them.

She sat on the edge of the bench and slipped her feet into the shoes. "Since I possessed the subtlety of a bulldozer this afternoon, blatant is the least hypocritical."

Was her attraction to Duncan a whim? she wondered suddenly. Or were there other factors at work she had yet to determine and categorize? She did question whether becoming involved with him was a good idea, but her concerns were more personal than professional. There were no substantial conflict of interest issues. Even his being a former agent posed no problem professionally since he hadn't been relieved of duty for cause or illegal activity. The Bureau had strict rules of conduct, and associating with criminals was out of the question.

But what about her heart if their mutual attraction drifted into deeper, more emotional territory? She knew from past experience her job would eventually become an issue. She worked long, sometimes odd hours and was often called away in the middle of the night. Depending on the case she was investigating, she might be required to travel with little or no notice. All of which put strain on a relationship.

Duncan had been an undercover operative so chances were he'd be more understanding than most in that regard, but could he handle the knowledge her life could be on the line? She might be assigned to the nonviolent criminal unit now where the risks were minimal, but how would he react once the danger dramatically increased if she transferred to ISU? Hunting down a sociopath capable of unspeakable horrors was a world away from chasing after a seducing scam artist.

She looked up at Georgia. "What am I doing?"

Her friend propped her shoulder against the doorjamb. "Uh-oh. What's wrong?"

Anxiety made breathing a concentrated effort. "I only met him this morning, and already I'm wildly attracted to him. Look." She held up her trembling hand. "What is this?"

Georgia lifted a slim shoulder in a partial shrug. "Adrenaline," she said. "You're hyped about seeing him. It's normal, Mac. It happens."

Not to her it didn't. She never rushed into relationships, and had once dated a guy three times before she'd had even a conscious thought about kissing him. With Duncan, she'd been counting the minutes until she could taste him again.

"He's a world-class kisser, incredibly good-looking, not to mention sexy," she said, justifying his attributes by ticking them off on her fingers. "Intelligent. His employees are certainly protective of him. A man doesn't inspire that kind of loyalty in people because he's a jerk."

Georgia's russet eyebrows pulled together in a frown. "And this is a problem?"

Sunny caught her bottom lip between her teeth. "I like him, Georgia," she said quietly. Her heart pounded so hard she feared it would burst right out of her chest. "He's the kind of guy…"

Understanding instantly lit the other woman's gaze. "That you could fall for," she finished wisely.

Sunny lifted her trembling hands in a gesture of self-defeat. "Don't start. I know what you're going to say." She stood, made an adjustment to the wide leather belt at her waist and stalked out of the bedroom. If she didn't leave now, she might chicken out and she hadn't spent a fortune on a new comforter set, pillows and a luxurious set of Pima cotton sheets because she'd planned to sleep in them alone.

Sunny waited for Georgia to join her in the ceramic-tiled foyer. "You're going to say, stop being an idiot, Mac," she said. She snagged her small black hobo bag from the table in the entryway and dug out her keys. "Take a chill pill, girlfriend. It's a date, not a commitment. Right?"

"Right," Georgia said.

Sunny gave a brisk nod of agreement. "Relax. Go with the flow." She turned on the lamp and engaged the alarm.

"Exactly," Georgia said, opening the door and stepping out into the corridor.

"And don't get bogged down in all the emotional crap," Sunny continued to rant as she locked the door. "Have fun for a change. Get loose. Get a grip. Get your money's worth out of all that…what did you call it?"

"Masculine-sensitive bedding?"

"Right. Put that masculine-sensitive bedding to good use."

"Oh, *absolutely*."

"Excellent advice, Georgia," Sunny said when they reached the elevator. Feeling somewhat calmer, she smiled. "I'd have to be a fool not to listen to you."

"I don't hand out all my best advice to just anyone, you know. Don't waste it."

Together they laughed and stepped into the elevator. By the time they reached the lobby, Sunny's anxiety was nearly nonexistent. Her excitement over spending an evening with Duncan, however, remained as strong as ever.

WITH THE HEAT index pushing into the triple digits, Glen Specht could think of much more pleasant locations to hole up in than a run-down apartment building on Chicago's South Side. Other cities where the air was cooler, cleaner and less thick with humidity. More aesthetically pleasing locales like the West Coast. Not a wise choice, considering he was wanted in Washington, Oregon and California. He was also wanted in Idaho, Colorado, Nevada, New Mexico and at least a half-dozen more states, as well.

No, he amended. Marcus Wood, Archibald Willoughby, Travis Reisner and the others were wanted. Glen Specht remained a nonentity, a nobody. Just as he'd planned.

Maybe he should've stayed on the east coast. Connecticut and Vermont had held a wealth of possibilities.

His lips almost twitched at the pun.

The microwave dinged, drawing him out of his brief moment of longing for more comfortable accommodations. Taking care not to scald his fingers, he set the plastic container of fried chicken, whipped potatoes and a sorry excuse for corn, which looked more gray than yellow, on the fake wood-grain serving tray.

He slowly peeled back the plastic film covering and watched the steam rise. Chicago boasted many a fine restaurant he could've enjoyed, but he chose to take his meals in the solitude of the furnished apartment rather than risk being seen in public too soon. Timing was everything in his line of work. He'd come too far to blow his chances because he'd developed a taste for the finer things that were becoming more and more difficult to ignore.

He tossed the filmy covering into the garbage can he kept under the sink. A trio of fat brown cockroaches scurried away, escaping the harsh glare cast over their hideaway from the single exposed lightbulb hanging by a rusted chain overhead. Other than an impatient press of his lips, he ignored the filthy creatures. He detested bugs, but his iron self-control, a skill he'd developed into an instrument of perfection, would never allow him to show a shred of weakness.

More than bugs, he detested weakness of any kind, yet he made his living exploiting the very thing he despised. The irony *almost* made him smile.

He poured himself a glass of iced tea, added the plastic

convenience store tumbler to the tray along with a paper plate of sliced tomatoes heaped with mayonnaise. Using care, he took his meal into the living room with its ratty used furniture and smoke-stained walls.

The furnished third-floor walk-up barely ranked above tenement standards, but other than the cockroaches he studiously ignored, the living arrangements currently suited his purpose. No one bothered him here. In the carefully selected neighborhoods where he chose to hide while prepping for his next job, what few residents he did come into contact with weren't the type to look a man in the eye. If questioned, they'd never remember him. He was afforded a sense of freedom without the threat of some pain-in-the-ass good Samaritan fingering him.

Not that he worried. Like a chameleon, he'd mastered the ability to fit in with his surroundings. Yet another skill that had served him well.

He sat in the threadbare recliner and positioned the tray in front of him. With the small color television he'd picked up from one of the many pawn shops he'd scoped out that morning, he tuned into the local news station. He turned up the television to drown out the sounds of the neighborhood, and listened as the news anchor set up the clip of a boating accident on Lake Michigan involving three teenagers earlier that day.

"So tragic," he murmured with feigned sympathy.

By the time the newscast ended, he'd finished his unimpressive meal and set the tray aside in favor of the thick manila envelope containing his evening's work. Slowly, he unfolded the newspaper clippings and placed them on the peeling surface of the walnut-veneer coffee table. Photographs, maps and a small spiral-bound notebook of handwritten notes followed, each item meticulously organized for the sole purpose of studying and memorizing every last detail of the mark.

Her name was Hope Templeton, the bereaved twenty-six-year-old widow of Darrin Templeton. He studied the pixel-blurred photograph of the lovely Mrs. Templeton on her wedding day. The voluptuous blonde smiled up at her new husband, the hint of a smirk on her full pink-frost-tinted lips.

Glen actually frowned as he stared at the photo. The former secretary turned trophy wife wasn't quite the classic bereaved widow, nor as emotionally vulnerable as he preferred his marks. The concern gave him a moment's pause. Had the young widow pulled off one of the oldest sweetheart scams around? Had she used her lush body to lure Templeton away from his wife of twenty years simply for his money? Perhaps Hope Bremer Templeton, formerly of Petal, Mississippi, wasn't his perfect pigeon, after all.

He drew the photograph closer. The Harry Winston diamond wreath clasped around the widow's neck made his decision all the more difficult. Valued in the millions, even at twenty-five cents on the dollar, the piece could garner a nice sum. Provided he could unload the necklace, of course. Even with his wide network of contacts, one-of-a-kind items were tougher to fence because they tended to draw unwanted attention.

He shifted his focus to the deceased. The Chicago lawyer had amassed a fortune suing corporate America on behalf of his clients. Drug companies, the big three automakers, sports equipment manufacturers and even a major school bus company had paid in the billions for their mistakes.

Templeton wasn't an unattractive man. Maybe the young widow had married for love. He didn't question

Templeton's motives, as they were obvious. Hope had been his young, beautiful trophy wife. "Ditch the bitch that helped you rise for the one that keeps it up."

He let out a sigh and returned the clipping to the table, picking up the notebook next. Settling back in the chair, he opened to the first page and began studying his notes. No detail about the mark was too small. In his opinion, his attention to detail marked the cornerstone of his success. He knew more about Hope's life than he suspected her dead husband ever had.

Two hours later, he'd committed every last detail to memory for the final time. He was ready.

Carrying the documents into the bathroom, he tossed them in the stained cast-iron bathtub and soaked them in lighter fluid. He struck a match, and the pungent tang of sulfur filled his nostrils. He dropped the lit match on the soaked documents and waited for the evidence to go up in flames.

When only black ashes remained, he washed the traces down the drain, not caring that portions of the institutional green-tiled walls of the tub enclosure were now blackened in places with soot. Tomorrow he would be gone from this hellhole, and Glen Specht would once again cease to exist…until Peter Seville swept Hope Templeton off her little feet and seduced her for all she was worth.

7

DUNCAN KNOCKED on the door to Colin's apartment. When his brother didn't immediately answer, he rang the bell. Twice.

Silence.

His concern climbed, along with his annoyance. He pounded on the door, harder this time, then rolled his shoulder to ease the discomfort. Muscle and bone protested the movement. Familiar pain sliced through him.

For a guy who prided himself on attention to detail, he was doing a good job of proving himself a sorry example. Case in point; forgetting to run by the drugstore for more ibuprofen when he knew the bottle he kept in the glove box of his SUV had been empty for a week. He wasn't one to make excuses, but busy didn't begin to describe his schedule of late.

He rang the bell again. Colin would have a selection of pain meds around the house. Preferably of the legal variety. Duncan loved his brother and thought he'd done a decent job of being supportive throughout the years, but pulling a disappearing act now, after all this time, pushed the limit on Duncan's patience. He didn't have time for Colin's crap, no matter how much he understood the demons that haunted his brother. What he did need was for Colin to get back on the wagon, stay clean or get the hell over whatever obsession currently ruled him.

Lucy had warned him weeks ago they were taking on too many new clients. Again, he hadn't paid attention. He blew off her concern and chose to concentrate on the fact that Colin's interest in the business had kept him out of, and away from, trouble. If he'd stepped back and looked more closely at the whole picture, he might've realized sooner that Colin's overwhelming success generating new business was yet another version of overkill, albeit less self-destructive than in the past.

To Duncan's knowledge, Colin hadn't had a drink in months, nor had he snorted, smoked, popped or free-based anything illegal. There'd been no late-night phone calls from his brother being stitched up in some emergency room because a couple of goons had beaten him to a pulp over unpaid gambling debts. In Duncan's book, that had spelled progress.

He blamed himself for sending Colin over the edge this time. If he hadn't been so wrapped up in his own problems and feeling the pressures at the agency, he would've seen the signs and just maybe he could've prevented Colin from taking off on another bender. Picking up the pieces had always been his role, not acting as trigger. Whatever route Colin's self-destructive behavior had taken this time, Duncan would help his brother clean up as he'd always done, whether that meant paying for another round of rehab or covering a gambling debt.

He lifted his right arm to pound on the door again, but it swung open before his fist connected. "Where the hell have you been?" he barked at his brother.

"Hey, Duncan," his brother greeted him cheerfully, ignoring Duncan's dark mood. "What brings you by? Come on in."

Duncan walked into the apartment and stared hard at his

brother. His hazel eyes showed no signs of intoxication, but were clear and bright if a bit weary. His hair damp, as if he'd just showered, was combed away from his face. Duncan could find nothing in his brother's appearance to hint at a weeklong bout of anything destructively hedonistic.

Not yet willing to concede his suspicions were unfounded, he walked into the living room. In the past, Colin's self-indulgence generally resulted in Duncan dragging him back from whatever edge he'd crawled. More times than he cared to recall, he'd had sift through the muck left over from days of partying to even find his brother.

"I came by to check up on you," he said, surprised by the pristine condition of the apartment. No overflowing ashtrays littered the coffee table, nor were there remnants of a bust waiting to happen. No suspicious, stale odors. Not even an array of empty pizza boxes, fast-food wrappers or shriveled French fries in sight.

He spied a glass on the end table and snagged it. Not bothering to hide his distrust, he sniffed the contents. Water? Vodka, yes, but water? Not what he'd been expecting.

He set the glass back on the table. "Got any aspirin?" he asked roughly. "This humidity is playing hell with my shoulder."

Colin's eyes narrowed slightly. "Sure," he said. "Have a seat."

He waited for Colin to leave the room, then performed a cursory search, with every intention of seizing whatever he might find. He checked behind pillows and under cushions but couldn't produce so much as a potato chip crumb. A quick drag of his foot under the sofa and loveseat didn't unearth a single dust bunny, let alone a hastily tossed stash or accompanying paraphernalia.

"Why haven't you returned my calls?" he called out to

his brother. He walked to the oak entertainment center and checked both media cabinets. All he found were Colin's extensive CD and DVD collections. No surprises in the tray of the DVD player or hidden around the stereo system. The cabinet doors beneath the wide-screen television stand housed only a pair of stereo headphones. Crossing the room into the alcove off the kitchen, he stopped suddenly by the dining table and looked down in surprise.

"A jigsaw puzzle?" he muttered, scratching the back of his head.

"Here you go." Colin set four unopened plastic bottles of various brands of pain relievers on the table. "Take your pick."

Duncan indicated the puzzle with a nod of his head. "What's this about?"

Colin's smile was sheepish. "They help me unwind," he said, sounding mildly embarrassed.

They. An indicator there were more somewhere. Dozens, more likely. Not sure what he was supposed to say, Duncan opened a bottle of ibuprofen and tossed back three caplets without water. "Why haven't you returned my calls?" he asked again.

Colin tucked the tips of his fingers into the front pockets of his jeans. "I didn't know you'd called." He indicated the wall phone behind Duncan. "I only got in a couple of hours ago and was busy. I haven't had a chance to check messages."

"In?" Duncan set the bottle on the table with a sharp snap. He glanced over his shoulder to the phone. Sure enough, the red message indicator light blinked rapidly. "Mind telling me from where?" he asked, looking back at his brother.

Irritation passed though Colin's eyes. "I was out of town for a couple of days."

"Out of town where?"

Colin let out a short, impatient breath. "Wait here."

Oh yeah, that made him feel better.

No way was he giving Colin a chance to flush his stash until Duncan knew exactly what he'd been taking. He took off after him, down the hallway to the spare bedroom. Duncan's heart sank when Colin flipped on the overhead light. He'd suspected his brother had been answering the siren song of another obsession, but for once he wouldn't have minded being wrong.

Large cardboard boxes filled the usually stark room, neatly arranged six deep and as many high along the back wall. He understood the cause of his brother's overkill tendencies. The brutally hard times they'd faced a few years after their father's death twenty years ago hadn't been easy, but they'd been especially hard on Colin. His brother's need to overcompensate made him feel safe, but in reality, all Colin had was chaos wrapped in illusion, created by a false sense of security.

When their dad had lost a long battle with cancer, Zach Chamberlain hadn't left his family destitute. There'd been life insurance, mortgage insurance, a home, some rental properties and substantial savings accounts. As a family, they'd mourned their loss, then moved on with their lives. From what Duncan remembered of those early days after his dad's death, other than missing his dad, not much had really changed in his life.

His mom didn't have to go out and look for a job when they were kids, there were still birthday and holiday celebrations, still Little League and Pop Warner games and trips to Galveston each summer. Until one day, five years after his father's death, the world suddenly collapsed around them without warning. The nest egg his dad had built to take care of his family had vanished when a smooth-talking con artist took his mother for every last cent.

Unlike Colin, Duncan didn't blame his mother. At seventeen, even he hadn't suspected the man his mother had married for what he was until it was too late. The kicker had come when the authorities did nothing, because no crime had been committed, at least not in the legal sense. Julianne Chamberlain-Morton had unwittingly given her new husband the means and opportunity to steal from her, leaving herself with no legal recourse all because she'd married without the benefit and protection of a prenuptial agreement.

Once the shock had worn off, Duncan had done whatever he could to help his mother and brother. Those first months had been the toughest of Duncan's life, but even more so on then twelve-year-old Colin. The rebellion that followed took many forms over the years, and Duncan couldn't help being grateful Colin hadn't ended up in prison or dead. There hadn't been much his brother hadn't tried, from booze to drugs. And of course, there were the obsessions.

Colin didn't purchase a single tube of toothpaste or only one can of shaving cream, box of cereal, whatever; he bought by the half dozen or more. He didn't pay the rent on his apartment one month in advance like most people, he paid six months in advance. The fear of being without, however based in reality it might've once been, was a mere sampling of Colin's obsessive behavior patterns.

Staring at the boxes lining the wall, dread filled Duncan. He let out a sigh and opened the flap of a nearby box to peer inside.

Comic books? "What the…"

"Well?" Colin asked, a distinct hint of pride in his voice. "What do you think?"

He thought his brother had really lost it this time. "Well what? Where'd they come from? Why on earth would you need all this?"

Colin frowned. "Hey, they aren't mine."

Great. Just what he *didn't* want to hear. He'd thought the theft phase of Colin's rebellion had ended more than a decade ago. "Why, Colin?" he asked wearily before letting out a long, heavy sigh. "What have you done?"

Colin's lips thinned, and he shook his head in a display of abject disappointment. He reached for a manila folder sitting on top of one of the cartons and shoved it impatiently at Duncan. "Egan Casualty insured the first edition, mint comic book collection of Oliver Vale for twenty-five grand. On the secondary market, they can go as high as four times that amount, if the right buyer comes along. Some of these babies are rare. Serious collectors will to pay premium dollar for a single edition. Vale's collection wasn't stolen, he sold it to a dealer in Maine, then filed a false police report to collect on the insurance."

Duncan vaguely recalled the low-priority claim. Guilt pricked his conscience. He should've had more faith in Colin, but history dictated otherwise. Besides, his brother had never worked recovery, nor had he expressed an interest in that side of the business. How was he supposed to know that had been the reason Colin had taken off suddenly.

He handed Colin back the file. "How'd you track them down?"

"I had a little help."

"Lucy," Duncan guessed.

Colin shook his head. "Marisa. She gave me the idea of putting a want-to-buy ad in the more widely distributed publications. I had a bite two days after the ad came out."

"So you drove up to Maine to recover the property?"

The smirk on Colin's face was one of satisfaction. "Yup."

A sliver of pride filled him at his brother's ingenuity, but it didn't completely erase his annoyance. "Why not let someone know where you were going? Why the big secret?"

"You know what you would've said if I'd told you? 'No, Colin, I'll handle it,'" he mimicked. "Well, I'm sick to death of you handling me. I thought I was your partner."

"You are my partner."

"Then, dammit, start treating me like one," Colin said forcefully. He slapped the file down on one of the cartons. "I've been clean since we opened the agency. Three years, Duncan. Three years and I haven't slipped once. Not one time, and you still have no faith in me. What else do I have to do to earn your trust?"

Colin stalked from the room.

Damn.

"You're my kid brother," Duncan argued when he found Colin in the living room. "I worry." The truth was, he hadn't wanted Colin working recovery jobs. They dealt in stolen merchandise. The caliber of people Duncan came in contact with weren't exactly upstanding citizens. He thought he'd been protecting his brother, doing what he could to keep him from finding trouble. Obviously, Colin didn't share his philosophy.

"Well, don't," Colin snapped. "Find yourself another hobby, okay? I can take care of myself."

"So what are you trying to tell me? You want more recovery assignments?"

"Yeah, I do. Let me work the smaller claims, the low-priority stuff to start. I'll still bring in new business, because I'm good at it."

"Too good," Duncan muttered, thinking of the mess

threatening to overtake his office. If Colin was seriously ready to cover some of their lighter weight jobs, that would free up Duncan to concentrate on heavy hitters like Wilder, Dearborn and Garfield. It would also get Lucy off his back, insofar as their financial status was concerned. At least until she found a new reason to nag him.

"All right," he conceded, praying he wasn't making a mistake. "You can start with the nickel-and-dime recoveries, but don't think because they're small jobs they're not important. They can be our bread and butter in between the big cases. I've asked Marisa to cover your meeting on Friday. That okay with you?"

"She'll do a good job," Colin said, his confidence in Marisa evident by his sudden grin. "I've been thinking we might want to consider redefining her position, anyway. Hire a new secretary, promote Marisa and maybe think about picking up some of her education expenses as a bonus."

Although he, too, had been considering officially expanding Marisa's job description, Duncan still hesitated agreeing outright with Colin. There was his conversation with Lucy to consider, as well, and he worried how his brother would handle the news that they were currently on shaky financial ground. Correction, *temporarily* on shaky financial ground.

You still have no faith in me…

Long habits died hard. That didn't mean he would stop worrying about his brother.

"We're having a cash flow problem, and can't afford to make any big changes right now." One step at a time, he thought, keeping the news they were dangerously close to laying off personnel to himself for the time being. "Lucy was all over my ass today about revenue."

Colin gave him a tolerant look. "Why do you think I took on the Vale file? Last month's financials were a nightmare."

"You knew?" Duncan asked, unable to mask his surprise. He had no idea Lucy kept his brother informed. He supposed it did make sense, though.

Colin chuckled. "You really don't read Lucy's status memos, do you?"

"No," Duncan admitted. "But I'm going to start." He checked his watch. "I've got to go. Meet me in the office at ten. We'll go over some files, get you started."

Colin walked him to the door. "Why so late? You're always in no later than seven."

Duncan shrugged. "Could be a late night," he answered evasively.

"You're working too hard. And here I was hoping you had a hot date," Colin teased.

Duncan tried to contain the smile threatening to erupt, and failed. "Who says I don't?"

"Wow!" Colin laughed. "With a girl?"

Duncan supposed it had been a while. A long while, now that he thought about it. Months, even.

"No, with a *woman*." One hell of an exciting woman he looked forward to seeing again with a great deal of anticipation.

"Anyone I know?" Colin asked. "That babe on the second floor gets all dreamy-eyed whenever she sees you in the elevator."

"It's no one you know."

"Guess you won't tell me about her, either, huh?"

Duncan's smile shifted into a full grin. "Not a chance, little brother."

He reached for the door, but stopped to look back at

Colin. "You're right. I should've trusted you," he offered by way of an apology. "It won't happen again."

The traffic was light as he drove across town from Colin's apartment to meet Sunny at Toucan Sam's. Fifteen minutes later, he pulled into the restaurant parking lot and was prepared to admit he had been in the wrong jumping to the conclusions he had about this brother. He'd been operating on assumptions which were based on history, not stopping to take into account not only the progress Colin had made, but how his brother had done nothing to elicit Duncan's suspicions.

Accepting Colin as a more active participant in every aspect of business would require some adjustments on Duncan's part. Carrying the burden had always been his role. Sharing responsibility was a foreign concept to him.

He made a sound of disgust as he killed the engine. Apparently Colin wasn't the only Chamberlain with a few scars from the past.

Fine. He could learn to let go, lessen his grip on the reins. A little. But there wasn't a chance in hell he would allow the business to fold, not when the difference between success and failure could mean an end to the progress his brother had made in turning his life around.

Failure was not an option.

No matter what it took.

8

IF THE QUAKING of Sunny's limbs were being monitored by
the Richter scale, she'd easily register a reading high
enough to flatten the greater D.C. area and beyond. All because she'd changed her sheets for something other than
laundry day? She hadn't been filled with this much nervous
excitement since the day she'd graduated from the academy at Quantico. Obviously she not only needed to get laid
more often, she needed a life.

Fearing hyperventilation if she didn't get a grip and
calm her rattled nerves, she took advantage of her early ar-
rival by closing her eyes and breathing deeply. Holding the
steering wheel of her Jeep Liberty in a death grip, she tried
to imagine herself lazing in the tall grass near the stream
on her parents' property. Blocking out the bustle of the busy
city around her, she imagined the soothing sound of water
flowing over rocks and lapping at the shoreline. In her
mind, the leaves of the trees fluttered softly overhead on
the warm, summer breeze. The sun beat down on her,
warming her skin as she catalogued the shifting shapes and
images formed from enormous, white cottony clouds.

The rhythm of the water changed suddenly, drawing her
attention away from the cloud pictures. Shielding her eyes
from the glare of the sun with her hand, she rose up on one
elbow to see a gloriously naked Duncan emerge from the

stream. The fresh, cool water clung to his deeply tanned skin, rivulets of moisture winding a sensual path through the hills and valleys of lean, hard muscle. Slowly, he moved toward her, a seductive grin on his face filled with such confidence her breath caught, making a mockery of her deep breathing technique. She followed the path of water sliding down his body. He was so big and…impressive. Everywhere.

A sigh escaped. A pathetically dreamy one that had her opening her eyes and frowning. Her fantasy made no sense. What was she thinking? Streams were too shallow for swimming, or even serious wading. Oh well, she thought with a tiny shrug. This was *her* fantasy, after all, she could imagine whatever she chose. And she liked where her imagination had ventured thus far. It heightened the anticipation of trying out all that new masculine-sensitive bedding on Duncan to see if reality was anywhere near as impressive as fantasy.

She closed her eyes, then snapped them open and frowned again. This was not supposed to be a fantasy, but an exercise in relaxation. Maybe her subconscious knew something she didn't? Oh God, she hoped so.

One last attempt had her lashes fluttering closed again. Her grip on the steering wheel slackened as she envisioned reaching her arms toward Duncan, welcoming him…

A light rap on the driver's side window made her shriek. She flinched so hard, her knee slammed into the steering wheel. One hand flew to her chest in a vain attempt to still the wild beating of her heart, while the other massaged her knee and what would no doubt be an ugly bruise come morning.

She turned her head to see Duncan shrug and offer an apologetic little half smile that did nothing to slow the pounding of her heart. In fact, she could've sworn her pulse picked up speed. So much for relaxing and getting a grip. She was more keyed up than when she'd gone wandering into fantasyland.

With one final deep, far-from-calming breath, she pulled her keys from the ignition. He opened the door for her and she snagged her bag from the passenger seat before sliding from the Jeep. Her feet hit the pavement. "You scared me half to death."

"Sorry 'bout that." He sounded about as contrite as the sexy tilt of his mouth had been apologetic. "I waved, but you didn't see me."

Oh, she had seen plenty. The image would remain etched on her conscience for eons. "I was…lost in thought," she murmured. *If you only knew.*

She pressed the lock button on her key ring to set the car alarm, then attempted to stuff her keys inside her bag. Unsure whether to blame her nerves, the fantasy or the man responsible for both, the keys slipped from her fingers and landed on the pavement with a clatter. She stared in fascination as he stooped to retrieve them for her. His onyx-black hair gleamed under the reddish hue of the setting sun, and his shoulders…oh my, she hadn't realized exactly how wide they really were. Her imagination went into overtime as she envisioned dragging her nails over his muscular flesh, along the sculpted landscape of his back to his rear end where her fingers pressed into the taut flesh, holding him to her….

He stood and held her keys out to her, a quizzical expression on his beautifully handsome face. "Are you okay? You're looking a little flushed."

It's called hot and bothered, honey. "I'm fine. It's just…uh…just the humidity," she stammered, then fanned herself with her hand while managing a nervous laugh. He probably thought she was an idiot. "Maybe we should go inside. You know. Air conditioning?"

Thankfully he took the hint, motioning for her to go ahead of him. She stepped over the curb to the concrete walkway and winced, unsure which caused her more agony, her sore knee or her feet, courtesy of the unaccustomed height of the four-inch spiked heels pinching her toes.

"You look incredible," he said when he came up beside her.

More heat crept into her cheeks, but she didn't mind the cause this time. "Thank you." She cast a sideways glance in his direction as they reached the entrance of the restaurant. He looked just as sexy and rumpled as when she'd left him hours ago. "You look…the same."

He chuckled, the sound warm and inviting. "Should I take that as compliment or criticism?"

"I'm sorry," she said in a rush as he held the door open for her. She hadn't meant to insult him. "Oh God, I didn't mean to imply…I mean, I never meant—"

He snagged her hand, sending a jolt to her system that stilled her rambling. Lacing their fingers together, he tugged gently until she faced him. Before she realized his intentions, he dipped his head and his mouth covered hers, hot and determined. His tongue pressed against the seam of her lips demanding entrance. The world around her faded as she welcomed him inside. A sigh rose in her throat and she leaned into him.

He ended the kiss just as abruptly, leaving her with a distinct sense of disappointment. She wanted more. A lot more. The sooner the better. And couldn't care less that they were in public.

He traced the outline of her jaw with a light brush of his fingertips against her skin, his touch impossibly gentle.

"Relax, Sunny," he said quietly. "Nothing is going to happen here that you don't want to happen, okay?"

Coherent thought took more effort than she could possibly muster, but she did manage a mute nod in response. The way her lips tingled and her insides kept twittering and jumping all over the place, she'd be lucky to ever have a rational thought again that didn't include Duncan and the way he so effortlessly reduced her to sheer idiocy with a mere kiss. Good Lord, she hated to think what would happen to her rationale when they had sex.

With her hand still clasped in his, they approached the hostess who gave them a knowing smile before leading them toward the rear of the restaurant. Sunny tried to take care as she maneuvered the rough-textured terra-cotta tiled flooring in her heels, but she couldn't get his that-you-don't-want-to-happen line out of her head.

She should tell him she wanted plenty to happen and be done with it. Be direct. Go after what she wanted. The only real question was timing.

The atmosphere was indeed casual as Georgia had suggested, but she hadn't been prepared for the outlandish decor of Toucan Sam's—trashy tropical with a big splash of jungle not-so-chic. Bright neon toucans protruded like street signs from posts made from the trunks of imitation palm trees. Ghastly yellow and lime Day-Glo-colored banner-type flags hung from the birds' beaks, directing customers to such imaginary locales as Rum Punch Pier, Captain Morgan's Cove, Tequila Sunrise Dunes and Bahama Mama Beach. Overhead beams resembling thick tree branches were draped in artificial vegetation of lush leaves, dangling vines and plumeria.

The hostess led them into the relatively secluded Captain Morgan's Cove. They were seated in the last vacant booth near an indoor waterfall decorated with jagged lava rock and more artificial plants. A pool at the base of the waterfall came complete with lily pads where fake frogs croaked and danced in time to reggae music playing in the background.

Sunny took the menus the hostess offered since Duncan's gaze was riveted in fascination on the chorus of frogs.

"I hear the food is supposed to be good," she said hopefully. She giggled, unable to contain her amusement when the frogs started bobbing up and down in animated enthusiasm.

"I sure hope so. This place looks like…" He shook his head and faced her. "Like…"

"The decorator fried a few too many brain cells in Margaritaville?" she finished for him.

"That would cover it," he said and chuckled. Plucking the drink menu from the rattan holder, he spread it open so they could view it together.

Sunny leaned forward, resting her arms on the glass tabletop. The mixed drink choices weren't quite as outrageous as the decor, offering the standard blended fare with a heavy tropical slant, a variety of intriguing shooter combinations, half of which she'd never heard of, and the usual mixed drinks.

A young waiter garbed in a Hawaiian shirt and a pair of frayed denim walking shorts approached to take their drink order and introduced himself as Joey. She half expected him to be sporting flip-flops, but thankfully there were health and safety codes dictating otherwise.

"Corona," Duncan told the waiter. "With lime."

Sunny flipped drink menu closed and returned it to the holder. "Make that two, please."

"A woman after my own heart," Duncan said once Joey

shuffled off in his canvas deck shoes, sans socks. "Never would've guessed you for the beer type, though."

She flicked the edge of the bright Hawaiian-print napkin with her fingernail. "Oh? And what *type* would you have guessed me for?"

He rested his forearms on the table and leaned slightly forward. "Exotic," he said simply.

Why that gave her heart a jolt, she couldn't say, but she liked the feeling as much as she enjoyed the electric intensity of his gaze as he looked at her. The deep, husky timbre of his voice wasn't bad, either. Definitely all of the above, she decided. When it came to her reaction to the man seated across from her, Anything Goes was quickly becoming her motto.

She cleared her throat and shifted uncomfortably under his stare. "Do you come here often?" she asked lamely. From his reaction, she was betting not.

The mock horror on his face confirmed her suspicions and she laughed. "Not exactly," he said, his tone filled with dry humor. "Lucy talks about it, but I think I should've checked it out first."

"It's not so bad." She glanced over at the frogs in heavy shake-your-booty mode. "They're kinda fun and cute, don't you think?"

"I didn't realize you had such a warped concept of what qualifies as fun and cute," he teased her. The corners of his eyes crinkled when his smile deepened. "Puppies, kittens, they're cute. Amusement parks, merry-go-rounds and a day at the beach. Now that's fun."

"You can keep the merry-go-round," she countered, "and put me down for Christmas instead."

Finding Duncan under the tree on Christmas morning could be loads of fun, she thought. Of course he'd be wear-

ing nothing but one of his heart-stopping smiles and a stra-
tegically placed red bow, waiting to be unwrapped solely
for her pleasure. A big red bow, too…at least according to
her imagination.

In desperate need of a distraction before she wound up
caught in the middle of another delicious fantasy, she
scanned the menu and decided on the grilled trout with rice
pilaf and a salad just as the beach-bum-clad Joey returned
with a pair of frosted glass mugs and two Coronas, a slice
of lime tucked into the neck of each bottle. He took their
order, promising to return soon with the appetizers Duncan ordered for them.

"This warped sense of humor," Duncan said. "A ge-
netic defect or an acquired skill?"

Humor touched his smile. She tried desperately not to
melt right there in the booth in front of him.

She let out an intentionally dramatic sigh. "Defect, I'm
afraid. What can I say?" She shrugged. "I'm the spawn of
a severely flawed gene pool."

"Explain to me how a person genetically predisposed to
humor becomes something as serious as an FBI agent.
Family tradition?"

"You wouldn't say that if you ever met my folks," she
told him dryly. "They're not what I'd call traditionalists."

"You realize a statement like that requires explanation."

She plucked the lime from the bottle and twisted the
juice into her mug while searching for the right words to
describe her unorthodox upbringing. "When my parents
weren't hauling my sister and me around with them to
anti-something marches, sit-ins or protests for the cause of
the week, a small horse ranch near the Alleghenies was
home. In between all that raising of social consciousness,
my sister and I were homeschooled until we were old

enough for high school, then sent off to public school strictly for the collegiate opportunities. Dad trained horses and worked as a farrier, and my mom was the poster child for über-homemaker before the concept was considered vogue."

A brief shadow passed through his eyes. "There are worse things in life," he said quietly.

Speaking from experience? she wondered. "Not when you're sixteen and all you want to do is fit in and be like everyone else. I bet your dad never staged a protest outside of your high school cafeteria in support of fair wages for migrant farm workers."

"No," he said. "I can't say that he did."

She poured beer into her glass and smiled at him. "I rest my case. It has been my parents' mission in life to serve up social consciousness with a double order of antiestablishment rhetoric on the side. Obviously I rebelled by becoming a federal agent."

"That must've gone over well."

"My dad nearly had a stroke." She laughed to soften the edge of cynicism in her voice. "It really wasn't as bad as I'm making it sound. They are proud of me, even if they didn't exactly celebrate my choices. But, they do support individuality so they accepted that I had made the right decision for me. When I went into the coast guard, they did flip out, which was nothing compared to when I announced I'd applied to the Bureau."

"What did you expect? You joined forces with the evil empire," he said, his smile deepening.

"That's one of the more PG-13 expressions my dad has used to describe the government, yes. I was raised to question authority if it went against my beliefs, fight the good fight in peaceful demonstration and to express myself and my thoughts freely without fear of censorship. That's not exactly what they teach us at the academy, is it?"

Duncan hadn't intended to discuss the Bureau or her investigation tonight. He wanted to know more about the woman who'd been a constant in his thoughts since this morning, but he was enjoying the glimpse she'd given him into her background. "Not when I passed through Quantico, they didn't." He lifted the bottle and took a long drink. "So," he said after a moment, "why *did* you become an agent?"

Her golden eyebrows winged upward. "Other than a burning desire to save the world from evildoers?" she asked in mock innocence.

"That would be the one I'm interested in, yes," he said and set the bottle back on the table.

The waiter returned with their appetizer, a platter overflowing with deep-fried coconut shrimp, pineapple spears, mango slices and a variety of dipping sauces. He vanished as silently as he'd appeared.

"I have a knack for solving puzzles."

He didn't miss the sudden sharpness of her tone, or how she lowered her gaze to concentrate on adding a selection of shrimp and tropical fruits to her plate. He knew how to spot a bullshit story when he stepped in one, and from her abrupt response, he guessed there was more than she felt comfortable divulging.

"I'll remember to call you next time I'm stumped by a crossword puzzle," he said, keeping it light.

She lifted her gaze to his. The hint of a smile teasing the edges of her mouth, had him wondering if he'd imagined the chill in her voice.

"Word searches are my forte," she said. "Or trivia. I'm a hopeless *Jeopardy* junkie."

"A wealth of useless information, is that it?"

"A whole lot about nothing." Her smile widened a fraction and the warmth slowly returned to her eyes.

He stared at her mouth, overwhelmed by the sudden urge to kiss her again. Grabbing hold of his fork, he stabbed a fat shrimp. "Having a wide base of knowledge is nothing to be ashamed of."

"It's not going to win me any awards." She popped a chunk of pineapple into her mouth. Sweet juice coated her lips and she used the tip of her tongue to collect the moisture.

He shifted on his side of the booth. Forget kisses. Kissing was highly overrated compared to the images flashing through his mind of exactly where he'd like to see her mouth and that pretty pink tongue. Much more interesting, erotic images that were sending his testosterone levels through the imitation thatched roof.

"It's not like there's a huge demand for agents with my particular talent," she added in the same dry tone she'd used earlier.

He'd bet she had plenty of skills the Bureau wouldn't be interested in, and the idea of him being the one to exploit those particular talents was making him hard. How was it that he had the feeling he'd known her forever, when in reality it'd been less than a day? He couldn't remember ever feeling so…so… He searched his mind for the right word. Connected, he decided.

He consciously shoved that eerily dangerous thought from his mind. "Criminal investigation requires a certain attention to detail," he said as conversationally as he could manage.

"I suppose." She popped a slice of mango into her mouth, seemingly oblivious to his train of thought. "Even if it wasn't exactly what I'd been hoping for, the promotion to CID was an important career step."

"Aiming for the director's job, are you?" he asked, before polishing off another shrimp. Ambition. A philosophy he understood and subscribed to himself.

"Not quite." She set her fork on her plate and reached for the mug of beer she'd poured. "I want ISU."

"Profiling?" he blurted. "You?"

She gave him a sharp glance. He hadn't meant to make it sound as if she weren't good enough to make ISU, but her admission took him by complete surprise. She wasn't much bigger than a mite and looked as if a stiff wind could blow her into the next county. ISU took a hard-core approach to hard-core crime, a survival tactic he imagined necessary for coping with the grisly details of the job.

"Why is that so hard to believe?" Defensiveness laced her voice. "Because I'm a woman?"

Not wanting to stomp all over her feminist toes, he considered his response carefully. The truth was, he just couldn't imagine her lasting for more than a year or two. A job like that got to a person. It was no secret the agent credited for making the unit what it was today eventually cracked under the strain. Hell, it had nearly killed the guy.

Duncan pushed his empty plate aside. Buying time, he took a long pull on his beer before answering. "Gender has nothing to do with it," he eventually said. "What are the longevity stats? The burnout ratio for unit personnel is probably the highest in the Bureau."

She set her fork on the edge of her plate. "Some profilers do last longer than others," she conceded. "But it's what I've always wanted and I intend to have it."

"But why?" he couldn't help asking, if for no other reason than to learn more about what made this woman tick. "If run-of-the-mill bad guys aren't enough of a challenge, transfer to organized crime. It's no safer, but at least you won't wake up screaming in the middle of the night."

Determination made her eyes glitter like hard green crystals. "The reason I wanted to be an agent was so I could become a profiler," she said, her tone as hard as the look in her eyes. "After I left the coast guard, I knew I needed a degree in criminal justice to be considered for employment, but that alone wouldn't be enough for ISU. I picked up a double in psych so I'd be a step ahead of the competition. I've made no secret of the fact that ISU is what I've always wanted. And, I'm a lot closer now. If I can bust the Seducer, that'll give me even more of an edge."

"Apparently you've given this a lot of thought." What else could he say? Far be it from him to burst her professional bubble, even if he did see her teetering on the verge of making a monumental mistake. He'd been there. Just from the time he'd spent with her, he knew she was as dedicated to the Bureau as he'd once been. ISU would burn her out, and then what would she have? Not that he had any right to voice his opinion. With his own less-than-sterling record, he was hardly in a position to offer her career advice.

"Yes, I have," she firmly stated. "I asked for SEDSCAM for a reason. Which reminds me…about those two cases you're handling in addition to Wilder—"

"Sunny?"

"Yes?"

"Let's not talk shop tonight, okay?" Locating the property stolen from the Seducer's victims was important to him, more so now than ever after his conversation with his brother, but now wasn't the time. Besides, he wasn't so wrapped up in lust for her that he'd feed her information without a guarantee he'd be in on her investigation, provided they did share more cases in common.

She let out a gentle sigh. "Sorry," she apologized. Her expression turned sheepish. "I tend to get overly passionate on occasion."

Passionate was good. Very good, in fact.

He reached across the table and settled his hand over hers. "So," he said, smoothing his thumb over the back of her hand. "Tell me what else makes you passionate."

9

"THIS IS HARDER than I thought it would be," Duncan complained good-naturedly.

Sunny gave him an encouraging smile. "Your technique is good." Better than good, she thought. The guy was nothing short of a pro. "Are you sure you haven't done this before?"

"Until you," he teased, "I was as pure as the driven snow."

She laughed heartily, as she'd been doing for most of the night. Whether it was the carnival atmosphere of the miniature golf course giving her a more lighthearted feeling than usual, or the company of the man she couldn't seem to stop touching at every opportunity, she didn't know, and quite frankly, she didn't much care.

"Somehow I doubt that," she said dryly.

His eyes filled with hunger when he looked at her, leaving her with the distinct impression they were no longer discussing his golf technique. A heaviness settled low in her tummy. She hadn't believed it possible for her to experience such insistent need for someone she'd only met, but from the look simmering in his eyes, the sentiment was decidedly mutual. By suggesting they play miniature golf after dinner when she had a perfectly good condo where they could've been alone, hadn't been her brightest idea. Whatever had she been thinking?

She knew exactly what she'd been thinking—while she might be wildly attracted to him, she really didn't know him all that well. Not wanting the evening to end too soon, the outdoor miniature golf complex, complete with a remote control racetrack, indoor arcade and the standard junk-food court, she'd passed on the way to the restaurant had seemed like a safe alternative. Not exactly the pleasurable pursuits she'd had in mind, but the time she'd spent with Duncan hadn't been a waste. In addition to discovering he had a younger brother who worked at the agency with him, she'd also learned he'd been born in Shreveport, but had spent much of his childhood in Fort Worth. When she'd asked him how he'd ended up in the D.C. area, he'd explained that once he'd left the Bureau, he'd relocated north to be near his mother and brother.

"Show me again," he said. "I have one shot left and I want it to count."

"Oh, all right." His helpless act had grown old over an hour ago, but she was bright enough at least to take advantage of the opportunity to get close to him again, to feel the texture of his skin under her hands, to breathe in his tantalizing masculine scent.

"Put your thumbs together lengthwise. Like this," she instructed. She moved in close and eased her hands slowly over his. "It'll strengthen your grip so your club won't slip when you stroke like it did the last time."

"We can't have that," he said.

The husky tenor of his voice, combined with the warm fan of breath against her ear sent a delightful shiver sliding down her spine. She turned her head to the side and stared at his mouth. "Just make sure you hold on…tight."

Desire flared in his eyes.

She was playing with fire and loving every second of it. When he looked at her that way, she couldn't think straight.

She stepped out of his way, not to give him room, but for her own sanity. The view of his backside as he bent over the club preparing to putt the golf ball through the lion's mouth had her curling her bare toes into the patch of Astroturf.

He took his shot and made it on the first try, as he'd been doing all night long. The grin on his face when he looked at her over his shoulder was nothing short of triumphant. "That's game, baby."

She folded her arms and tilted her hip slightly to the side. "For someone who claims to have never played miniature golf," she said skeptically, "you certainly beat the pants off me with no problem."

"Now you're talking." He walked toward her, a definite predatory light in his gaze that sent her pulse careening. "Care to have another go and make it interesting this time?"

"Not a chance. You've played before. Come on, Duncan. Admit it."

He took a step back, then with the putter gripped in his hands, he adjusted his stance as if he were stepping up to a tee on the back nine. She gasped when he swung the club with the precision form of a seasoned pro. "You're a liar. How long have you been playing?"

"Tonight was my first time." His heart-stopping grin was anything but innocent when he wrapped his arm around her waist and hauled her against him. "But I've played *real* golf for years."

Every nerve ending in her body came instantly and even more vibrantly alive at the contact. Her breasts swelled, and the sharp tug of desire in her belly made her damp with need. "You cheated," she said, but the whispered words sounded more like an invitation than the playful accusation she'd intended.

Ducking his head, he brushed his lips over hers in a feathery kiss before letting her go. "I did, didn't I?"

"You're shameless." Needing to catch her breath, she scooted away from him to the stone bench where she'd dropped her shoes upon entering the final obstacle of the miniature golf course. She slipped her feet back into her shoes while watching him retrieve their discarded clubs, attempting to recall when she'd last enjoyed herself so thoroughly—with a man or otherwise.

Enjoying a night of fun, laughing, acting silly and simply connecting with another human on a purely personal level had been very long overdue, she decided. And there was the chemistry Duncan kept referring to which definitely continued to sizzle. She'd be a fool not to acknowledge the heightening awareness building between them in that regard, either.

But there was more and every time she tried to pinpoint the exact cause, the emotion she couldn't name became even more elusive. For reasons that defied explanation, she suspected Duncan was at the root of the cause.

In no hurry to return to her place—alone—she leaned back on her hands and stretched her legs out in front of her as he joined her on the bench. Laughter and the hum of conversation from other golfers drifted toward them on the warm summer breeze. The revving of an engine from a hopped-up car sounded in the distance. Some teenage boy probably showing off in front of a pretty girl, she thought and smiled. What she wouldn't give to recapture that time of innocence.

Duncan rested his elbows on his knees and leaned forward, the putters clasped loosely between his palms in front of him. "Tonight was fun. Thank you."

"I just had that very same thought."

Shouts from a group of teenagers near the outdoor entrance to the arcade across the way drew her attention. "Do you remember what it was like being that young?" she asked Duncan. "When your biggest worry was a term paper or keeping your room clean enough so your mom wouldn't nag you?"

"We couldn't wait to grow up, could we? Convinced we'd do it differently. Better." He let out a caustic bark of laughter. "We were so arrogant, thinking we could accomplish the impossible. Life is complicated. By responsibilities, ambitions, even fear."

Realization slammed into her with the force of a freight train, leaving her momentarily breathless. The elusive emotion she'd been struggling to pinpoint suddenly became amazingly clear. The constant presence of fear she carried with her had mysteriously vanished.

Being with Duncan had accomplished what nothing, not the extra locks on her doors and windows, not the alarm systems or the precautions she took to ensure her safety, had done. With him, she felt safe, a sensation she hadn't experienced with any degree of honesty in almost a decade. No wonder she didn't immediately recognize it. The feeling had all but become foreign to her.

The how's or why's she couldn't begin to hazard a guess. In time the answer would come to her, of that she had no concern. She was, after all, a whiz at solving puzzles.

The thought of puzzles instantly brought SEDSCAM to mind. However illogical, the idea of her and Duncan enjoying each other's company tonight seemed almost obscene while the Seducer was still on the loose. The UNSUB was out there, somewhere, and so far she remained powerless in bringing an end to his cons. While she'd been flirting and engaging in age-old mating rituals, the UNSUB could already be setting up his next mark.

She let out a long sigh filled with frustration. "Duncan?"

"Hmm?" he answered lazily.

"I know you said you weren't interested in talking shop, but I need to ask you a question. There's something I have to know."

Under the bright stadium lights of the outdoor complex, she had no trouble mistaking his hesitation, or his suddenly guarded expression. She forged ahead, anyway. "We've been trying to establish a geographic pattern for the Seducer, but haven't had much luck," she said. "It could be helpful to us if you told me which cities are involved in the claims you're investigating."

He shifted his attention back to the group of teenagers. She waited patiently, but had to wonder what he was thinking.

"Dallas and Miami," he finally said, after a few moments of silence.

"Thank you." Considering she'd allowed him to sit in on her interview with Margo Wilder, she'd expected him to give her what she wanted. The fact that he'd hesitated, even momentarily, annoyed her.

"Now will you tell me something?" he asked.

"If I can," she hedged. The Bureau wasn't exactly the most user-friendly investigative agency when it came to jurisdiction or sharing evidence with nongovernmental agencies. Still, he had provided her with a piece of information which could prove invaluable once Georgia ran Dallas through the computers.

"Has your UNSUB shown up in either one of those locations?"

"Miami," she told him. To her knowledge, once the UNSUB pulled his scam, he moved on to a new city, but that deduction was based solely on the information available to her. There were clearly other victims she didn't know about yet and if acknowledging that she and Duncan did have a case in common, so be it. "Does the name Ian Banyon have a familiar ring to it?"

Duncan straightened. "It's very familiar to Celine Garfield."

No question about it, she *needed* to review his files. For now, though, she elected not to pursue the issue. Her decision had nothing whatsoever to do with her personal relationship with Duncan, but because she had no intention of compromising her investigation by putting the integrity of any evidence she might collect at risk. Tomorrow would be soon enough, when she could go through proper channels by making an official Bureau request. Since he'd been present during the Wilder interview, explaining how she'd learned of his agency's involvement wasn't at issue, so she definitely had her butt covered in that area. When she nailed the UNSUB, she wanted the charges to stick, and didn't want the judge to have any reason to throw the case out on a technicality because she hadn't followed procedure in obtaining evidence.

As they walked toward the parking lot after returning their clubs, her earlier nervousness slowly returned. For all her big talk with Georgia about going with the flow, and whatever happens, happens, regardless of how antiquated, she didn't want to give Duncan the impression she was the kind of woman that jumped in the sack with a guy on the first date.

They reached her vehicle, and she pulled her keys from the front pocket of her jeans. She'd left her bag hidden under the seat and had locked it in the Jeep so she wouldn't have to keep an eye on her purse while they'd golfed.

Duncan took the keys from her, then unlocked and opened the door for her. Would he ask or would he leave it up to her to issue the your place or mine invitation?

Nothing is going to happen here that you don't want to happen.

The words he'd whispered to her at the restaurant clamored through her mind. That was her problem. She *did* want something to happen, something sexy and exciting and fulfilling.

He stepped forward, sandwiching her between the thick wall of his chest and the interior of her four-wheel drive. Heat engulfed her from head to toe, but it had nothing to do with the weather, and everything to do with sex.

He settled his big hands low on her hips, sparking myriad sensual, erotic images. His hands on her bare hips, guiding her over him as she slid down the thick length of his shaft. Touching. Exploring. Tasting.

She looked into his eyes and her breath caught at the heat swirling in the depths of his gaze, igniting a flame that burned her deep inside. Her feminine senses were already spinning out of control and they hadn't even kissed.

He drew her closer until her breasts brushed against him. The air crackled with pent-up, sexual energy, and her nipples beaded into tight buds, rasping against the lace cups of her demi bra. She wanted to feel the warmth of his hands on her breasts, the heat of his mouth as he tasted her, the pull of need in her belly as he suckled her.

Wreathing her arms around his neck brought their bodies even closer. Applying the slightest amount of pressure, she urged his head down for a hot openmouthed kiss. If she couldn't find the words to tell him what she wanted, then she'd just have to show him. He tasted like heaven, warm and purely masculine. Hot. Demanding. Intoxicating. *Safe.*

Her fingertips teased the wavy strands of hair brushing the collar of his shirt, then she dug her hands into the thick mass and boldly explored him. She plastered her body to his and felt the distinct ridge of his erect penis. Moving against him, she was rewarded with a moan of pleasure.

She skimmed her hand over the fly of his khakis and issued a moan all her own at such a delicious discovery. The reality of him put her fantasies to shame and she was suddenly glad of the dark shadows of the parking lot.

His mouth left hers to skim her jaw, his lips trailing a steamy path down the side of her neck. Sensation shot through her with lightning speed and she lost her balance, stumbling backward. He caught her and pressed her up against the side of the Jeep, surrounding her with his heat, his need. Beneath his trousers, she felt the throbbing length of his penis. Her own sex pulsed in response and she ached for his touch as much as she craved the feel of him hot and heavy in her hand.

Without shame or regret, she took what she wanted. Unzipping his fly, she slipped her hand beneath the fabric. Wrapping her fingers around his rock-hard length, she gently stroked the velvety smoothness of him.

He sucked in a sharp hiss of breath, and brought his mouth down hard on hers. Need raked her insides. Skimming his hands along her sides to her waist, his fingers then worked her belt buckle and the button fly of her jeans. Warm, sultry air brushed her skin. His fingers dipped beneath the lace of her panties and her world spun. Nerve endings she'd forgotten existed burst into flames at the first bold slide of his fingers over her dewy folds.

She wanted Duncan. Here. Now.

Desire pulsed through her veins. Her skin grew tighter, hotter. Her frustration mounted. She wanted Duncan in a way she hadn't ever experienced and it frightened her as much as it exhilarated her. Wanted him inside her, craved the weight of his body over hers, the length of him stroking her deeply, consuming her.

His fingers bit into her hips and he set her away from him, ending what they'd started far too soon. He rested his forehead against hers, his breathing as ragged as her own. At least she was granted a modicum of satisfaction on that front, although a far cry from the satisfaction her body demanded.

"I think we'd better say good night." His voice was tight. "We could get arrested if this goes any further."

Disappointment filled her, yet failed to completely quell the delicious sensations still vividly humming inside her. "Probably a good idea," she reluctantly agreed, although for the life of her, she couldn't summon a single argument in support of the decision, threat of arrest notwithstanding. "I do have an early day tomorrow."

He placed one final, hard kiss on her lips, then moved back and waited for her to climb into the Jeep before he closed the door. With trembling fingers, she managed to slip the keys into the ignition and start the vehicle so she could lower the window.

With one hand resting on the roof, he leaned toward her. "How does Friday night look to you?"

She gave him her most sultry smile. "Very promising," she whispered huskily, then indulged in one last taste. She made it good, too, so he'd have no trouble mistaking exactly what she had in mind come Friday night. Not that she'd left much to his imagination already.

"Do you want me to follow you home?" he asked when they eventually came up for air.

"I'll be fine," she said automatically, then realized her mistake. *Smooth move, dummy,* she thought. She snapped her seat belt into place, unable to believe she'd blown a perfectly good opportunity to finish what she hadn't wanted to end.

He moved away from the Jeep. "I'll call you, and we'll make plans."

She disengaged the emergency brake, shifted into reverse and pulled out of the parking space. She didn't bother to tell him the only plans they'd be making concerned which side of the bed he preferred.

Thirty minutes later she pulled into the underground garage of her condominium complex. The bright teal digits of the clock indicated the time was a few minutes shy of midnight. She did have an early day tomorrow. Once she served the search warrants on the gallery and theater owners first thing in the morning, two teams of lab technicians would begin the slow, painstaking process of combing the crime scenes for evidence.

Once back in her condo, she reset the alarm for the night, turned off the lamp in the entry and headed down the hall toward her bedroom. She stopped midway, thunderstruck by a realization that shocked her. She had been a kiss away from inviting Duncan to her place, a man she didn't really know all that well, when she knew what could happen to a woman who was foolish enough to bring a stranger into her home.

Instead of berating herself for missing out on what promised to be very intense experience, she should be thanking her subconscious for keeping her from making what could've been a horrible mistake. Lust was not a license for carelessness. Taking chances with her safety, possibly with her life, was nothing short of an act of pure stupidity.

A cold chill crept over her. She hurried into the bedroom and turned on the lights. For the flash of an instant, she wasn't standing in her bedroom, but in the corridor of a small apartment building in Norfolk, watching in abject horror as the county coroner closed the zipper of a thick black body bag.

She shook her head to erase the image. "Stop it." Duncan was not some twisted whack job. He was ex-FBI, for crying out loud. A man that inspired fierce loyalty in his employees. "He is *not* a sociopath."

Nor was she as careless as her friend and neighbor Abby Monroe had been. But then, Sunny doubted Abby had believed Gary John Wilton had been the Norfolk Stalker when she'd invited him back to her place after meeting him at a local dance club.

A shudder passed through Sunny and she snagged the remote control from the nightstand and flipped on the television. She avoided the news and settled on a late-night talk show. A sorry substitute for human contact, but it was enough so she didn't feel quite so alone, even if the background noise failed to completely ease the vulnerability plaguing her tonight.

She wasn't particularly fond of the word *paranoia,* but she did have a certain fondness for *cautious.* The Bureau shrink she was required to visit during the recertification process had labeled her mildly paranoid. She didn't agree. There was nothing wrong with taking extra precautions with her safety, so long as her need for security didn't cripple her emotionally or prevent her from doing her job.

She dropped onto the edge of the mattress and stared unseeing at the television set. She'd wanted Duncan. Had she used the antiquated no-first-date-sex rule as an excuse to mask some other psychological factor?

She frowned, unsure if she wanted to know the answer.

The violent death of a friend was bound to have a lasting effect on a person, especially an innocent twenty-year-old. Sunny had been in the coast guard, stationed in Norfolk, Virginia, and living on her own for the first time. She'd been friendly with the neighbors in the small apartment building where she'd lived, but she and Abby, who'd lived across the hall, were close in age and had become good friends. They'd go to the occasional movie, have lunch or just hang out in one or the other's apartment, drinking a few beers and engaging in girl-talk.

From different backgrounds, Sunny valued structure in her life, an element that had been missing during her childhood, while Abby had reveled in the freedom of her newfound independence away from her parents' strict rules. Compared to Abby, Sunny knew she'd come off as downright stuffy, to which Abby had often joked they'd been born to the wrong families.

Unlike Abby, Sunny had never been comfortable with the whole one-night stand concept. In her opinion, Abby had often taken chances that had made Sunny uncomfortable, so she occasionally avoided going out with her friend. And then one night, Abby had met the wrong guy. The price had been her life.

Gary John Wilton was what the ISU called an organized killer, in that he hunted a specific, as opposed to a random, type of victim. Abby, with her long, dark hair and tall, svelte frame had been Wilton's ideal prey. Open, friendly and just a little promiscuous, she'd unwittingly fed into Wilton's twisted fantasy. He'd picked her up at a local dance club, she'd invited him back to her place. What was supposed to be a fun, no-strings-attached evening turned out to be a nightmare.

Sunny had heard nothing, and hadn't even realized something was wrong until the cops had knocked on her door the next day. Abby was supposed to have met her parents for brunch, and when she didn't show, her folks had come to Abby's apartment. The door had been left ajar, and when they'd walked in, they'd found their daughter's body.

Sunny never forgot the helplessness she'd felt that day, or the accompanying fear that had consumed her afterward. Standing in the hallway being questioned by a pair of homicide detectives, she'd been frustrated by her inability to provide them with any assistance in identifying Abby's killer. One of the detectives had excused himself, and when he'd walked away, Sunny had a clear view into Abby's apartment, right at the moment the coroner was closing the bag containing Abby's body. That image of her friend's face frozen in terror had remained with Sunny forever.

Her life had been irrevocably altered, but she'd come away with a clear vision of her future. She didn't suffer from a superhero complex, nor was she arrogant enough to believe she held the power to single-handedly bring about the end of violence in society. She didn't operate under the misguided assumption that for every piece of scum she put behind bars, she was saving Abby in the metaphorical sense. But, she did know with absolute certainty that given the opportunity, she could bring the worst of the bad guys down one by one.

The sudden rise in volume courtesy of a television commercial jolted her back to the present. She shook off the morbidity of the past as best she could and went through the motions of her nightly routine.

Fifteen minutes later she crawled into bed, and didn't even consider turning off the television.

10

SUNNY GLARED at the telephone on her desk, willing it to ring. The silence was really beginning to grate on her nerves.

With the warrants served and the lab techs collecting evidence, there was no reason for her to hang around the crime scenes where she'd only drive the techs nuts with her questions. From experience she knew she'd gain more cooperation from them if she left them alone and waited for word should they turn up anything of interest.

The owner of the Fifth Street Art Center had offered her nothing of value when she'd questioned him, nor had the theater employees or the box owner been of any assistance whatsoever. The gallery owner and his wife had returned from an extended vacation in Europe only two days ago, and until Sunny and Ned had shown up this morning to serve the search warrants, they hadn't any idea a break-in had even occurred.

Upon arriving back in her office around noon, Sunny had immediately placed a call to the special agent in charge in the Dallas field office, but he had yet to return her call. She needed an agent to visit the local police stations to inquire about crimes related to SEDSCAM, but she had to go through proper channels since she didn't know anyone in the Dallas office she could call on for a favor. At the very least the victim must have filed a police report for insurance purposes, else Duncan's office wouldn't even have the claim. She could call the local police herself, but she'd only get the runaround, whereas an agent physically breathing down their neck had a better chance of producing results.

For roughly two seconds she considered calling Duncan. He'd been assigned to the Dallas office and could probably supply her with the name of an agent, but she discarded the idea just as quickly. Until she obtained his files in an official capacity, she didn't want to run the risk of raising questions she wasn't prepared to answer.

"Ring, dammit," she muttered.

The phone remained as silent as a tomb.

With a frustration-filled sigh, she picked up the receiver and dialed Georgia's cell phone. The call immediately clicked over to her voice mail. Georgia couldn't possibly be at the estate after all this time, Sunny thought. The meeting with Wilder and the sketch artist had been scheduled for ten o'clock. It was now nearing three in the afternoon, and Sunny still hadn't heard from the junior agent.

After leaving a message for Georgia to call her, she tried Jack Caruso next. He, at least, answered on the second ring.

"Caruso," he practically barked into the phone.

"It's Mac." She cut right to the chase. "I'm looking for Agent Tremont. Has she left the estate yet?"

"Why how are you, Mac? Me? I'm doing fine. Just goddamned peachy. Thank you for asking."

Her lips twitched as she shook her head at his sarcasm. "I'd ask you how it's hanging, but I'm afraid you'd tell me."

"Well, now that you ask—"

"I didn't." She snagged a pen from her drawer and twirled it around. "Tremont?" she reminded him.

"The redhead? With the legs?"

"You're a sexual harassment suit waiting to happen," she chided him. Jack Caruso was a good agent, but he certainly enjoyed jerking her chain. Always one to bluster and complain, his sometimes crude, often surly attitude didn't change the fact that he had the instincts of a bloodhound when it came to investigation techniques. Unfortunately, he had a tendency to piss off the wrong people, and as a result, had never advanced in his career beyond field agent.

"You tell her for me she wants to harass somebody, ol' Jackie-boy's her guy."

She leaned back in the desk chair and started tapping the capped end of the pen on the arm. "You could really benefit from a gender-sensitivity training seminar, you know that?"

"I'm a real sensitive guy." He emitted a raspy chuckle. "Just ask my wife."

"Jack?" Her patience began to wear thin. "Tremont? Have you seen her?"

"She cut out of here a couple of hours ago," he said. "Problems?"

"No, no problems." Only concern, she thought and frowned. "Did she happen to say where she was going?"

"Sorry, can't help you there."

She thanked him and hung up the phone. It wasn't like Georgia to not check in, and Sunny could think of no good reason for her to be delayed.

The phone on her desk rang. "About time," she muttered, and picked up the receiver again. "Mac, here."

"Agent MacGregor?"

She straightened at the sound of a deep voice she didn't immediately recognize. "This is Special Agent MacGregor," she said cautiously.

"Reece Klabo," the caller said. "ISU."

Her heart nearly burst out of her chest. Reece Klabo was the number one man in the Investigative Support Unit and number two man of the National Center for Analysis of Violent Crime, or NCAVC. Unlike the head of NCAVC, Klabo remained an active profiler.

"How can I help you?" There was only one reason she could think of for him to call her. Any agent interested in joining ISU knew Klabo was the man to impress. If he said "Jump," every wannabe-profiler within hearing distance asked, "How high?"

"Can you be at Quantico within the hour?"

"Yes, sir," Sunny said, not about to become an exception. "I'll be there."

"Good. I'll be expecting you."

The line went dead.

She hung up the phone, afraid to move for fear she might wake up from what could be a dream about to come true. The rumor mill had been grinding the past few weeks about a possible spot opening up in ISU, and she hadn't hesitated to make a point of informing her unit chief, Clint Burrows, she wanted consideration for the position. Her boss hadn't been the least bit encouraging. All she'd received had been a dismissive response of "duly noted."

She cleared off her desk and locked the SEDSCAM files in her desk drawer. Not wanting to suffer disappointment later, she tried not to read too much into Klabo's request to see her, but the hope that she may be moments away from becoming not only a member of the elite team of profilers, but also the youngest woman in the Bureau's long history to ever hold the post, was simply too hard to resist.

THE WINDOWLESS offices of the National Center for the Analysis of Violent Crime at Quantico, were located sixty feet below ground. Only the best in law enforcement were allowed within these subterranean walls.

Sunny glanced into the empty offices she passed, her body humming with excitement. She caught glimpses of varying degrees of clutter, from organized chaos to plain messy and disordered. Every available flat surface was littered with mountainous stacks of case files. Corkboards, easels and in some cases, the cinderblock walls themselves, were peppered with newspaper headlines, grisly shots of crime scenes and the brutal reality of victim autopsy photographs. She didn't shrink from the horrific images, but viewed them with the dispassionate eyes of a professional.

At the end of the corridor, she turned right, coming to a stop outside Klabo's office. The door stood open, but the office was deserted. Since she'd been instructed by the armed Marine guard at the front desk to wait inside, she walked into what she considered sacred ground, the hallowed domain of legendary criminologist, Reece Klabo.

Rather than taking up space in a power-position, the plain government-issue, gray metal desk was crammed into one corner of the office. A bookcase overflowing with books, files and documents sat behind the desk, serving as a makeshift credenza. The leather sofa on the opposite wall was old and weathered from years of use in what, she imagined, were many late-night sessions developing profiles of the country's most notorious killers.

The walls of Klabo's office were decorated with a series of charts and a South Carolina state map, flagged with colored pushpins indicating several cities around the Charleston area. Above the map and charts, a long row of seven eight-by-tens with the faces of pretty young girls, ranging in age from late teens to early twenties, smiled innocently at her.

She read the bold headlines tacked to the wall with blue adhesive putty to the right of the map. She understood the headlines had been designed to sell newsprint, but in her opinion, the press had gone overboard when they'd gruesomely dubbed the killer the Charleston Carver.

She shifted her attention to the worktable next to the sofa and the neatly arranged columns of photographs. A composite drawing sat off to the left of what she assumed was the unknown subject.

"Give me your first impression."

Sunny spun around at the unexpected sound of Klabo's voice. He wasn't an old man, in fact he was only fourteen years her senior, but he looked beyond his years due to the constant stress of the job. The deep lines of his face were those of a much older man, and his thinning, light brown hair was peppered heavily with gray at the temples. Not a big man, she estimated his height a couple inches shy of six feet, but he was fit, as evidenced by the ease with which he moved.

On the drive from her office to Quantico, she'd imagined various scenarios for this meeting, so she wasn't too surprised he was testing her abilities. She was more than ready for the challenge.

Returning the drawing to the table, she gave him a direct look. "White male, mid- to late-thirties," she said confidently. "Impulsive. Short-tempered."

Klabo walked to the front of the desk and leaned against the edge. He crossed his ankles and folded his arms over his chest. "Not bad," he said with a nod of approval. "Go on."

She scanned the headlines again, followed by a study of the crime scene photos of the seven victims spread over the table. The first thing she noticed was the similarities in the scenery. "The UNSUB uses a dumpsite to dispose of his victims," she said. "The damage he does to them takes time. These aren't the murder scenes. They're too public."

She continued to study the photos. "He's using force to overwhelm his victims," she said. "He wants to be an organized killer, but he lacks the patience to be truly successful. Sometimes he goes too far, though, and ends up killing the vic before he can complete the fantasy."

She picked up two particularly chilling postmortem photographs and carried them over to Klabo. "His impatience frustrates him," she continued without hesitation. "This angers him. It explains, if you'll excuse the term, the overkill evidenced in these vics. He's not arrogant, so you won't find him hanging around the investigation like most organized killers. And he's becoming more desperate, more deeply frustrated. His impatience will cause him to make mistakes."

Klabo set the two photographs facedown on the desk behind him. "Why mid- to late-thirties?" he questioned her.

"Two reasons," she said, walking back to the table. "The impatience of his kills indicates he hasn't reached an older man's maturity. Second, the hair."

She picked up the composite and handed it to Klabo, indicating the UNSUB's hairline. "It's thinning on top and receding. Hair loss at an earlier age is a possibility, but the deeper lines on the forehead provide a more accurate estimate of his age. The problem is that composites aren't a reliable source since no two witnesses will view the UNSUB the same way," she concluded, speaking from her own experience with the SEDSCAM investigation.

Klabo looked impressed, which boosted her confidence a few more notches. She'd been born to do this job.

"Why do you think the UNSUB is impulsive and short-tempered?" he asked.

"The shape of the nose is crooked and the bridge flat," she said. "That would indicate it's been broken, probably from fights. Says short fuse to me."

Another approving nod. "Is that why he overwhelms the vics?"

"No," she said. "Women don't find him attractive. The eyes are too cold. He doesn't have the kind of charm Bundy or Wilton had with women. I don't see any woman going with this UNSUB willingly."

"He could be hunting prostitutes," Klabo suggested.

Sunny shook her head and hitched her thumb to indicate the row of photographs on the wall. "We know he's not after prostitutes," she said. "Even if he were, he'd still have to overpower them. They're more streetwise, so it wouldn't take them long to realize something isn't right with this guy. They'd reject him, which would only infuriate him more because his prey hasn't cooperated. His temper would kick in and his attack would be over the top."

She glanced pointedly at the overturned photographs on Klabo's desk. "I suspect that's what happened because of the excessive damage in those two vics. He killed them before he could fulfill the fantasy. He blamed the vics and took out his rage on them. Even without studying the medical examiners' findings, I'm willing to bet his recent vics have shown more postmortem mutilation than his earlier kills."

She held her breath and waited.

Klabo tossed the composite on the desk with the photos. "Have a seat, MacGregor." He indicated the worn sofa. "You can breathe now. You impressed me. That was well thought out and methodical. A damned good analysis, even with the limited evidence available to you."

"Thank you, sir." She couldn't help but feel a huge sense of accomplishment. Klabo wasn't only a legendary criminologist, he also had a reputation for being impossible to please.

"You just profiled one of my agents, MacGregor." The lines of Klabo's face deepened when he smiled at her. "That drawing was someone's idea of a joke. There is no composite of the UNSUB in this case."

Her confidence fled as she sank into the brown leather. So much for a good impression. "I'm sorry," she said. "I didn't realize."

He waved away her apology. "Your analysis of the scene photos is what interests me. That was eerily accurate, MacGregor. How is it an agent from nonviolent crime can pull off what has taken some of my own agents months of intensive training to accomplish?"

She wasn't certain whether he'd just praised her or issued a veiled criticism. "I'm not sure what you mean."

"You don't have a lot of experience working violent crime," he said. "Your work in the D.C. field office consisted of background checks, the occasional surveillance and backup when necessary. Until two years ago when your involvement in the Romine incident resulted in the end of the careers of several agents, including the former assistant director of the Bureau, you were just another badge in a blue suit." He regarded her with a direct stare. "Your move to CID has produced some exemplary investigation work, but it's a hell of a lot different than what we do here."

"I'm aware my experience is limited in the violent crime area, but—"

He silenced her with a wave of his hand, then grabbed one of the photos she'd handed him during her analysis.

He stalked across the office and thrust the photo in front of her. "Take a good look, Agent MacGregor," he said in a harsh, biting tone. "That's the kind of sick shit we see down here every single day, sometimes it's a hell of a lot worse. Sometimes it's kids in this condition. I've watched seasoned agents under my command puke all over their shoes at less.

"This isn't exactly a Hallmark card," he continued, his dark brown eyes were as hard as his voice. "This is the handiwork of a sociopath with no regard for human life. How can you look at the mutilated corpse of a nineteen-year-old college student and not so much as blink?"

"If I blink, I might miss something," she said without missing a beat. This was her big chance, and she didn't want to screw it up by blowing smoke up his ass, telling him what she thought he wanted to hear. She went with her instincts, and that meant being completely honest. "Emotional involvement is a luxury that can cloud the truth. If you can't see clearly, then how many more nineteen-year-old college students will end up in this condition?"

He offered her a brisk nod, then walked back to the desk to resume his previous stance. "This job will eat at you until there's nothing left," he said. "The divorce rate in this unit is high. Burnout is even higher. Why do you want to work for me when you can stay in CID, move up the ranks to unit chief in maybe another ten to fifteen years?"

"Waiting it out in a cushy job until it's time to draw my pension doesn't interest me." She had a good idea where the conversation was headed and it pissed her off that he hadn't come right out and asked her about it.

She stood and faced him. "You've read my personnel file. I wouldn't be here if you hadn't already had me thoroughly checked out," she said, surprising herself by the steadiness of her voice. "What you want to know is what kind of Freudian bullshit is behind my wanting to join ISU. If the fact that a friend of mine was one of Gary John Wilton's victims will have an adverse effect on my performance. The answer to both is no, but it is the reason I became an agent."

"Think you can save the world from all the monsters hiding under the bed, do you?"

"No, sir," she said firmly, wondering when he was going to tell her to hit the pavement. Now, or after he ripped her a new one for her impassioned speech. "Not all. Just the worst of them."

He nodded approvingly. "Fair enough." He circled the desk and sat, the chair creaking under his weight.

"Relax, MacGregor," he said. "You're under consideration for the job. I will personally be monitoring your progress on SEDSCAM. I know it doesn't fall under my jurisdiction, but you can't be spared to run a test case out of this office. I discussed it with Burrows. He assures me the circumstances surrounding SEDSCAM are similar enough in theory to what we do here in NCACV for the case to be an effective gauge of your talent."

Great, she thought, careful to keep her opinion to herself. She was going to be judged on the case with zero leads.

He looked at her sharply. "Does it bother you that I'll be watching?"

"No, not at all." *Liar, liar, pants on fire.* "My job is to solve the case."

"You'll have someone constantly looking over your shoulder if you're going to be working for me. You better get used to it."

Great, she thought again. Or as Caruso would say, just goddamn peachy.

11

SUNNY WALKED into her office, closed the door and sagged against the smooth wood surface.

Just like that, she thought, thumping the back of her head against the door, she was one bad guy away from her chances of ever trying out her new masculine-sensitive bedding. At this rate, she'd never have sex.

She banged her head against the door again. And again before she winced and rubbed at the now tender spot. No way could she continue exploring the possibility of a relationship with Duncan. Not with the top cop she needed to impress breathing down her neck. With the SEDSCAM investigation under close scrutiny she couldn't afford so much as a whisper of impropriety. One wrong word blown in Klabo's direction and her shot at transferring to ISU would be history.

She'd already screwed up. First, she'd allowed him to partake in the interview of a material witness, then to further complicate matters, she not only confirmed his suspicions about the Miami incident, by revealing one of the aliases used by the UNSUB, she'd totally ignored the rules in order to gain information from him. Under no circumstances did the Bureau release information regarding a suspect to a nongovernmental entity.

She didn't break rules, she upheld them. Order, structure, those were the words etched on her badge of honor. A badge she'd just gone and tarnished. And for what? So she could have hot, sweaty sex with a guy that set her on fire with a look, an unconscious touch or the sound of his deep, velvety smooth voice?

Her head met the door for each, "Stupid, stupid, stupid," she muttered.

She pushed off the door before she caused herself serious brain damage. As much as it pained her neglected libido, she'd just have to cancel her date with Duncan for tomorrow night. What else could she do? Once she concluded the SEDSCAM investigation, perhaps they could get involved, but why? Just so she could have her heart trampled later rather than sooner? Eventually he'd end up resenting her job, and if she did receive the transfer, her life would become even more complicated. Klabo had told her the divorce rate in the unit was the highest in the Bureau. She imagined budding relationships didn't stand a chance with those odds.

Shrugging out of the dark-olive linen blazer she'd worn over the matching sleeveless sheath, she hung the jacket on the hook on the back of the door, then slipped off her shoulder holster and locked it in the file cabinet. She heard a soft knock before the door opened tentatively.

Georgia and Ned stood in the doorway, both looking at her expectantly.

"What?" she said a tad too snappish. Good grief, if she was already getting cranky, by the time she closed SED-SCAM she was sure to be a raging bitch. Duncan was to blame. Him and his effortless ability to awaken her hibernating hormones. "Stop looking at me like that."

Georgia rolled her eyes and pushed her way into Sunny's office. Ned followed on her heels. "How'd it go at ISU?" Georgia demanded.

Sunny glared at Ned. "Big mouth," she complained and closed the door again. She'd obviously made another mistake by trusting Ned to keep his yap shut about her meeting with Klabo. With an active investigation underway, she'd felt obligated to inform at least one member of her small team of her whereabouts. Georgia would've been her first choice because she knew the other woman could at least keep a secret. But since Georgia had been unavailable, she'd needed Ned around to take the call from the Dallas field office if it came in during her absence.

"If the Russians get hold of you, our national security doesn't stand a chance," she griped at Ned.

"Russia's no longer the enemy."

He dared to grin at her when she was in the middle of a snit. She seriously considered giving him a good swift kick in his designer-covered backside with the pointed toe of her low-heeled black pumps.

"I don't think she's read a newspaper in the last century," he said to Georgia, his grin widening.

She decided to ignore him.

"And where have you been?" she asked Georgia.

"Uh-huh." Georgia set a sheaf of papers on Sunny's desk then took the chair on the right while Ned occupied the left. "Tell us about the meeting with Klabo first."

Sunny walked around her desk and sat, giving the hem of her dress a sharp tug. She let out a sigh. They did deserve to know since they were a part of her team. She kept the details of her discussion with Klabo to a minimum then explained he'd be watching over their shoulders because she was now under consideration for a position with ISU.

"This means we have even more pressure to put a stop to the UNSUB," she concluded, then looked pointedly at Georgia. "Which reminds me, the three of us should always know where to find one another. No disappearing for hours without letting either me or Ned know where you can be found."

"I was doing research," Georgia explained. "I *might* have a theory, but we're going to need more data to be one-hundred percent."

Considering how much evidence she *didn't* have in this case, Sunny wouldn't be averse to asking a psychic for help at this point. *Oh, Miss Cleo, where are you now?*

Georgia rifled through the papers she'd set on Sunny's desk. "You were right about Wilder's interpretation of the UNSUB. There's definitely an artsy look to Abbott. But take a look at this and tell me what you think." She handed Sunny and Ned photocopies of the composite sketch taken that morning.

Sunny studied the drawing and did a visual comparison to the other composites still tacked to her wall. She saw the UNSUB, same as she did in all the other sketches, just a slightly modified version to fit the persona he'd portrayed to Wilder. She looked at Georgia and shrugged.

"Ever hear of Albrecht Dürer?" Georgia asked.

"German painter, big into the Venetians." Ned slid his glasses back up his nose as he looked down at the sketch in his hands. "Yeah, I see what you mean."

Sunny propped her elbow on her desk, dropped her head into her hand and rubbed at her temple. "What I know about fine art wouldn't cover the head of a pin," she complained.

"I know," Georgia said mildly sympathetic. "Picasso could smack you with a blue guitar and it'd do no good."

"Whatever you say."

"Dürer was an early sixteenth-century artist," Georgia explained. "He has some paintings to his credit, but he's primarily known for his engravings. Between 1513 and 1515 he produced his three most important works in the genre. A lot of ink has been spilled by art historians on these works, but take a look at this particular engraving."

She produced a photocopy of what appeared to Sunny to be a black-and-white drawing of an old, unattractive knight on an old, unattractive horse in the midst of a chaotic menagerie. The drawing, or engraving, she corrected, held a certain morbidity she found mildly disturbing.

"The earliest of the three engravings is this one, *Knight, Death and the Devil*," Georgia continued. "See the knight's calm determination?"

Sunny peered closer. "Okay," she said and shrugged.

"This piece reflects the contemporary religious preoccupations of the time," Georgia explained patiently. "Remember, this was all done during the Reformation, Martin Luther, that era. Almost all art during the Reformation contained symbolism, some more complicated than others. So Dürer's use of the knight in this instance is symbolic. See the dog running alongside the horse?"

At Sunny's nod, she continued. "Here, the dog is representative of untiring devotion. So, even the appearance of the Devil can't shake the knight's steadfast beliefs because he knows if he does, then the end result is Death."

Sunny blew out a stream of frustrated breath and rubbed more enthusiastically at her temple. "Georgia, get to the point. Please?"

"Remember yesterday when you said the UNSUB appears differently to each of his vics? We think—"

"But can't prove," Ned interjected.

"Right. We *think* this is intentional. He creates a persona and essentially becomes that persona. Well, what if he's trying to tell us something?"

"So far, we've been successful in keeping this case out of the press, so he isn't even aware that we're on to him," Sunny replied. For how much longer, though, she couldn't be sure. Wilder had drawn a lot of local media attention and she expected the journalistic vultures to start swarming any day now once they learned the feds had taken over jurisdiction on the case.

"I asked Wilder today what she and the UNSUB had talked about when they were together. Of course, she said, they often discussed art. She indicated the UNSUB had told her of his fascination with Albrecht Dürer. He'd even commented on this particular engraving, which is on display at the Met in New York City. Apparently, according to Wilder, he used to sit for hours at the gallery imagining what it had been like as a Christian knight so fierce in determination he could resist the temptation offered by the Devil."

"That's not so unusual," Ned told Georgia. "When I see Renoir's *Le Moulin de la Galette,* I can almost hear the murmur of conversation in the background. Can't you?" He looked to Sunny for confirmation.

She shrugged. "If you say so."

"While I was sitting through the session with Wilder this morning, it clicked. I went to the library afterward to do some research, which is where I was all afternoon." She produced another photocopy and set it on the desk next to the Wilder composite of Justin Abbott. "Uncanny, isn't it?"

Sunny stood and circled the desk so the three of them had a clear view of the two renditions. "I take it this is Dürer?" she asked, indicating the last photocopy Georgia had provided.

Georgia nodded. "It's called *Self Portrait.* Quite the hunk, isn't he?"

"Maybe if you're into six-hundred-year-old men," Ned added.

Sunny braced her hands on the desk and peered more closely at the two copies. "It's the eyes," she said slowly. "They both appear almost…lofty."

"I agree," Georgia said. "They underscore the solemn, almost religious feel, in an odd sort of way. Which, by the way, most art historians agree the Christ-like appearance was Dürer's intention."

Sunny straightened and folded her arms, still keeping her attention on the two photocopies. "Wilder and Abbott discussed art at length. Dürer is his favorite, so because Wilder's so familiar with the art world, she sees Dürer in her mind when she thinks about Abbott, and relates this to our sketch artist. So what does it tell us? That the UNSUB's seduction goes beyond sexual?"

Georgia gave her a look overflowing with confidence. "I hadn't thought of that. But I did come up with three possibilities. First look at the symbolism in the engraving. Devotion. Nothing will distract the knight from his true path. Temptation. The Devil trying unsuccessfully to steer the knight from his steadfast devotion. And finally Death. Not in the literal call-the-coroner sense, but symbolic death. The knight won't succumb to temptation because it will mean the end of his faith."

"The UNSUB is devoted to his task," Ned suggested. "He's staying the course and won't stop until we stop him."

"Exactly," Georgia said. "Second, what if he laid the groundwork so Wilder would subconsciously associate him with Dürer. You can pick up any art history text and find what I did today. I think he's taunting us, Mac."

Sunny admitted Georgia's theory could have merit, at least on the surface. "This is only one case," she warned.

"Granted, it's an interesting theory, but it might not hold up against the other cases."

The phone on Sunny's desk rang. "What was the third thing?" she asked, absently reaching for the phone.

Georgia's smile widened. "I think our UNSUB is from New York."

"MAC, HERE."

Duncan smiled at the sound of Sunny's voice. "If Mac were here, I could kiss her."

"Uh, hello." She didn't sound particularly welcoming. "What can I do for you?"

The coolness of her tone disappointed him. He'd been anticipating the sweet, intoxicating sound of her laughter, or a husky double-edged reply that would make him hard because he'd been unable to stop thinking about her. "That's a loaded question, babe. If you're alone, I'll be more than happy to tell you."

"No, I'm not."

He definitely detected an unmistakable chill in her voice, no question. Because he'd caught her off guard, or because he'd called her at work? "Bad time?"

"I'm sort of in the middle of something."

Ah, he thought, his ego marginally restored. "This'll be quick. Got a pen handy? Friday. My place. Forty-two, twenty-four—"

"Uh…about that. I'll have to pass."

Not exactly the enthusiastic response he'd been hoping to hear. What happened to the woman he'd held in his arms last night? The one who hadn't been shy in letting him know exactly what she wanted from him? *That* was the woman he wanted to talk to, the one he wanted in his bed, not this cold, distant impersonator. "Maybe we should—"

"No," she blurted. "It's just…I really can't. I'm sorry. It's not a good idea. Goodbye."

The line went dead.

Goodbye?

Duncan frowned and hung up the phone. That definitely had not been a polite end to a conversation goodbye. In fact, it sounded more like…

"Goodbye?" he muttered to himself. "What the hell was that all about?"

Marisa breezed into his office. "What was what all about?"

"It's nothing," he said, but his gut told him it was definitely *some*thing. If Sunny thought she could blow him off without an explanation, then she'd better start thinking again. He couldn't come up with a single reason for such a drastic change in her personality between last night and this afternoon, but he was determined to find out what had gone wrong.

"Have Rick get me the address for Sunny MacGregor," he asked Marisa. Tonight sounded like a good idea to him. "Somewhere in the D.C. area."

"The agent who was here yesterday?"

"One and the same." Or maybe there were two of them, he thought. The woman he'd just spoken to was a complete one-eighty from the one who'd left him standing in the parking lot in desperate need of a cold shower last night. She'd been an incredibly sexy temptress one minute, then a sweet, innocent flirt the next. She'd had him twisted in so many knots, he hadn't been able to think straight.

"Rick's out serving subpoenas again," Marisa said, heading for the door. "I'll ask Lucy, then I need you to clarify some points for me for my presentation tomorrow."

As he waited for Marisa to return, he tried to concentrate on the initial police report taken in the Wilder case, but his thoughts kept returning to Sunny and her mysterious behavior. He pushed the file away in disgust.

Maybe she simply wasn't interested in pursuing a relationship? If he were talking about another woman, he could buy that excuse, but this was Sunny. He didn't believe it for a second. He wasn't some teenaged virgin. A woman didn't nearly come unglued in his arms if she wasn't hot for him.

Something had spooked her, he decided. But what?

His determination to find the answer stemmed from more than wanting her in his bed. Now, more than ever, he needed to ensure the agency's success. His meeting this morning with Colin had shown him that his brother was serious about expanding his interests in the agency. Not only had Colin relieved him of nearly a third of the files that had been crammed in his office, he'd blown Duncan away when he'd handed over a sizeable check to help cover operating expenses until they were back on their feet financially and consistently generating revenue again.

Duncan had questioned him on where he'd gotten the money, of course, but thankfully Colin hadn't taken offense. He'd just smiled and told him when a guy didn't use his money to run after bad habits, he could save up an amazing amount of cash.

No way could Duncan ignore that kind of enthusiasm, especially when only three years ago Colin had been as close as he could get to rock bottom. The thought of watching his brother crawl back into the gutter made his stomach churn. Every time an addict fell off the wagon, the odds were against them making it back again. For that reason, Duncan knew he'd do whatever was necessary to ensure Colin's continued success.

And that, he decided, included finding out what had spooked Sunny and had her running in the opposite direction. He needed her and the information she had at her disposal that could lead him to the property stolen from Dearborn, Garfield and Wilder.

After his meeting with Colin he'd placed a few calls to his contacts in Miami and Dallas, but as he'd suspected, all he'd done was rack up more long distance charges. He'd hit the streets afterward and even his shadier contacts hadn't heard a word about a new cache of hot gemstones. The property had to be somewhere, but where? Unfortunately there was only one person who could answer that question—the Seducer.

Marisa returned and he spent the next hour going over the presentation with her. With the extra money that had come in and Colin's decision to take on a more active role, Duncan had decided to go ahead and offer Marisa the promotion after her meeting tomorrow. He and Colin had considered telling her today, but the kid was already giving nervous a whole new dimension. Lucy had been so thrilled with the hefty deposit she hadn't uttered a word of protest when Duncan instructed her to run an ad for a new administrative assistant and to initiate the paperwork for Marisa's pay to reflect her new position.

"Stop worrying," he told Marisa. He stood to help her carry her presentation materials into the conference room. "You'll ace it."

Her smile was tentative, but hopeful. "From your lips," she said with a nervous giggle.

Lucy barged into his office. "Well, now you've done it," she said in an accusatory tone. "I told you no good would come of you playing footsie with that fibbie."

"What are you talking about?"

"This!" Lucy thrust a sheaf of papers in front of him.

Duncan let out a sigh and took the fax from her. "It's

only a demand to produce documents," he said, scanning the cover letter signed by S. R. MacGregor on official FBI letterhead. "Not a big deal."

She could just be covering her ass, he thought. The Bureau invented the dotting of *i*'s and crossing of *t*'s, and he would've done the same thing. Except for her cool dismissal on the phone earlier, he might've believed the argument.

"I'm going to need the Garfield and Dearborn files copied before you leave tonight," he told Marisa. Sunny wanted his files, then he'd make damn sure she had them, but not without getting something in return. By one means or another, he'd find a way into her investigation, no matter what it took.

"I sent them out to a copy service," Marisa said. "The copier's broken, remember? The files won't be ready until tomorrow morning."

Damn.

He glanced at the clock on the edge of his desk, which he could actually see now that it was no longer covered by a mountain of files. Ten after six. "And they're probably closed by now."

"At five-thirty," Marisa told him.

He turned to Lucy. "Can you stop on your way in tomorrow and pick up the files? I've got a meeting downtown that's going to eat up half of my day."

"Consider it done," Lucy said and wrote a note to herself on a bright red square of paper. "I'll courier them over to Miss Fibbie as soon as I get in the office."

"No," he said and grinned. "Don't. I'll be delivering them to Special Agent MacGregor personally." Friday night sounded like a *very promising* time to him.

Lucy looked at Marisa over the rim of her bifocals. "Is

it just me," she started before shifting her gaze in Duncan's direction, "or do you see a full-blown pissing contest about to happen?"

12

SUNNY RETRIEVED her mail from the miniscule lock box located off the main lobby of her condominium complex. Without bothering to look at them, she dropped the small stack of envelopes into the heavy shopping bag weighing down her arm. The mail could wait. All she cared about at the moment was slipping under the stinging spray of a hot shower. An even hotter pastrami sandwich delivered by the local deli she kept on speed dial, and an icy bottle of Corona with a twist of lime would come next, followed by a night in front of the television while boning up on art history from the text she'd purchased at the Georgetown University bookstore on her way home from the office.

A damned sorry excuse for the Friday night she'd been eagerly anticipating. She'd made the right decision in calling off her date with Duncan and refused to succumb to guilt, depression or even regret.

Too much, anyway.

She hadn't heard from him since late yesterday afternoon, not that she blamed him after how rude she'd been during their very brief phone conversation. Her twenty-four-hour internal debate on whether or not to call him back and explain why she'd changed her mind continued to wage a bitter battle inside her. The thought of hearing his voice again, though, when she knew what she'd be missing was just too depressing. She had enough regrets, like not inviting him back to her place when she'd had the chance.

She managed a halfhearted wave of greeting to Burton, the doorman seated behind the faux-marble horseshoe counter, on her way to the bank of elevators. In the shiny brass panels of the alcove, she caught a disturbing glimpse of her reflection and winced. Good thing her only hot prospect tonight was sole possession of the remote control and the ten-pound textbook. She looked about as appealing as something one of her family's barn cats buried under the petunias. What little makeup she did wear had long ago faded, leaving her skin pale and bland. The two-week-old perm she'd let Georgia talk her into was a limp, tangled mess. What had been a crisp black linen skirt suit when she'd pulled it from her closet this morning was more wrinkled than a champion shar-pei.

Oh yeah, she had sex kitten written all over her, she thought sarcastically as she stepped into the elevator. Her voice mail would be demanding overtime pay for collecting all the enticing offers.

Not!

The elevator reached her floor and Sunny walked into the corridor only to wrinkle her nose when she caught a whiff of the lingering odor of newly painted walls. She'd been one of the first to purchase a unit when the condo complex had gone up six months ago. She would've thought she'd be accustomed to the unpleasant paint smell by now, but with new tenants still moving in on a regular basis and anxious to decorate their homes, it was unavoidable. Not a single one of the brief glimpses she'd caught of the other units on her floor revealed the boring, standardized eggshell-white walls of her condo. She'd spied brilliant splashes of color, wallpaper designs in rich hues and even mosaic-tiled walls in the small foyer of the condo belonging to the gay couple across the hall. In comparison her place was…well, boring.

Just like her love life, she thought. She had only herself to blame. Opportunity had come along in the form of a major hottie and what did she do? Gave him the kiss-off. Since she wouldn't be having sex anytime soon, perhaps she should consider sprucing up her living space. Go for bold and exciting.

She'd rather have bold and exciting sex. With Duncan.

She pulled her keys from the pocket of her blazer when she reached her door and fingered the key for the top dead-bolt. She didn't know what was wrong with her tonight. With less than a month until her thirtieth birthday, she had everything in life she could possibly want. Professionally she had no complaints, and even the job of her dreams was within reach. On a personal level, her accomplishments surpassed those of many single women her age. She owned her own home and just last week she'd made the final payment on her Jeep Liberty. Other than a couple of credit card balances that were more than manageable, she wasn't bogged down in debt, either, even with her new mortgage payment. Unlike her sister, Dale, who went through money like water, Sunny didn't live paycheck to paycheck, and after deducting her down payment on the condo, her savings account remained moderately respectable. Already thinking ahead to her golden years, she'd even invested in a couple of low-risk mutual funds.

If every aspect of her life was going so well, then why did she suddenly feel so…incomplete?

Duncan Chamberlain, that's why.

She rammed a key into the second lock. She may have

been living like a nun for the past few months, but no one could ever accuse of her practicing to become one. She'd been drawn to a number of men in her lifetime, so why hadn't a single one of them ever invaded her thoughts with the same consistency as Duncan?

Probably because none of them *were* Duncan.

She blew out a stream of breath, finished off the last lock and opened the door. Juggling her purse, the weighty shopping bag and her briefcase, she disengaged the alarm system, reset the locks and lugged her packages into the small pentagon-shaped dining room. Careful not to scratch the glass-topped table, she set her things on the clear surface and snagged the cordless phone from the holder she kept on the antique buffet. She sank into one of the taupe jacquard chairs, toed off her pumps and punched in the speed dial code for the local deli, only to be instantly placed on hold.

She flicked a speck of lint from the silk plant on the center of the dining table before dropping her chin into her hand. Duncan's effect on her could have something to do with the sinfully sexy tilt of his mouth and the way he certainly knew how to use it. Or maybe her obsession stemmed from the way his big masculine body had felt against hers. The directness of his gaze when he spoke to her, or the way his eyes darkened to a soft warm gray when he was aroused certainly did a number on her. And how could she forget the rich sound of his deep, velvety-smooth voice? Or the way he made her laugh in a way she hadn't done in ages.

Try all of the above, dummy.

Still waiting for the clerk to come back on the line, she slid out of the chair and headed for the kitchen and the ice-cold beer she'd been thinking about on the way home from work. She cut up a lime then twisted the juice from a section into the neck of the bottle before taking a long drink. Good, but nowhere near as satisfying as she'd hoped.

Returning to the table, she pulled her mail from the shopping bag. Bank statement, a couple of utility bills, a credit card statement, the quarterly reminder that her car insurance was coming due and a thick white linen envelope from her folks. She smiled wryly at their hypocrisy, wondering if her nontraditionalist parents even realized the irony of a formal invitation to celebrate something as traditional as thirty years of marriage. An anniversary which just happened to fall the day before her thirtieth birthday.

The clerk finally picked up the line and Sunny placed her order. She included Tiramisu with her pastrami, then decided she needed even more comfort food, adding a pasta salad and a side of marinated mushrooms. The clerk promised to be at her door in forty-five to sixty minutes, which gave her more than enough time to shower.

After calling downstairs to let the doorman know she was expecting a delivery, she slipped a twenty from her wallet and set it on the table in the entry before heading for the shower. She emerged fifteen minutes later refreshed, but that incomplete feeling continued to plague her.

She dried off, then pampered herself in a feminine ritual she generally refrained from during the work week by smoothing tangerine-mango-scented lotion over her skin. The thought of a bra held zero appeal, but until the deli dude made an appearance, she decided against letting the girls roam free for the time being. With optimum comfort still at the forefront of her mind, she slipped into a white lace bra and a matching pair of panties. Tugging a loose-fitting white cotton tank top over her head, she settled on a pair of pale yellow French terry shorts. After coating her damp curls with the goopy stuff the hairstylist at the salon made her promise she'd use religiously, she padded across the earth-toned Berber carpet to her dresser for a pair of socks. The temperature could soar to one hundred and fifty degrees and her feet would still be cold.

Before she could sit on the dusty teal comforter to pull on her socks, the doorbell rang. She hadn't realized she'd been in the shower that long.

Rushing down the hall, socks still in hand, she snatched the twenty off the table. Without bothering to peer through the peephole, she unlocked the two deadbolts followed by the useless, insecure lock inside the knob, then swung open the door.

Shock rumbled through her. The lively staccato rhythm in her chest beat like a frantic drum. A knot formed in her stomach, then slowly drifted south, creating a warmth inside her in a way only one man possibly could ignite. Duncan.

Damn, he looked good. And so much more appetizing than the food she'd been expecting. He wore a pair of dark jeans lightly faded in all the right places that clung to his lean hips. The sleeves of his white, gauzy button-down shirt were rolled back to reveal those mouthwatering forearms. He looked deliciously appealing, and way out of her price range.

She blinked. Once. Twice. Three times before she remembered to frown at him. "What are you doing here?" she demanded.

His gaze swept over her, slowly, meticulously. Not at all unlike what she'd spent far too many hours imagining he'd be doing with his hands tonight if she hadn't come to her senses.

"It's Friday. We had a date, remember?" The promise of a smile teased his lips.

Her imagination sparked.

The temptation to throw her arms around him and apologize for being stupid and stubborn and rude overwhelmed her. Unfortunately, there'd be no acting out of that particularly fantasy anytime soon.

Disappointment that he was off limits jockeyed for position against relief that she still possessed enough intelligence to understand her actions came with consequences she wasn't willing to take.

Her gaze traveled down the length of him. Disappointment beat the pants off relief by a mile.

"Mind if I come in?" he asked.

Yes, she minded. She minded a lot. While she was at it, she also took issue that he'd been occupying her thoughts since they'd met when she needed to concentrate on how to capture a seducing, thieving scammer. Duncan's mere presence made her question the wholeness of her life, and that bothered her, too. And if she was honest, then she had to admit that what she really wanted was to forget all her silly concerns and lead him straight into her bedroom where they could make love until nothing else mattered except mindless pleasure.

Against her better judgment, she stepped back and waved him inside. "How did you find me?" she asked once he closed the door behind him. "I'm not listed."

He turned the power of that damned smile on full-blast. "When I want something, I go after it."

Her knees went weak. Forget the bedroom. The sterile, boring white tiles in the entry were looking better by the second.

She set her socks and the twenty on the hall table, then rested her backside against the edge before wrapping her fingers over the edge of the smooth wood. *Not* to test its durability, either, but because being so impossibly close to him stretched the limits of her resistance. "What do you want, Duncan?"

"We'll get to what I want later," he said, boldly taunting her. He set a thick envelope she hadn't even realized he'd been carrying next to her. "You wanted copies of my files, remember?"

He was certainly asking a lot since she could barely recall her own name.

His knuckle grazed her hip. Her breasts tightened, followed by the most delightful tremor that chased down her spine. He didn't appear to even notice the distress she was under.

She cleared her throat. "You should've sent them to my office."

"I was coming here, anyway," he said and shrugged.

"Apparently I didn't make myself clear that we wouldn't be seeing each other tonight." The man was far from obtuse. Arrogant? Without a doubt, his presence offered her enough proof to solidify that belief. But dense? Hardly. He'd simply chosen to ignore her decision.

Rather than moving away so she could breathe, he deliberately invaded her space. Bracing his hands on the surface of the table, he bracketed her hips and leaned toward her, holding her captive.

An unwilling prisoner? She hadn't yet decided, but no seemed as good an answer as any.

"I wasn't sure who I spoke to yesterday." A devilish light entered his gaze and her heart started hammering all over again. "It sure didn't sound like the Sunny I know."

No, she probably hadn't, she thought guiltily. "The Sunny you thought you knew is currently unavailable. At least until this Sunny wraps up SEDSCAM."

Was it her imagination or did he just lean in closer? Since she'd just admitted to multiple personalities, she didn't think she was in a position to objectively assess the situation.

"What changed between Wednesday night and Thursday afternoon?"

Nothing. Everything.

He did deserve an explanation. Georgia and Ned had been in her office when he'd called and she'd gladly opted for the coward's way out by taking advantage of their presence to avoid having to quantify her decision.

"Sunny?" he pressed.

She let out a breath, wishing he'd back off, but wanting him closer at the same time. "I'm being watched," she told him. "SEDSCAM has become my test case for a position in ISU. Klabo himself is monitoring my progress on this one, and that means I can't afford so much as a whiff of impropriety."

He shrugged. "So?"

"You obviously don't understand what a chance like this means to me."

"No, I get it." He removed one hand from the table and drew his fingers lightly down the length of her leg, from the hem of her shorts to her knee, then back up again. "But one has nothing to do with the other."

She struggled to ignore the heat uncurling in her belly and concentrate on their conversation. The sudden dampness of her panties when the heat of his palm slid more boldly down her leg made a mockery of her attempted lucidity.

"Don't be ridiculous." Her breath caught. "Of course it does." She reassessed her earlier position on dense. His or hers, she couldn't begin to fathom. "You of all people should know you don't stop being an agent at five o'clock.

Remember the oath we swore to uphold? The one that talks about integrity? Well, that just happens to hold meaning for me, okay?"

"What we do after hours is our business." The tips of his fingers slipped beneath the hem of her shorts, drawing enticing, distracting patterns beneath the fabric along her thigh. "I don't think we'll have any trouble separating business from…"

His lazy smile widened when he dipped his finger along the inside of her thigh. She shifted, easing her legs slightly apart to give him plenty of room.

"Pleasure," he finished.

He really didn't need to stare at her mouth like that. She had no trouble whatsoever discerning his meaning. "There's nothing *to* separate." Except maybe Duncan from his clothes.

He dipped his head and nuzzled the side of her neck. A rush of breath left her when his tongue nailed the sensitive spot between her shoulder and neck.

"Besides, what's the point?" She tipped her head to the side. "Once I join ISU, it isn't like I'll even have the energy for a personal life. Longer hours, constant travel, not to mention the drain—"

He gently nipped at her skin, stilling her argument before he soothed the spot with his tongue. "Sounds like a convenient excuse to me."

"It's reality. My reality." Between his fingers gently massaging her inner thigh and the delightful little love nips against her throat, her current reality was becoming difficult to ignore.

"Trust me, it'll get ugly." She tightened her grip on the edge table. "Been there before and hated that."

"Ugly?" He tongued the hollow of her throat. "I doubt that," he said against her skin.

She tipped her head back, thrusting her breasts forward, willing him to touch her, to cup the weight in his palm, to take her into his mouth. "You'll eventually resent my career," she continued to ramble, "which will turn me into an intolerable bitch, who will drive you away. We'll say mean things to each other, you'll break my heart and it'll end badly. Who needs the headache?"

He lifted his head and looked down at her with those get-lost-in-me eyes that had changed to a deep, smoky gray with just a tad too much arrogance. "I'll break your heart, huh?" He pried her fingers from the table and lifted her arms over her head, then whipped off her tank top and tossed it on the floor.

Appreciation filled his gaze as he looked at her. Her heart took a dive off a cliff when she caught sight of the barely discernable tremble in his hands as he lightly drew his fingers over the slope of her breasts.

"I think you could." In fact, she was sure he would, provided she was dumb enough to fall for him. He'd easily shatter her heart into a million irreparable pieces. Then what would she have? Boring walls *and* a broken heart.

His thumb circled her nipple. "You think too much."

The tug of desire was so sharp she couldn't think straight. "Just a sampling of my bad habits. See? It's starting already."

"Babe, we haven't even begun."

She knew without an ounce of doubt he was referring to something far more incredible. His hands found the waistband of her shorts and she didn't consider not standing so he could push them over her hips. She barely managed to kick them aside with her foot when he took hold of her hips and lifted her fully onto the hall table. She reached for him, but he ignored her silent plea to bring their bodies together. Instead, he hooked his hand under one of her knees, lifting her leg to rest her foot on the edge of the table. If it weren't for the flimsy lace panties, she'd be completely open and exposed to him. Vulnerable. With her hands on his shoulders to steady herself, she understood her trust in him exceeded any she'd ever given to anyone before.

He lifted her hands from his shoulders, then placed them behind her, narrowing the space between them. With his fingers laced through hers, he held her immobile, then dipped his head and kissed her. His mouth was hot, demanding, the kiss bordering on fierce in its intensity. This was what she would be giving up, and she wasn't sure she had the strength. Was she really willing to risk everything she'd ever worked for, for a few nights of what promised to be unbelievably memorable sex?

She tore her mouth from his. "Duncan, wait."

He didn't. Instead he set her skin on fire, placing kisses along her jaw, trailing a fiery path down the column of her throat to the slope of her breasts.

"What if we get caught?" she asked.

He lifted his head to look at her. Desire burned in his eyes. Oh hell, the way he was looking at her, she decided she didn't give a rat's ass if her condo was bugged with a direct link to Klabo's office. No way was she letting this man out of her sight until they finished what he'd started. She'd deal with tomorrow, tomorrow. Or the day after that. Or…

"Forget I said anything," she said.

A crooked half smile canted his lips. He removed his hands from hers and settled them on her waist, his thumbs dipping teasingly beneath the lace of her already damp panties. "The threat of discovery is a powerful aphrodisiac. Heightens the pleasure."

"As if we need any help in that—" The rest of her statement stilled on her tongue as he drew the length of his finger lightly over her exposed core. His touch, combined with the press of lace against her sensitive flesh created one of the most erotic sensations she'd ever experienced. "Area," she finally finished. "Oooh, do that again."

He did, applying the slightest amount of pressure. Her hips bucked against his hand. "You like that, don't you?"

"Hmmm," she murmured, dropping her head back against the wall. She closed her eyes, arched her back and surrendered the fight to a battle she had no desire to win. She sighed with pleasure when the warmth of his mouth, closed over her breast, the heat of his tongue flicking against her nipple through the lace of her bra. She wanted him, needed him in a way she couldn't remember ever wanting another man. More than her next breath or the next beat of her heart.

He gave equal attention to her other breast. Stroking her, he increased the pressure by the slightest degree just enough to push her closer to the edge of no return.

"What about this?" The warmth of his breath fanned her ear. He pushed aside the lace, exposing all of her, before easing his finger deep inside her. A moan bubbled up from inside her at the delicious intrusion of him pushing into her body. He withdrew slowly, spreading the moisture he collected over her folds, taking reverent care in caressing her swollen, throbbing clit. "Do you like it this way?" he asked her, his voice ragged.

"More," she whispered, lifting her hips. She wanted much more. She wanted all of him, filling her, pleasuring her, and she never wanted the moment to end.

He answered her demand, slipping two fingers inside her.

"Yes." The word came out on a hiss of breath. She lifted

her hips even higher, pulling him more deeply inside her body. It wasn't enough. "More," she whimpered.

"Oh, my…yes." She felt her body give to accommodate him, felt the liquid heat of her own arousal and it still wasn't enough to quell the pressure building inside her. She arched her back, then opened her eyes to look down at his incredibly talented hands giving her pleasure, marveling at the sight of him inside her body. With both feet on the table supporting her, she lifted her hips and took him as far as her body would allow.

His other hand held her bottom to steady her, his fingers kneading her flesh. Her head fell back and she cried out as she inched closer and closer to the center of exquisite pleasure.

"Come for me, babe," he whispered.

Her body trembled. She cried out, but the release she sought remained out of her grasp. "Take me there." She managed to rasp the words around the tightening of her throat.

His hand moved from her bottom, but she didn't much care once he caught her clit between his fingers. More pressure. More pleasure.

She rode him hard, stroking, reaching, searching for blessed release. Her moans grew louder, more insistent the closer he carried her toward the edge.

"That's it, baby," he encouraged her. "Take it all." He thrust harder and faster.

She whimpered. Her body trembling, straining closer… so close.

"You're so wet," he said roughly and kicked the pressure on her clit up a notch. "So hot and slick."

The first electrifying sparks burst within her with a force she'd never known before. "Duncan!" she called out as her world tilted.

"I'm here," he said, reassuring her. "Let it go, babe. I'll keep you safe."

Her eyes flew open and she looked at him in wonder as another explosion of pleasure ripped through her. She cried out and reached for him, her fingers digging into his shoulders as she rode wave after wave of the rush of molten heat.

She clung to him, trusting him to keep his word. Trusting him to keep her safe.

The world slowly righted. Somehow his arms were around her, holding her against him, his hand smoothing her hair away from her face. The beat of his heart against her ear comforted her. The heat of his body warmed her. The tenderness in the way he held her touched her so deeply she feared she'd weep.

The ringing of the doorbell startled her. "Damn," she muttered. Her dinner. She'd completely forgotten.

Duncan pulled back to look down at her. "Expecting someone else?" he asked.

She managed a weak smile shook her head. "Deli delivery," she said. "Oh God, I can't move." She didn't want to move, either, but she didn't see much difference at this point. Want. Can't. She didn't care so long as he continued to hold and stroke her with such sweet gentleness.

With more reluctance than she would've ever believed possible, she slipped out of his embrace and searched for the twenty that had been on the hall table. She found it tangled in her discarded clothes and forgotten socks, scooped them all up and handed him the money. "Here," she said, then reached up to plant a quick kiss on his lips. "I'll be right back."

The wicked grin on his face had her pulse revving all over again. "I'll find you."

She nodded and took off toward the bedroom, dropping

her top, then her shorts in the hallway. She unhooked her bra and left it near the bedroom door, then slipped out of her panties and hung them on the doorknob. She didn't want him to have any trouble finding her.

As far as she was concerned, once he stepped into her bedroom, tomorrow would be a long time coming...at least for this weekend.

13

DUNCAN STOOD with his hands braced on the faux marble counter in Sunny's kitchen, fighting to regain control of his libido despite the ridiculous impossibility of the task. He'd come to Sunny's apartment with a solid, crystal-clear agenda, but for the life of him, he was having a hell of time remembering exactly what that had been. Work, obviously, but that was the last thing on his mind at the moment, not when there was a woman—hopefully naked—waiting for him to join her in the next room.

The tantalizing aroma of spices from whatever Sunny had delivered wafted from the plastic sack he'd set on the counter, drawing his attention. He set the bag inside the refrigerator and reached for one of the bottles of water. Food may be the least of his priorities, but the bottle of sparkling wine on one of the lower shelves held definite possibilities.

He walked to the edge of the kitchen. "How about some wine?" he called out to Sunny.

"That's fine," she answered from the bedroom. "Glasses are in the top cabinet on the left by the sink."

He located a pair of frighteningly delicate champagne flutes and set them on the counter. A search of her neatly arranged cabinets didn't produce an ice bucket, so he improvised with the largest bowl he could scrounge up, filled it with ice, then wrapped a kitchen towel around the bottle before removing the cork.

With the makeshift ice bucket and flutes in hand, he headed for the hallway she'd disappeared down. A pair of yellow shorts marked the entrance to the short corridor, followed by a filmy tank top and two thick, fuzzy socks and finally her lace bra, leading the way to her bedroom door. The lace panties that had nearly had him requiring respiratory therapy when he'd removed her shorts, hung from the knob like the final clue leading the way to the prize beyond.

"What took you so long?"

His eyes slowly adjusted to the dimness of the room, cast in shadows from the soft, flickering candlelight. Several fat pillar-style candles were scattered throughout the room, on the long dresser, the tall bureau and one on each nightstand beside a queen-size bed with the covers drawn back. But no Sunny. "I had to navigate an obstacle course," he said. "Where are you?"

"Waiting."

He turned toward the sound of her soft voice. She emerged from what he suspected to be the master bathroom, stepping into the light where he could finally see her.

"For you," she added.

She crossed the room toward him, predatory and beautiful. Her lips, still swollen from his kisses, were curved into the beguiling smile of a woman confident in what she wanted and unafraid to make her demands known. He appreciated her boldness, liked that she didn't try to play coy, and loved how close she'd come to mindless earlier. He wondered if her confidence would wane if she knew that had been only the beginning of where he planned to take her tonight.

If his hands hadn't been full, he'd have hauled her up

against him and kissed her senseless. The need to touch her, to smooth his hands over her curves, to explore every luscious inch of her body, had his dick throbbing painfully. He'd never wanted to thoroughly possess a woman, not in the way he longed to make Sunny his.

The realization gave him a moment's pause, wondering exactly how complicated a relationship would be for them. For her especially, now that she was close to achieving her goal. He was well aware his connection to SEDSCAM could cause problems for her, and he couldn't ignore the nudge from his conscience that any involvement with him might hurt her chances for a transfer to ISU.

If he told her the truth about his leaving the Bureau, there'd be no way in hell she'd let him near her investigation. That aspect alone had already been compromised with her news the big shot in ISU was personally monitoring her progress on the case. Convincing her to let him in now would take some fancy maneuvering on his part, but he felt confident she'd let him play inside her sandbox. If he came clean about being relieved from duty for misconduct, not only could he blow his three biggest cases, but he'd place the business and his brother's continued success in jeopardy.

Bravery, fidelity, integrity. The bravery and fidelity portions weren't an issue. But he knew for damned sure Sunny would make a federal case out of the integrity part of the Bureau's motto, and nights like tonight would be nothing but a fond memory.

She took the bowl from him and carried it to the nightstand. "Left or right?"

"Excuse me?"

"The bed," she said. "Do you sleep on the left or the right?"

He walked over to the nightstand and set the glassware beside the bowl. A strip of half-dozen gold foil packets lay next to the lamp. Such blind faith, he thought and smiled.

Her hands drifted over his back, slowly winding around his waist until her slender body brushed up against his back, her cheek pressed against his spine. He looked down at her hands splayed across his abdomen. No way in hell could he walk away from her.

Deciding to take his chances, he loosened her hold on him and turned to face her. "Who says we'll be sleeping?"

Her smile broadened. "Ambitious men are so sexy," she purred wickedly.

He smoothed his hands over the bare skin, down her back to her rounded bottom and urged her close. He dipped his head, kissing her thoroughly and sealing his fate with the first sweep of his tongue inside the sweet warmth of her mouth.

For now, he elected not to think about the future. No purpose would be served worrying about what would come during the light of day or what vital parts of his anatomy Sunny would divest him of once she discovered the truth. Instead, he shoved his reservations deep into the shadows. For tonight, all that mattered was Sunny, sensual exploration and mutual pleasure.

She made short work of the buttons on his shirt, then shoved the fabric down his arms. With her face cupped gently in his palms, he made love to her mouth while she unfastened the buckle of his belt and the button-fly of his jeans. Her hand dipped beneath the waistband of his briefs, boldly wrapping her slender fingers around his length. His hips jerked, and she moaned softly in his mouth.

She broke contact, then used her lips, her teeth and her tongue to kiss, nip and lave his chest. He let go of her long enough to remove his shirt. Before it hit the floor, her hands were suddenly everywhere—on his abdomen, at his waist, shoving his jeans down his legs, kneading his ass, teasing his inner thighs. The warmth of her breath fanned his cock, and he sucked in a sharp breath as she cupped his balls in her hand.

"Hmm, so heavy," she murmured, then drew her tongue up the length of his dick with agonizing slowness. Her lips brushed against the head before her tongue lapped at the moisture gathered on the tip.

"Not for long if you keep that up," he said tightly.

Her laughter was low, husky and so seductive he had to count to ten to maintain control. "I don't think we'll have any problem keeping you up."

If she kept talking that way, he'd be over the edge in no time. She'd already pushed him too close for comfort.

She settled to her knees in front of him, and his stomach bottomed out as she slowly slid her warm, moist lips over the head of his cock. With the tips of his fingers on her shoulders, he braced his feet slightly apart and lowered his gaze, watching her love him with her mouth in long, slow, wet strokes.

The pressure built fast. Too fast. He gritted his teeth and looked away only to catch their reflection in the antique mirror angled in the corner of the room. The view was even more erotic. Her knees were slightly parted, and her shapely backside raised upward as her hips slowly rocked back, then forward with each deep stroke of her mouth, giving him a perfect, clear view of her center from behind. Under the warm glow of the candlelight, he stared in amazement at their reflection, his gaze zeroing in on the dewy moisture glistening between her legs.

The revelation that her going down on him was making

her wet pushed him past the limits of his control. Unable to withstand another nanosecond of her exquisite brand of sensual torture, he reached for her. She dipped her shoulders to escape his grasp and her hands flew to his ass, gripping him firmly with both hands, the edge of her fingernails biting into his flesh. She pumped him harder, faster with her mouth, but it was the whimper of need in her throat, vibrating around his cock that proved his downfall.

His control shattered and he flew over the edge into sweet oblivion with a velocity that rocked his core. A growl ripped from his chest. His knees threatened to buckle from the force of his release, yet she still refused to relinquish him, milking him and pushing him further into the abyss as the aftershocks of ecstasy rolled through him.

His heart pounded in his chest until he thought it would burst. The ringing in his ears was even more deafening as he struggled to regulate his breathing. Damn, he hadn't meant for *that* to happen quite so fast.

Slowly, Sunny rose to her feet, placing biting little kisses over his flesh. She took his hand and laced their fingers together, then slid their joined hands down to her damp curls. Parting her legs slightly, she guided him to her heated core. "You made me all wet," she rasped, her breathing nearly as hard as his own. "I almost came giving you head."

She released his hand and wrapped her fingers around his biceps. Her head tipped back and her lips opened as she rocked against his hand while keeping her half-lidded, desire-filled gaze locked with his.

"Tell me what you want," he demanded, his voice rough from lack of oxygen.

He pressed his thumb against her clit then circled the tender, swollen flesh. Her eyes darkened to the color of rich jade, and she drew in a sharp breath through her teeth. Her lips turned into a sexy pout and she moaned, the sound incredibly arousing. "I want you inside me," she whispered. She pressed down and tightened her slick, hot sheath around the length of his fingers buried inside her.

He needed a little time before he could satisfy that particular demand. With her already nearing the point of total mindlessness, he had a good feeling the wait wouldn't be a long one. Especially when there were so many other ways he wanted to bring her pleasure.

Needing to catch his breath, but not wanting to give her a chance to cool, he gently urged her down onto the bed. Sliding his body over hers, he tasted her skin, explored her curves at his leisure despite her whimpers of protest and the urgency of her hands demanding he speed up the process.

He had no intention of rushing things. Rising above her, he supported his weight on his elbows, then lightly brushed the hair from her face. "Shhh," he murmured, then kissed the frown marring her porcelain complexion. "We have all night. All weekend for that matter. What's the rush, babe?"

"I want you," she whispered. She looped her arms around his neck. Uncertainty entered her gaze. "So much it's scaring me."

"There's nothing to be afraid of." Except maybe him following through on her prediction of breaking her heart when she found out he hadn't been completely honest with her. "I'm not going anywhere." God help him, he meant every last word.

"Then make love to me," she said before lifting her lips to his. Her kiss was fierce, hot and demanding.

He palmed her breast and she arched into his hand when he dragged his thumb lazily over the tight peak. Her fingers sank into his hair and she urged his head down. Taking her breast into his mouth had her hips rolling up to meet his.

He left her long enough to snag one of the pillows gathered against the headboard. "Lift your hips," he gently ordered, then adjusted the pillow beneath her bottom to elevate her. He gently pressed her thighs open, exposing her hot, wet center.

He dotted the tender flesh of her abdomen with kisses while rhythmically stroking her slick folds with his finger until she let out a soft moan and stretched her arms over her head, palms up. She closed her eyes, offering her sweet body to his will. He wondered if she had any idea how he treasured the precious gift she gave to him so freely.

He shifted his weight and settled between her thighs, awed by the sight of her petal-soft feminine flesh slick with the evidence her arousal. Carefully, he spread her folds, exposing her core and the tight swollen clit he ached to taste. Tracing the opening with the tip of his finger, he slipped inside to collect and smooth the thick, wet heat over the pink, throbbing bud. Her hips bucked when he touched the ultratender flesh, followed by a low, deep groan so sultry his dick began to throb.

He wanted her so mindless with passion, so caught up in need that all that mattered to her was the pleasure he could give her. And then he took her there.

He pushed her, teased her closer to the edge until she was tossing her head from side to side, her hands gripping the sheets. The orgasm she sought, he intentionally kept just out of her reach.

He pushed inside her and felt her muscles contract around his fingers. Stroking her, long, slow, then changing the pace when he felt her close to coming apart, only to slow her down again. Her cries of frustration grew louder, her breathing hard. His own arousal reached the point of pain, but he wanted her wild for him before he took her and made her completely his.

Dipping his head, he tasted her. With her hips elevated, he lapped her need with his tongue. Her cries turned to deep groans of intense pleasure. He continued to stroke her deeply and suckled her throbbing clit. She came hard, crying his name, her body convulsing around his hand as the waves of pleasure crashed through her.

Remembering the sparkling wine on the nightstand, he retrieved the bottle from the ice bucket. He took a drink, then settled his mouth over her hot center, allowing the wine he held in his mouth to mingle with the moisture pooled inside her. Then he drank from her.

Sunny was certain she'd just imploded. From the inside out, sensations overlapped, intersecting and becoming confused in her mind. Cool. Hot. Slick. Wet. His mouth. His hands. The effervescence of the sparkling wine on his tongue, inside her.

Too much, she thought. It was all too much and the cry that tore from her lips was long and forceful as another orgasm crashed into her before she could recover from the last one or even catch her breath. Powerless to calm the riotous explosions, helpless against the intense pleasure convulsing through her, all she could think of was that she wanted more, more, more.

She wanted Duncan inside her, to feel his long, hard length deep within her body, stroking her, filling her. He drove her positively insane, made her crazy from the steady stream of shockwaves rocking her.

The pillow disappeared, and she felt the strong grip of his hands tugging her toward the edge of the bed. With great care, he turned her over onto her stomach, then eased her onto her knees. She lifted her hips and he entered her from behind, connecting their bodies in one, long swift thrust. His hands held her hips as he withdrew, then pushed into her again, this time with such agonizing slowness she thought she'd die from the new wave of incredible sensation setting her body on fire. Using her arms to support herself, she widened her stance to take him deeper and lifted her bottom higher, wanting every glorious inch of him to fill her. Each stroke of his body increased the pressure building up inside her again. She hadn't believed it physically possible for another orgasm to be within her reach so quickly.

He increased the tempo of his thrusts. The wild moan that escaped her lips only made him drive into her harder. The tension inside her grew. When he reached his hand between her legs and caught her clit between his fingers, the orgasm slammed into her with the force of a meteor. She flew apart and grabbed his wrist, pressing his hand more firmly against her mound, riding the wave of ecstasy with a wildness unlike any she'd ever known. He'd done this to her, made her feel raw, primitive. Somewhere in the back of her mind she heard a deep, primal growl and was shocked to realize the sound had come from her.

She felt Duncan thrust into her one last time. The hand still clasping her hip bit into her flesh as the force of his own release overtook him. Never in her life had she experienced anything so exquisite, so pure and beautiful as pleasure coursing through their bodies simultaneously. Physically, she didn't know if she'd ever recover, but she couldn't wait to experience the emotional oneness again.

"Oh God," she muttered breathlessly and slid down onto the mattress as if liquefied. She rolled onto her side and watched in fascination as he discarded a condom she hadn't even realized he'd worn.

"You were, uh…occupied at the time." His lips tipped upward into a grin that under normal circumstances would have started her pulse pounding. Since he'd already cornered the market in that area considering her pulse rate threatened cardiac arrest, she figured he'd just gotten a two-for-one bargain.

How on earth he had the strength to move, let alone take the few steps necessary to reach the waste can she kept by the nightstand, was beyond her. He joined her on the bed seconds later, and she mustered up the last of her energy reserves to scoot next to him.

He pulled the sheet over them to ward off the chill as their sweat-drenched bodies cooled. Wrapping his arms around her, he effortlessly hauled her halfway up his body so she lay draped across his chest. She let out a very contented sigh and closed her eyes, lulled by the rhythm of his heart beating against her ear.

"The right," he said suddenly.

His voice sounded raspy, sleepy, and she smiled, feeling a tad egotistical about her role in the whole thing. "What's right?" she murmured.

"The bed." He attempted to stifle a yawn and failed. "Which side I prefer. The right."

She lifted her head and looked at him. "I should hope so. If you'd said left, you'd have to tough it out, honey. Nothing could move me now."

He chuckled. "Nothing, huh?" The arrogance in his gaze made her a wee bit nervous as he smoothed his hand down her spine and past her bottom. The tips of his fingers lightly teased her inner thigh.

The first stirring of desire slowly uncoiled in her belly.

She parted her legs and he lazily stroked her, leisurely stoking the embers into a low simmering flame. "Can't resist a challenge, can you?"

"I can't resist you," he said quietly.

Her heart lurched at the emotion shining in his eyes. She wasn't foolish enough to believe it might actually be love, but regardless of the label, she knew without a doubt the feeling was mutual.

14

ALONE IN THE DARKNESS, Duncan sat on the edge of the bed, elbows braced on his knees, head lowered into his hands. He never thought he could be so completely blindsided. He was the one who always did his best to be prepared for any possible outcome.

He hadn't even seen this one coming.

Lust he understood; he'd been prepared for and could handle it. He could even accept that he cared about Sunny after such a short time. What he hadn't considered was the tightening in his chest threatening his oxygen levels when he thought about not having Sunny in his life.

"Damn it," he muttered. He rubbed at the knot of tension forming at the base of his neck, but found no relief.

How the hell had it happened? And so quickly? And to *him*?

They'd known each other for exactly two days and he was what…seriously considering something long-term? Forget the complications and conflicts of her job, the threat to his bachelorhood had him scared spitless.

He straightened. He had nothing to fear. All he'd done was confuse lust and the aftereffects of amazing, mind-blowing sex with…with that other *L* word. God, if he couldn't even think the word, how was he supposed to say it?

He reached around in the dark for his jeans, then stood and slipped into them. He was freaking out for no good reason. What could he possibly have to worry about? Once his misconduct issues were out of the bag, she'd plant those hot CFM shoes she'd worn the other night on his backside and boot him right out of her life. Problem solved. Bachelorhood saved.

After he found his way to the master bath, he headed toward the kitchen to join Sunny. The clatter of dishware, the ding of some kitchen appliance and the unmistakable rhythm of rock music softly playing drifted toward him. Sunny stood facing the counter, her back to him. The ruffled hem of the cotton-candy pink chemise she wore barely covered her ass, which she was busy swaying in time to the upbeat song. The filmy fabric skimmed her curves, leaving little to his imagination.

His dick was hard in under two-point-five seconds. Convinced he'd lost all reason and no longer possessed an ounce of self-control, he came up behind her to slip his arms around her waist and bent down to nuzzle the hollow between her neck and shoulder. Her hair was damp, and she smelled like fresh mangos, rather than the musky scent of sex he'd been anticipating.

She wiggled her backside against his crotch. "Hungry?"

"For you?" He gently took her earlobe between his teeth. "Always," he growled in her ear.

"I was thinking food." She turned in his arms and wreathed her arms around his neck, rubbing sinuously against him. "First."

His hands coasted down her spine and over her curvy bottom to the hem of her nightie. He skirted his hands beneath the silky material and came into direct contact with satiny smooth skin, no scraps of lace or silk to impede a much more intimate exploration. "Are you suggesting I rebuild my strength?"

"With what I have in mind for dessert, you're going to need it." She dragged her tongue slowly along her plump bottom lip, her meaning unmistakable. "Hmmm," she murmured, then flicked her tongue over his flat nipple.

She would be the death of him yet, but he had to have her. With his hands on her rump, he lifted her up and she wrapped her legs around his waist. Feeling her thighs clench his hips almost made him lose control. Better to go out with a bang than a whimper, he thought.

The counter was cluttered with dishware and take-out containers, so he spun them around and backed her up against the closest wall. He had his jeans unfastened and was buried to the hilt inside her sleek, moist sheath within seconds. Her breath expelled on a throaty groan so low and sultry he nearly came out of his skin.

She clung to him, making the most erotic little sounds of pleasure mingled with each hard pant of breath she expelled. His fingers bit into the soft flesh of her ass as he thrust, withdrew, harder, faster, again and again. She was hot, wet, and he lost himself in the raw openness of their lovemaking.

Her moans grew louder, more demanding until she emitted one long shouted, "Yessss..." Her body tightened around him, and she flew apart.

With one final deep thrust, he came in a heated rush and followed her into blissful oblivion on his own powerful release...without the protection of a condom, his conscience reminded him, just a tad too late.

SUNNY STABBED the last marinated mushroom on her plate with her fork and popped it into her mouth. For someone hung up on safety, she'd certainly taken a huge risk. The worst of it was, she hadn't even realized what she'd done until Duncan had apologized. He didn't deserve all the blame. She'd been just as swept away by the uncontrollable, purely spontaneous passion, and was equally irresponsible. Since she was in the safe zone of her cycle, she was fairly confident they'd dodged a bullet—this time. First thing Monday morning, she was making an appointment with her gynecologist for birth control.

"I've been thinking…" he said, and pushed aside his empty plate.

"Uh-oh," she teased. Shifting in the padded chair, she kicked her icy feet onto his lap, searching for warmth. "Did it hurt?"

"Cute." He smiled, not the least offended. "Comedienne, are you?"

"I have my moments." She nudged his hand with her toe, and he wrapped his fingers around the ball of her foot. "Ah, thank you," she said, soaking up the heat from his hands. "Okay, now tell me what had you exercising your mind."

"Your transfer to ISU hinges on your success with SED-SCAM, right?"

"Klabo didn't use those exact words, but that's the gist of it." She set her fork on the edge of her plate and reached for her glass of soda, curious where this was all leading. "Why?"

"I could help you get that transfer."

He'd already produced his files, which had understandably slipped her mind, but she had the distinct impression he wasn't referring to any official documentation. Solving SEDSCAM would give her the transfer she wanted, but putting an end to the Seducer's career and making sure the charges stuck were equally important. "How exactly?" she finally asked him.

He released his hold on her foot. Leaning forward, he braced his arms on the table and gave her a direct stare. "By helping you nail the UNSUB."

"No." She shook her head. "No, Duncan. Out of the question."

"Hear me out," he argued.

"Are you insane?" For a man who was losing it, she thought he did a good job of appearing quite rational. She lowered her feet to the floor and sat up straight. "You of all people know that—"

"No nongovernmental entity shall be privy to evidence or other information gathered in connection with an ongoing FBI investigation," he recited by rote.

"For the explicit purpose of protecting the civil liberties of any person or persons of said investigation," she finished. "That would include the UNSUB, in case you were wondering."

His expression bordered on impatient. "Sunny—"

She lifted her hand to still his argument. "No. There are nine men and women sitting on the Supreme Court who'll back me up on this one. They've kinda, you know…" she leaned toward him "…*made it a law.*"

Frowning, he let out a sigh filled with frustration. "Would you just listen to what I have to say?"

She folded her arms over her chest and frowned right back at him. "If you're going to ask me to break the law, forget it."

"I can help you nail him, Sunny. Legally."

What if he could? *Legally.* She chewed her thumbnail and carefully weighed the consequences of her participation in this conversation.

SEDSCAM wasn't about her, or even the transfer she so desperately wanted, but about several women who'd suffered the humiliation of being taken in by a swindler. They deserved vindication. There may even be more victims who hadn't come forward out of shame, but weren't any less deserving. Didn't Sunny owe it to each of those victims to do everything in her power to bring the UNSUB to justice?

She couldn't ignore the victims. They were the reason she'd become an agent in the first place. If she put her own needs, wants and desires before the victims, then she didn't deserve her job and might as well resign from the Bureau.

She looked at Duncan. While she had an idea what drove him, she still had to ask. "What's in it for you?"

"A quarter of a mil in recovery fees," he said without hesitation. "Once he's in your custody, my chances of getting to the property are small. He's stashing the stuff somewhere and if he's smart, which we know he is, he'll try to use returning stolen goods to plead down to a lesser charge. You give me a chance to question him without the Bureau crawling up my ass, I get what I want, and you have a perp with no bargaining power."

"How is that legal?" she asked incredulously. "For one, if we get a line on his location and I tell you, my butt's on the line for involving a civilian. I already said too much when I confirmed the UNSUB's Ian Banyon alias. Second, I don't want to think about the laws you'd be breaking trying to get information from him. And third, do you have a clue what they do to cops in prison?"

He had the audacity to chuckle. "You can't provide me with information on an ongoing investigation, but that doesn't mean you can't discuss documented evidence related to it. If it can be verified, it can be admitted."

He did have a point. Except for one small detail. "I

can't advise you of the UNSUB's location if we catch him, Duncan. There's no way around that one."

"I'll have figured it out on my own, and you're in the clear."

"Then why do you need me?" she asked, thoroughly confused.

"Because you're going to lead me to him," he said.

A chill brushed her spine and she trembled as his meaning became clear. Her ego took a bruising from the humiliation that she'd played right into his hands.

"You son of a bitch," she said coldly. She shot to her feet with her hands fisted at her sides. "You'd resort to having me followed? I guess it's not that tough to do when your tail is in the same bed."

He came out of the chair. "Sunny, wait a—"

She stormed off down the hall and slammed the bedroom door. There was no reason for the ache in her chest. Okay, fine, so he had no compunctions about taking advantage of their having become lovers. That still wasn't reason enough for her to feel as if her ego had been kicked.

He didn't want *her*, he wanted to get the Seducer before she did so he could find the stolen goods and collect his recovery fees.

He knocked on the door. The man obviously had a death wish.

"Get out, Duncan," she shouted through the door. "Go. And take your goddamn files with you."

He barged in, his expression only half as thunderous as her temper. "Just hold it right there," he said, his voice rising. "Have you tailed? What kind of bastard do you take me for? I want to *help* you figure out how you're going to locate the UNSUB." He scrubbed his hand down his face. "Of all the…"

Stupid. Asinine. Idiotic. She had at least a dozen more adjectives she could supply him. Judgmental also sprang to mind.

She dropped onto the bench at the foot of her bed and winced when she landed with a thud. Now she *really* felt like a fool. A first-class, blue-ribbon fool. Her defense was even more silly. She'd given herself to him completely, no barriers. That kind of total exposure was bound to leave a girl emotionally vulnerable.

"I'm sorry," she apologized. "I was…" Oh God, she had to say the word. "Wrong."

"Do you really think that's what all this has been about?"

"I jumped to the wrong conclusion," she admitted, sounding rather petulant. "I said I was sorry. Can we just drop the subject, please?" She'd had enough humiliation— imagined and real—for one night.

He walked toward her, then crouched in front of her. "Yeah, you did. A real wrong conclusion," he said gently, settling his hands on her knees. "We might have met because of this case, but that's not why I'm here now. Do you understand?"

She could only nod because a boulder-sized lump had wedged itself in her throat. The tenderness in his eyes when he looked at her had her heart squeezing in her chest, for the right reason. She'd known he was trouble from the first moment she'd laid eyes on him, but she hadn't realized the true extent until this very moment. He hadn't said he loved her, and she wouldn't have believed him if he had because it was too soon. Yet, regardless of how stupid she'd been, she was smart enough to understand that whatever he hadn't said echoed what she suspected was already in her heart.

FOR AS LONG as Sunny could remember, Saturday had always been her fun day. She rarely made solid plans, just did whatever she decided sounded like a good idea.

Some days she'd putter around the condo in her pj's until noon, or maybe spend the day watching old movies or reading a book. Occasionally she'd drive out to see her parents, or just get in her Jeep and drive with no particular destination in mind. The day had always been hers to do with as she pleased, and while she rarely shared them, she liked the idea of having Duncan hanging around on her fun day.

By mutual agreement, they'd tabled their earlier discussion until they were both rested. Still, it'd been hours before they'd fallen asleep. As a result of all that late-night lovemaking, she'd risen much later than usual and had been surprised to see it was after noon when she'd finally climbed out of bed.

Showered and dressed in her favorite pair of jeans and a cotton tank top, she'd spent the past hour reading through the files he'd delivered to her last night while he continued to sleep. She found new information on the Garfield incident in Miami, which surprised her. A necklace had been stolen which hadn't been included in the police report Sunny had. A second report had been filed five days later, which she'd been unaware of until now. In order to file an insurance claim, the loss had to be reported to the authorities. Garfield claimed she hadn't realized the necklace was missing, but Sunny wasn't certain she believed the vic. The necklace— a stunning Egyptian design made of a platinum amulet encrusted with rubies, sapphires and diamonds—was worth a small fortune. A chain fashioned of more gemstones, circled the neck. A piece of that caliber wasn't something a person could easily overlook, especially when reporting a theft.

The interview Sunny had conducted with Celine Garfield had revealed the UNSUB had approached the victim for the purpose of acquiring Egyptian artifacts. She wondered if Garfield had been wearing the necklace when the UNSUB made initial contact. If so, then Sunny had a good idea of why he'd chosen Garfield as a mark. She made a note to ask Garfield when she'd last worn the piece, but she didn't expect the woman to be much help.

Sunny set aside the photo of the necklace and reached for her coffee. As much as she'd like to better understand the vics, their attitude toward the Seducer had her stumped. None of them had been all that helpful. Oh sure, they'd cooperated fully with her investigation, but they'd all appeared more concerned with the return of their property than in aiding in the Seducer's apprehension.

Sex could definitely change a person's outlook, she thought, thinking momentarily of the naked man sleeping in her bed. But was it enough to completely alter an individual's perspective of right and wrong? Each of the vics she'd interviewed thus far had commented on the Seducer's prowess in the bedroom. Wilder had claimed him a master of foreplay. Maddie Bryson had reported a very intriguing encounter with a wine bottle that had made Sunny uncomfortable, as had Joy Tweed's revelation of the sensual self-awareness she'd discovered under his tutelage. Bettina Manchester had been extremely forthright in relating her tale of the UNSUB's seduction, and Sunny still couldn't read through the recorded statement without blushing. She might fantasize about having sex with Duncan beside a stream, but she wasn't sure she'd have the nerve to actually live out the fantasy as Manchester had done with the Seducer while out on an afternoon hike in the mountains.

Duncan's file on Wilder basically mirrored her own, although hers contained more detail. The Dallas claim for Alicia Dearborn had been more enlightening and was similar to Wilder's in that Dearborn was another patron of the arts. The UNSUB hadn't pulled anything as extreme as what he had on Wilder with the art gallery, but a painting had been stolen, along with more cash and a fur coat. The coat was a new one, but the valuable art and cash were all too familiar. Even without official confirmation and based solely on the circumstances surrounding the case, she felt confident Eric Vossler was the Seducer. Now that she had the basic facts, she'd fax the information to Larry Henley in the Dallas field office, which might speed up the process. When she'd finally spoken to the Dallas SAC Friday morning, he'd been helpful and had promised to have one his agents look into the matter as soon as he had a body he could spare. Because SEDSCAM was a nonviolent crime, she understood why it held a lower priority, but that didn't lessen her frustration.

She'd been hopeful Duncan's files would provide a link to substantiate Georgia's theory that the UNSUB could be from New York. Sunny hadn't found a shred of evidence to support the argument, but she agreed with Georgia in that a believable con required the right blend of fact and fabrication. They knew the Seducer had an affinity for fine arts and may have indeed spent time in the galleries at the metropolitan museum as he'd related to Wilder, but to Sunny it wasn't enough to spend taxpayer dollars on a manhunt of the New York area. Still, Georgia had a hunch, and Sunny wasn't willing to discount the younger agent's theory completely.

She scooped up the documents she'd spread over the dining room table and returned them to the thick, padded envelope. As important as the case was to her, there wasn't much else she could do until Monday when she'd make arrangements to travel to Dallas for an interview with Alicia Dearborn.

Besides, she thought with a grin as she tossed the envelope on the buffet, she did have other pressing matters to attend to—and taking advantage of the gorgeous, naked man currently in her bed topped her list.

"SHALL I CALL YOU when your car is ready, Mr. Seville?"

"That won't be necessary, I'll be down momentarily." Peter Seville pressed a crisp one hundred dollar bill into the butler's hand. Glen Specht wouldn't have given the snooty bastard a nickel for his trouble.

"The lady will be checking out tomorrow afternoon," Peter said in a perfectly modulated voice. "Please see that she isn't disturbed."

"I will see to it personally, sir." The butler tipped his head politely then discretely disappeared from the suite on the heels of the bellman.

Alone, Peter quietly crossed the ostentatious living room to the enormous, beautifully appointed bedroom. His stay at the Drake Hotel had been far too brief to suit him. Unfortunately, he'd been forced to call an end to his business in Chicago much earlier than anticipated.

Slowly, he crept toward the bed, not that he expected the blonde to awaken. By the time the effects of the sleeping pills he'd given her wore off, Peter Seville would have vanished into thin air, and Specht would have returned in time to curse the sweltering heat and humidity of New Orleans. His work in Chicago was nearly finished, and it was time for Glen to prepare for Farley Madison's introduction to Elizabeth Southern.

For Farley's sake, he certainly hoped for a more challenging business venture than what he'd experienced with Hope Templeton. His pigeon had turned out to be a stupid, classless cow and far too simple-minded to be of more than an unremarkable amusement. He had been far more fortunate with Margo. She was a beautiful woman, one who possessed class, breeding and exquisite taste.

He cast one final glance at Hope and his stomach lurched. "How utterly pathetic you are, my dear." He spoke softly, not because he feared she could hear him, but because he could hardly hear himself think over the resonating snores pouring from her pasty lips. No, his soft-spoken nature belonged solely to Peter Seville, a refined man who appreciated the finer things. A professional respected in his field, a superior counselor at law.

Resting his knee on the mattress, he leaned over Hope and caressed her round cheek with the tip of his index finger, then tapped it twice on her pouty bottom lip. *"Je t'ai sous la peau,"* he whispered.

He had one last errand to attend to before the exchange at O'Hare. He had to make the best of what little time remained before Specht's return. That was the agreement, and despite Peter's disappointment, the time had come for him to depart the Windy City.

Two hours later, Peter Seville walked into the busiest men's room in the Delta terminal at O'Hare Airport, and disappeared.

15

"IT'S SUNSHINE, isn't it?"

"What part of no don't you understand?"

Sunny squirmed beneath him, but Duncan only tightened his hold on her wrists. He kept his legs tangled with hers, despite the torture she caused him every time she wiggled, her body coming into direct, highly distracting contact with his erection.

"The part about why you're in denial. It's nothing to be ashamed of," he teased her. He could get used to waking up like this every morning and had for the past four days. Making love to her was one hell of a way to start the day, and he wasn't happy that tomorrow he'd not have that luxury since she was leaving for Texas for a couple of days. He consoled himself with the fact they had a few hours together before her noon flight to DFW.

She narrowed her eyes, and he kissed her before she had a chance to tell him no again. His tongue tangled with hers. The tension left her body as she kissed him back, but he was on to her game. The second he let his guard down, she'd try to slip away from him again the way she had the last time.

He lifted his head. Desire filled her green eyes. The taut peaks of her breasts teased his chest. She was murder on his concentration. "Tell me," he coaxed before she distracted him and he made love to her again.

He couldn't get enough of her, had serious doubts he'd ever completely have his fill, but he'd come to the conclusion he'd better learn to live with it. Sunny hadn't only gotten under his skin, she'd sneaked into his heart and there wasn't a damned thing he wanted to do about it, either.

She remained stubbornly tight-lipped.

"Okay, if that's the way you want to play it." He lowered his head and nipped lightly at the tender skin beneath her breast. "I have ways to make you talk." With her hands still trapped within his above her head, he dotting her rib cage with kisses and flicks of his tongue, slowly charting a path to where he knew she was wildly ticklish.

"Never," she said and giggled. "You'll never get it out of me."

He swirled his tongue over her skin. When he reached the side of her breast, she erupted in laughter.

"Okay, okay," she said when she'd had enough. "Stop and I'll tell you."

"Sunshine."

"No."

He blew a stream of breath against the side of her breast and moved closer to his target.

"But you're close. You're close," she said the words in a rush before he could make good on his threat.

"I'm waiting."

She let out a melodramatic sigh. "If you laugh, I'll hurt you. Don't think I can't do it, either. I'm trained to kill, you know."

"Big deal," he countered. "So was I. I'm waiting…"

"You know, I bet we had some of the same instructors."

"You're stalling."

She rolled her eyes and gave him her I'm-so-bored-with-this look he knew was bull. "Sunrise."

He didn't laugh. The effort just about killed him, but he wouldn't laugh when she was so obviously sensitive about the fact that her quasi-hippie parents had named her Sunrise. "Sunny makes sense then," he said, struggling to keep a straight face. "But what's the *R.* stand for?"

"Rise."

His lips twitched. Hers didn't. "Sunrise Rise?"

Her expression turned serious. "Sun. Rise. Two words."

He cleared his throat, but he was in danger of losing it. "What were your parents smoking at the time?" he asked, letting go of her hands.

"I've been afraid to ask," she said in that wry tone he learned she often used whenever the subject of her folks came up in conversation. She looped her arms around his neck. "But it had to be mild compared whatever they were doing when my sister, Dale, was born."

He rolled to his back and took her with him. She rose to her knees and straddled his hips. Settling her bottom on his thighs, she took him in her hand and positioned the condom she'd been clasping when she'd refused to tell him what her initials had stood for.

"Let me guess," he said, needing a distraction. After nearly having his control shattered last night when he'd been mesmerized watching her apply a condom, he'd learned his lesson. The sight of her hands on him was more than he could withstand. He studied her face, instead. "Day Light."

Her forehead puckered as she concentrated on her task. He counted backward from one hundred. In two's.

"Dandelion," she said, her voice tinged with laughter. "One word."

"Babe, you do realize dandelions are weeds."

"Yes, I know," she said and let go of another sigh. "How much you want to bet there's irony involved?

"There we go," she said brightly, and he chuckled. She sounded as if she'd just put the finishing touches on a Christmas package. He had a present for her, one that was self-serving but dually pleasurable.

On her knees, she moved forward until her slick center was poised over him. With her bottom lip caught between her teeth, she wrapped her hand around his length and lowered her hips. She kept him from entering her, taunting him instead so the head of his dick teased her opening.

"Now I want you to do something for me." She released him, but still held him back, denying what his body naturally strained toward.

"Tell me, and it's yours."

She held his gaze, then moistened her lips with the tip of her tongue. In a gentle motion, she rolled her hips just enough to drive him crazy. She mouthed a silent two word demand that had him taking hold of her hips and easing her down the length of his shaft, just like she'd told him to do.

A WEEK LATER Duncan hadn't made any more progress than Sunny in regard to SEDSCAM. He'd come no closer to locating the stolen goods and his frustration was mounting. As far as his relationship with Sunny, however, *dissatisfaction* didn't exist in his vocabulary.

They'd been seeing each other for nearly two weeks, and although they hadn't exchanged keys yet, other than the few days she'd been in Texas last week, they'd spent every night together at her place.

Sitting in her living room, he perused the business section of the Tuesday paper, while she watched the latest reality show to hit the airwaves. Once the program ended, she flipped off the set and looked at him expectantly. "We need to talk," she said.

"Sounds serious." Not that he was too worried, but any conversation that began with "we need to talk" usually didn't end well.

"It is," she said. "I've been trying to piece together a profile, but I'm not having much luck. I started thinking about how much you know about pulling cons, and I'm wondering, exactly how did you become so knowledgeable on the subject?"

He'd been careful about not discussing the case with her unless she initiated the conversation, having no desire of being reminded of those tense moments in the beginning when she'd misconstrued his intentions. It still stung his pride that she'd had such a low opinion of him, but he understood they'd been chartering foreign territory and had been working under a new relationship handicap with a sharp learning curve. He'd rather avoid the subject altogether.

He folded the paper and tossed it on the coffee table. He'd promised to help her understand how a con artist worked and she hadn't been shy in taking advantage of his knowledge. He'd grown used to her constant battery of questions, and realized with every query, she came closer to the truth. The line he'd chosen to walk when he'd told her he could help her catch the UNSUB was a narrow one, but he'd navigated thinner. He'd once been a paid chameleon for the government, and although the skills might show a little rust from nonuse, they were deeply ingrained in his soul. A talent that had enabled him to keep the truth from her for as long as he had.

"Are you sure?" he asked her. "You might not like what you hear."

She laced her fingers with his. "I'm sure," she said, then gave his hand a reassuring squeeze, as if he were the one in need of encouragement.

"If you think about it," he said, "an undercover operative is nothing more than a legal con artist."

"Maybe on the surface," she concluded. "But a con is ruled by greed. He takes what he wants, because it's easier than making an honest living. But a con doesn't completely change his persona the way my guy does, so the textbook profile of a thief doesn't fit. You were undercover, you know what it takes to psychologically become a different person. That's what I need to understand."

He released her hand to turn to face her more fully. "What do you mean his personality changes?" he asked. This was news to him, and made the case all the more dangerous if her UNSUB was playing a mind game as she suggested. "And why haven't you told me this before now?"

She shrugged, unconcerned. "I just assumed you knew."

"No, you didn't. What if this guy comes unhinged?" He knew what could go wrong at any given moment, and he wanted her to fully understand what she could be up against. She didn't have his experience working violent crime. When she came face-to-face with the UNSUB, if she wasn't prepared to handle the worst, he didn't want to think about what could happen to her.

"This is a confidence man, a con artist, grifter, swindler, take your pick. Some are born, some made, but the best are a combination, like him. They're born into the life, taught their trade by elders. They don't live by the same rules we do, and their societal hierarchy isn't open for public inspection."

"Duncan," she said, her voice laced with impatience. "I already know all this. That's not—"

"And when was your last undercover assignment into a network of scum that you have so much experience? You're threatening this guy's livelihood, Sunny. He's running a highly profitable scam, so don't think it won't turn ugly really fast," he snapped irritably. He scrubbed his hand over his face. Frustration and fear for her safety bit into him hard. "Fired your weapon lately, Agent MacGregor? Other than on the firing range?"

She glared at him, but he didn't give a damn. Let her get pissed at him. He'd gladly take the heat if it kept her alive. "Been a while, hasn't it?" he intentionally taunted her.

"I don't know what just crawled up your ass, but don't even think you can—"

"When was the last time you fired your weapon?" he demanded hotly.

She crossed her arms and gave him a go-to-hell look before she turned away from him.

"When, Sunny?"

"Two years," she answered, still not looking at him.

"That recent, huh?"

"In nonviolent crime?" She stared at him, hurt lining her gaze. "What do you think?"

He leaned toward her and cupped her face in his hands. "It's not what I think, babe," he said, gentling his tone. "It's what I don't want to think about that has me worried."

She closed her eyes and pulled way from him, but not before he saw the abject disappointment in her gaze. "Duncan, please, this is what—"

"What you do, I know. The job doesn't bother me," he said, moderately twisting the truth. It bothered him—a lot—because he feared for her safety. God, if anything ever happened to her…

"You have to be ready for the worst when you go after this guy, especially if he's unstable. And we don't know that he isn't."

She nodded her understanding. He hoped she did, for her sake.

"You've already determined he isn't your average street scammer gone big time, checked the database for networks or clans for the highly skilled cons on record?"

"Yes, and paroled offenders, too," she said. "He's never been in the prison system. What I'm seeing is a variation of the classic sweetheart scam," he said. "Because the vics are too embarrassed to admit they've been bilked and abandoned, or they're in denial about what's really going on, they rarely report the crime. This tells me the UNSUB has had the advantage of time to gain more experience and perfect his craft."

"I've considered the possibility of a sweetheart scam, but the profile isn't there." She paused and glanced down at the newspaper cluttering the coffee table, then lifted her eyes back to his. "The vics aren't exactly doddering old coots."

"No, they're not, but based on the police reports, the fundamental elements of the incidents do match. The vics are marked, their asset potential determined, sex is exchanged and then the rip-off comes and the perp jumps."

She considered his argument. "Possibly," she said after a moment, "but traditionally these scams require at minimum, two perpetrators, and the marks are commonly old men, not women. The initial contact and set up is done by one of them, then another comes in and takes dear old Uncle Herbie to the cleaners. Even your files only contain evidence of one perp, which doesn't lead me to the conclusion of a sweetheart scam artist."

"When I was an agent, the Bureau sent me undercover to bust up a network of con artists pulling scams across state lines, which gave us federal jurisdiction. If you're as close as I was, for as long as I was, you learn the operation, how they set up the scams and chose their marks. This case is a variation, Sunny. Take my word for it."

"How long were you under?"

"Almost two years.

Her eyes widened in surprised. "And you lived among these people the entire time?"

"Pretty much." At least he had until his cover had been blown.

"No wonder you know so much." She eliminated the distance between them when she rose up on her knees and negotiated the cushion separating them. Bracketing his hips, she sat on his lap, then unbuttoned his shirt and carefully pushed the material aside. A frown creased her forehead as she gingerly ran her fingers over the puckered flesh from the wound that served as a constant reminder of what ambition had cost him.

She pressed her lips to the wound as if she alone had the power to make it all better. The tender reverence of her touch combined with the fear of knowing what could happen to her, made his heart constrict in his chest.

She straightened his shirt and lifted her compassionate gaze to his. "This is the case that ended your career, isn't it?"

He drew in a long unsteady breath, then released it slowly. "My cover had been blown." He didn't tell her he'd been aware of that fact, or how his handler had given him a direct order he'd disobeyed all because he'd been a slave to ambition.

"This was a sophisticated network operation we had infiltrated. It took months of work pulling off penny-ante scams so I'd be noticed by this particular group."

"You broke the law?" she asked incredulously.

"No," he said. He wasn't proud of his actions and regretted the results, but other than bending a few rules or regulations, he hadn't committed a crime. "We had informants, so when we'd get a line on where their people would be, then we'd work the same area. We had it set up so I pulled street cons, three-card monte, pigeon drops on other agents until I finally drew the attention of the right people."

She started to rise, but he grasped her hips and urged her back down to his lap, unwilling to let her go.

"Once you were in," she asked, settling back down, "how'd you keep up the pretense without risking the integrity of the investigation?"

"When the government is footing the bill, looking like a skilled grifter that earns big is easy. I insisted on working solo. These people wanted me earning for them, so that gave me leverage. My way or else. As long as I showed up with the take, no one questioned where it came from. If one guy brought in four grand, the next day my take was five. It worked because after a year of this, the man at the top level we were after asked me to show his son the ropes."

"And you agreed, to gain his trust," she correctly surmised.

"The operation objective was to get close enough to access the top level. You lop off the head of the monster—"

"And the monster falls," she finished.

"I had prearranged locations from the Bureau to pull construction cons. For about a month, I'm saddled with this guy's kid—"

"What was he like?"

"The kid?" At her nod, he said, "A walking oxymoron. Personable, could be a real charmer, but also arrogant. Ambitious. Very detached—scary detached—but he soaked up any attention I threw his way. He was eager to please, too."

"Disassociative disorder," Sunny said. "Separated or rejected by his mother at a young age is common. Being raised in a patriarchal society like the one you've described contributes to it, as well. He most likely had a material influence of some kind in his life, but my guess is it was minimal, otherwise he couldn't have related to you the way he did. Has probably had difficulty in relationships with women. His eagerness to please is most likely attributed to a domineering male figure since the maternal influence is all but missing." She gave him a cocky little smirk. "Impressed?"

"You nailed him all right," he said. "The kid did talk about a grandmother who lived in Hoboken, New Jersey, but I never heard him mention a mother. How'd you do that?"

"Abnormal psychology." She wiggled her eyebrows. "Comes in handy for profilers. Too bad I can't nail the profile of the Seducer as easily. Go on, I want to hear the rest of this."

"About a month in, we're at a prearranged location by the Bureau, and one day, the kid disappears on me. Before I realized what was happening, he's off down the road pulling a con solo. There wasn't anything I could do without risking close to two years of deep cover. We were close to the top and maybe weeks away from a bust, so I had to go along with it. A couple of days later, I went back, told the homeowners a cock-and-bull story about the kid being new and using the wrong materials and I gave them back their money. I don't know if the kid was following me or if I'd been spotted meeting with my handler, but my cover was blown. A few days later, I was pulled in on a vacation con, and just figured it was my reward for teaching the kid the game."

"I'm not familiar with vacation scams."

"You ever see those displays that say Win a Vacation

with a pad of entry forms? They're usually at the check-out counter. Independent retailers, hair salons, auto repair shops, small places mostly," he explained.

She nodded. "I see them all over the place."

"Don't fill out the form," he said wryly. "Some are honest, but for the most part, they're cons. The mark fills out the form and a few days later, gets a call he's won a prize. Naturally, it's never the vacation, or even a second or third prize. When the mark shows up to collect, he has to sit through a high-pressure sales pitch before he'll receive his prize. It's one of the more lucrative cons.

"Very sophisticated," he continued. "Rented office space, furnishings, even staff. The average person never knows it's a scam until it's too late. A pitch for a resort time-share with a below-industry-standard down payment to open an escrow that will never happen. By the time the mark figures out he's been conned, the perps have closed up shop and jumped. A lot of identity theft comes out of these scams, too. The marks think the deal's legit, so they fill out the paperwork without thinking twice."

"It's frightening when you think about the blind trust we place in strangers," she said. "We do our best to inform the public, but it constantly amazes me how many people still fall for that kind of thing."

He shrugged. "It's easy for con artists to operate when everybody's looking for a bargain."

She leaned forward and tucked her head against his shoulder. "So I take it you were being set up with this vacation scam?"

"Yeah, I was set up," he said quietly. Smoothing his hands over her back, he turned his gaze to the sliding glass door. The evening sun had already begun to set, casting shadows on the balcony. A fat red planter with wilted pansies fluttered limply on a hot summer wind that reached the balcony floor.

Peaceful, he thought. A concept which had been an illusion in his life for a long while. He knew in his gut unless he told Sunny the whole truth, peace would continue to evade him. He'd always be waiting for her to find out he'd lied to her about why he'd been relieved of duty. Two weeks ago it hadn't mattered that he hadn't been honest with her, but everything had changed. Until he came clean, the past would always be between them, even if she remained unaware of his duplicity, it'd be there, haunting the present. Their future, too.

The thin line he'd been negotiating snapped. "When I made contact with my handler, he told me to come in because my cover was blown."

She must've noticed a change in his voice, because she sat up and looked at him curiously. "Go on," she said quietly.

"I ignored the order," he admitted. "Instead I went after the bad guys."

"And?" she prompted. "How did that go?"

"Not as well as my ego and ambition led me to believe. The kid put a hole in me, and we almost lost one of the agents sent in to bring me out."

"And the network?" she asked in the same quiet tone.

He wished she'd give him a hint as to what she was thinking. "A few got away, but I did take out the bastard we'd been after. The rest are enjoying the hospitality of correctional facilities in Texas, Arkansas and Oklahoma."

She shoved her fingers through her hair and pursed her lips. She stared at him and said nothing. The central air conditioning hummed. A clock in the kitchen ticked. Like a time bomb.

He couldn't take another second of the silence. "Say something."

She blew out a breath and raked her fingers through her curls again. "So you weren't relieved from duty because you were wounded. And the failure to pass your firearms recertification was just a load of crap. Do I have it right?"

"Not exactly."

"Then how exactly is it, Duncan?"

Now she clearly sounded ticked. He didn't like it, but at least he knew where he stood. In deep shit up to his elbows and not a tow rope in sight.

"I didn't lie to you about the firearms recertification. Took it three times and failed each one. It's on the termination report."

"And you knew I couldn't access your service record because it's classified and I don't have clearance," she said sharply. "I trusted you to be honest with me, and when I asked you about it, you lied to me. So what isn't on the report?"

He dropped his head back against the cushion and stared at the ceiling. The boring white acoustic tile was a lot easier to look at than the distrust in her green eyes.

"I broke the cardinal rule. Failure to follow a direct order."

"You were fired for misconduct."

"The firearms recert was the excuse they were looking for to get rid of me."

"Why the classification?"

"All deep cover agents' service records are classified," he said. "The Bureau isn't impenetrable. The wrong person obtains certain information and a lot of agents end up dead."

"You should have told me this when I asked you about it the first time."

"A letter of censure for disobeying a direct order that resulted in an another agent being wounded isn't something I'm proud of. Besides, I didn't think we'd be involved, either." He ran his hands down her bare arms and gave her a teasing grin. "Two weeks ago I was just hoping to get laid."

He laced their fingers together and squeezed lightly. "I'm sorry I wasn't up-front with you."

The barest hint of a smile touched her lips, softening her expression. He had a pretty good idea he was falling in love with her, and suspected she felt the same. But it was too soon, and he understood that for the time being, just knowing was enough for both of them.

She nodded her acceptance of her apology and sagged against him. "Duncan?"

"Hmm," he murmured, enjoying the sense of peace finally settling within him.

"If you ever lie to me again," she said, "you can forget getting laid in this lifetime."

16

MIDMORNING THE FOLLOWING day, Sunny hung up the phone just as Georgia walked into her office with an armload of documents. "Well, that was a waste of time," Sunny told her. "Duncan was right. Celine Garfield is a total head case. She just told me the only reason she reported the theft to the police was to reimbursed by the insurance company. Getting her property back doesn't matter. I'm really beginning to wonder if she didn't give the UNSUB the stuff willingly."

She left her desk and joined Georgia at the round table she'd requisitioned for additional workspace. Two weeks ago she'd been pulling out her hair in frustration trying to understand the Seducer's victims. Although she couldn't relate to Celine Garfield's denial, she could admit to a better understanding of why most of the victims felt a need to protect the UNSUB—it came with the territory when you loved someone.

"I hope you've had better luck than I've been having with the profile," she said to Georgia.

"A big fat nothing," Georgia said, her disappointment obvious. She flattened her palms on the table and leaned forward, scanning the documents she'd set out for review. "My New York theory is going nowhere. I know it's here, but I can't prove a thing." She pointed to the eight-by-ten glossy of Celine Garfield's Egyptian-styled necklace. "Nice piece, but so what? The information from Chamberlain Recovery gives me more to work with, but not enough to find the proof I need. The UNSUB could still be from New York City, but without a more positive ID, we have nothing solid, only more supposition."

"Trust your gut, Georgia," Sunny encouraged her. "That's what I do when I can't see the 'it' thing when I know it's there. You just haven't seen it yet. How about the database check on recent inheritances? Any luck?"

Georgia shook her head. "Not really. I have tons of names within the age group we discussed, but Ned was right. Needles and haystacks."

Ned burst into her office, his face flushed with excitement, his glasses slightly off balance as he skidded to a halt. "Would you like to kiss my ring now, or later?"

Georgia turned and perched on the edge of the table. "I'm dying here and Agent Megabyte gets gold?" She folded her arms in a huff. "There is no justice in my world."

"Read it and weep." He took a place beside Georgia at the table. Nudging her with his shoulder, he said smugly, "I cracked Atlanta."

Sunny took the report from Ned and grinned at him. "It's about time we got a break in this case."

Ned beamed and adjusted his glasses. "When the UNSUB was posing as Adam Hunt, he impersonated the accounting manager of Manchester Rod 'N Reel to initiate six separate wire transfers to accounts in six different Manhattan banks. He did it by phone with a new teller he specifically asked for. He had to have cased the bank for a mark."

"Video," Georgia said. "Banks use cameras."

Ned shook his head. "No good. It's the main branch,

busy, hundreds of customers every day. Even if they did see someone how would they know it was the UNSUB?"

Sunny looked at Ned. "Someone had to see a strange guy hanging around the bank, especially if he's scoping tellers to find someone to do his dirty work for him. If he asked for this teller specifically, then he was definitely there. Go down to Atlanta and interview the bank employees. This guy's M.O. is seduction. He probably came on to one of the employees using the account manager's name to establish the relationship. That way when he calls to do the transfers, she won't question them."

"Will do," he said. "But it gets better. Two days after the wire transfers, the six Manhattan accounts were closed via another wire transfer to a single off-shore account. No name, naturally, just a numbered account, but I've got the details."

"Manhattan." Georgia slapped her hands against her legs. "Another connection, but nothing to connect it to. This isn't fair."

"It's a piece of the bigger puzzle, Georgia. Be patient," Sunny reassured her. "Ned, this is great work. Go through channels to have that account seized as soon as possible." Even with the enactment of the Patriot Act, off-shore accounts were still a jurisdictional nightmare and it could take weeks before they could seize the account.

"I'm already on it. Oh!" He snapped his fingers. "I heard back on that forged check from Bryson. Nothing remarkable whatsoever, so we have one more dead end."

"What about the Manhattan accounts?" Georgia asked. "Anything useful there?"

"You'll be eating your heart out when you hear this, buddy."

"Gee, thanks, pal."

"Three of the accounts belong to names we know—Banyon, Kaufmann and Abbott," Ned explained. "Peter Seville, Farley Madison and Jefferson Wright were the other three. I ran them through the database, but there were no hits on Madison or Wright."

"Seville?" Sunny asked hopefully.

Ned grinned, looking mighty proud of himself.

"If you have fingerprints and a positive ID, I will kiss your feet."

"Don't pucker up just yet, Mac. You're gonna love this. Peter Seville is a big-time lawyer out of Los Angeles. The ID on file at the bank matches Seville's ID. But, it's no match to any of the descriptions or the composites we have the UNSUB."

"What did the computer spit out on Seville?" Georgia asked skeptically. "Unpaid parking tickets?"

"No. A theft report *filed* by Peter Seville."

"That makes no sense." Sunny rubbed the spot above her eyebrows with her thumbs. "The UNSUB's vics have all been women."

Georgia shrugged. "Not if he's bisexual. A man wouldn't be as likely to come forward as a woman and admit he'd been suckered by a smooth-talking seducer."

Ned waved his hands back and forth in front of his face and looked as if he just gotten a whiff of something foul. "Hey, hey, hey. Time out. You're way off base here. I just heard back from the L.A. field office. Seville is eight months in on a year-long sabbatical. He reported his wallet stolen two weeks before the UNSUB hit Atlanta. Seville was vacationing in Dallas around the time of the Alicia Dearborn incident."

"Vossler," Sunny and Georgia said simultaneously, referring to the Seducer's Dallas alias.

Ned looked relieved. "Seville thinks he lost it in the men's room at some place called Billy Bob's, but I'm guessing it was lifted by the UNSUB. Pickpocketed, maybe."

"Why resort to petty theft when he has all the cash he's taken from the vics?" Georgia asked.

"He doesn't have to need it," Sunny clarified. "It's the fact that he can do it and not get caught. The rush he gets from it."

Georgia snapped her fingers. "We've got him," she said. "If he's used Seville's credit cards, paper trail."

Ned shook his head. "Guys, wait—"

"He wouldn't use the cards," Sunny told Georgia. "He's too smart for that, he knows we'd be on him in no time. Besides, Seville would've cancelled the cards as soon as he learned his wallet was missing."

"If you'd let—"

"He could have applied for credit under Seville's name from different banks. It takes time for those cards to come in, so there could be something recent," Georgia said.

"They have to send those cards somewhere. We might get lucky," Sunny added.

"Please let it be a New York address," Georgia said.

Ned loudly cleared his throat and glared at Georgia.

"I'm sorry, Ned," she said. "What were you going to say?"

He pushed his glasses back up his nose. "Watch closely, my friend. This is the part where Mac kisses my ring."

The phone on Sunny's desk rang. She still hadn't heard back from the lab on their final findings at the art gallery and theater and it'd been almost two weeks. "Hold that thought," she told Ned before reaching across her desk for the phone. "Mac, here."

"Tell me you're alone so we can have phone sex."

Warmth spread instantly through her at the sound of Duncan's voice. He'd been using that line every time he called her. It was his way of asking if he'd called at a bad time, but it never failed to make her pulse race just a little bit faster.

"I'm in the middle of a meeting. But I'd be happy to schedule you an appointment?"

Georgia nudged Ned with her elbow. "It's him," she said loud enough for Sunny to hear.

Ned tilted his head to the side, reminding Sunny of a curious cat working out a puzzle. "Is she blushing?"

"Every time *he* calls."

Sunny rolled her eyes and turned her back on Ned and Georgia, although her cheeks did feel hot suddenly. She was entitled to blush. She and Duncan hadn't been seeing each other that long.

"Pack a suitcase, babe," he said. "We're going to Chicago."

"Sounds tempting," she told him. "I can't. We're getting close." She didn't need to explain closer to what, he'd know she meant the UNSUB.

"I can get you close," he said and chuckled in a way that had her folding her arms over her chest to hide her tightening nipples.

"This is *not* a good time," she whispered desperately into the phone.

"Lucy's faxing you a new claim that came in about ten minutes ago," he said, his tone sobering. "It's your UNSUB, Sunny. He hit twelve days ago. Call your field office to get verification on a police report filed by a Hope Templeton in Lake Forest. Meet me in Chicago."

Her stomach bottomed out. Twelve days ago meant the UNSUB was long gone, to only who knew where. Again. "I'm on it," she said, and jotted down the pertinent information. "Thank you, Duncan. I appreciate this."

"You can show your appreciation later." His voice went all deep and husky on her again. She felt the vibration clear to her toes, among other places.

"My flight leaves in a couple of hours," he said. "I'll be at the Sheraton."

"I'll have to wait for confirmation, but I'll call you when we get in."

"We?"

As much as she would like nothing more than to spend time with him, this wasn't a lovers' getaway for her. "Georgia and Ned will be with me." She tried not sound too disappointed in front of her audience.

"Well, we'll figure something out so we can be alone. Watch your back, babe."

"Always." She hung up the phone and turned back to Georgia and Ned. "See if you can get the three of us on a flight leaving Dulles around six or seven tonight," she told Georgia. "Ned, Atlanta will have to wait until next Monday."

Georgia and Ned both stood.

"Sure thing," Georgia said. "I'm always ready for a change of scenery. Where to?"

"Chicago," Sunny told them. "The UNSUB hit twelve days ago."

"I've been upstaged." Ned let out a sigh, his expression crestfallen. He looked at Georgia. "There is no justice in my world, either."

"At least you had something," Georgia said gathering the documents she'd brought with her.

"I bet she kisses his ring," he muttered to Georgia as they turned to leave.

"Trust me, Ned," Georgia said. "You wouldn't want to know what she'll be kissing."

"I'm PROBABLY in violation of, at minimum, a dozen Bureau policies and procedures right now and I don't care," Sunny said and stretched her arms over her head. "This is worth it."

Duncan's hands smoothed over her breasts and down her belly. "Since when did you start living dangerously?" he asked.

"Exactly two weeks ago today." She slipped slightly forward in the Jacuzzi tub, but he banded his arm around her waist and hauled her up against him. She laid her head back against his shoulder. "You've corrupted me. Now I'll be canned for misconduct. Whatever will we do with all that spare time on our hands?"

"We'll see how proud you are being drummed out of the Bureau for a hot bath."

She let out a sigh and turned so she faced him. "You're much too hard on yourself." She placed her fingers over his lips when he tried to argue with her. "Yes, you made a mistake. A big one by Bureau standards, but if you'd been physically capable of passing your firearms certification, that letter of censure would've been the end of it. You aren't the first agent to screw up and you aren't the last."

He didn't look any more convinced than he had the last time she'd told him, but there wasn't anything more she could do. She knew from her own experiences, it was really up to him when he could let it go.

The sound of muffled voices followed by a loud thud in the hotel corridor made Sunny gasp. She grabbed for the side of the tub to stand, but her hand slipped on the wide ceramic tile base. Duncan steadied her, and she crouched not sure which direction she was supposed to go.

"What is it?" he asked her.

"The door." Her heart began to race. "Did you lock the door? The safety clasp. I forgot to check."

"It's taken care of," he said, his voice calm and reasonable, unlike her sharp, clipped tones.

She slowly released her death grip of the side of the tub and settled in with her back against Duncan's chest again. "You're sure?" she asked after her heart rate slowed to a more reasonable pace.

She could feel him watching her, and it only increased her unease.

"I'm sure."

She let out a quick breath, more like a whistle with no sound than an actual breath. Her hands trembled and she shook them hard to steady herself.

"You have lock issues, babe."

She wasn't fooled by the casualness of his tone or the way he tried to distract her by sliding his hands up and down the outside of her thighs. "Busted." She aimed for bright, but ended up closer to brittle.

"Were you robbed?" he asked. "Have a break-in?"

If only, she thought. She supposed in a way she had been robbed. Of a friendship, maybe even her wide-eyed innocence. "The Bureau shrink thinks I'm mildly paranoid. What do you think?"

"What matters is what *you* think."

She really did like that about him. "I prefer cautious, but you know, everybody has their favorite label."

He tipped his head forward to get a better look at her.

She studied the water as it sloshed against the side of the tub as if it were the most fascinating thing she'd ever seen.

"Are you going to tell me or do I have to drag it out of you?" He saw right through her flippancy. She really didn't like that about him.

"I get spooked sometimes," she admitted.

"I noticed."

He put his arms around her and pulled her tighter against him. She closed her eyes, feeling safe. Almost protected, wrapped in the warm strength of his embrace. As if she finally had someone who could watch her back once in a while, giving her time to catch her breath.

In addition to his adorable way of asking if he'd caught her at a bad time when he called, she realized he never actually said goodbye. He always told her to watch her back, as if reminding her she only needed to do it when he wasn't around to watch it for her. She didn't need a big, strong guy to protect her or shield her from the world, but she did like knowing Duncan was there, wanting to, because he cared about what happened to her.

She drew in a steadying breath, then spent the next twenty minutes explaining to him the reasons she took extra precautions with her safety. She didn't hold back, and told him of how frightened she'd been and all the *what-if* scenarios she'd tortured herself with and still carried around with her. What if she'd gone with Abby that night? What if she'd stayed up to watch a movie, had actually heard something and ignored it? But no matter which *what-if* scenario she played in her head, reality told her the outcome could never be changed. And that only reminded her of how little power she possessed.

"I don't care how Freudian it sounds, that night was my great defining moment when I knew precisely what it was I wanted," she told him. "The ISU agents who interviewed me were big and tough and a little scary. People stood back when they came into the room and nobody messed with them. Maybe it was because I was feeling very vulnerable at the time, but I knew I wanted to be big and tough and a little scary, too. I was desperate to have that security of knowing people wouldn't mess with me, either."

"I'm sorry you had to go through what you did. But sometimes good things come out of the bad. Even as bad as what happened to your friend Abby."

"Somebody I know should practice what he preaches," she said dryly, referring to his unwillingness to let go of his own past. "So locks became my life metaphor. Keep everything locked up safe inside and keep out what can come in to hurt you."

"You know the problem with doors and locks? If you keep them locked, nothing can get in *or* out."

"I go out."

"Only when you're sure it's safe." His arms tightened around her. "I'm not safe, Sunny. Don't think for a minute that I am."

"That's ridiculous." She rose up, turned and wrapped her legs firmly around his waist. "I've never felt safer than when I'm with you."

His lips tightened into a thin line. He took her hand and placed it over his chest, carefully splaying her fingers wide. His heart beat beneath her palm. Strong. Sure. Just like him.

"If you stay locked behind the door where you think you're safe, how are you going to know what's in here?" His fingers tightened over hers. "This is where I want you, Sunny. But you have to open that door and not be afraid of what happens once you get there."

She shook her head. "No. No. No. No." She tugged free to take his face in her hands. "You're wrong. You have to be, because I know you're already in my heart. You couldn't be there if I hadn't left the door open."

Emotion wedged in her throat, but she was so positive of the definition, this time she had no trouble finding the right label to apply. "I love you," she told him. "How could I feel that way if I was afraid of you?"

He slipped his arms around her and tugged her closer. Her breasts brushed his chest, her nipples tightening into tight beads.

"You should be," he said gently. "Because I'm scared to death."

She laced her fingers behind his neck and gave him a sassy smile. "I'll protect you. I've been trained to kill, you know. You're safe with me."

"I love you so much, Sunny." The intensity of his blue-gray eyes heightened, along with the swelling of her heart. "But you already knew that, didn't you?"

A smile she couldn't contain lifted her lips. "Yeah," she said. "I knew."

He rested his forehead against hers. "And you took pleasure in torturing me, too, hmm?"

"I'd prefer to torture you with pleasure." She rocked against him. The length of his shaft slid sinuously along her clit. Desire flowed instantly through her and she trembled.

"Or you could torture me with pleasure," she said, moving again. "Just be warned, I might like it and then—" she shrugged "—you'd have to do it all the time. Think about how exhausting that could be."

"There you go again, worrying about my stamina." His hands were on her bottom, gently kneading as she continued to rub herself along his length. In the cooling water, she felt the heat pulsing from him.

She moaned as the most delicious sensation rippled over her skin. His fingers found her opening and parted her folds, exposing her throbbing clit to rub unshielded against him. The pressure slowly built inside her, coiling tight, tighter as she reached for that pinnacle where she would explode and he'd be there to catch her.

"Not so fast, babe," he whispered, his breath hot against her ear. He caught her lobe between his teeth and gently bit down. "Make it last, and you'll come twice as hard."

"No." She pressed down, wanting to feel him against her.

He lifted her and the glorious feeling dimmed and clawed at her at the same time. Standing, he carried her from the bath to the big king-size bed where he gently laid her soaking wet body.

"What are you doing?" she asked him. The cool air hit her damp skin, and she shivered. "Just when things were going so well."

"It'll get better real soon, I promise."

He went to the closet where they'd stowed their luggage. "Duncan?" The sound of the zipper of his suitcase rent the air. She frowned and rose up on her elbows. "This whole making love thing? It works much better when you're over here with me."

She heard the rustling of paper and craned her neck to try to catch a glimpse. His wide back shielded her view. Nice view, but she wanted to know what he was up to because he was starting to make her nervous.

Finally he stood and came back to her, a bright pink-and-white striped bag in his hands. "Uh…exactly what do you have planned?"

He joined her on the bed and tossed the bag behind him where she couldn't see it. Now he was *really* making her nervous. "Duncan?"

"Do you trust me?"

"Yes," she answered slowly and with a moderate amount of caution.

"I'll never do anything you don't want, and I'll never

hurt you." His hand smoothed over her belly and upward to cup her breast in his palm. "Do you trust me?" he asked her again.

"Yes," she said, without an ounce of hesitation.

He drew his fingers through her damp curls and loomed over her to kiss her thoroughly. Parting her legs for him, she pushed his hand lower, her hips rising to meet him.

"That's much better," she purred when he lifted his head. He suckled her breasts and the glorious pressure she'd been craving returned full force—until the delicious strumming stilled. She opened one eye. "What do you think you're doing?"

The most wicked smile she'd ever seen tilted his mouth, making him look dangerous in a good way. He dipped his head and nuzzled the side of her neck. "I'm going to make you come so hard, you scream—" he flicked his tongue against her ear "—my name."

His words had the most profound effect on her. Her breasts swelled, her nipples grew tighter and she ached for him, feeling moisture gather between her legs. "Oh my," she managed in a whisper around the sudden clogging sensation in the back of her throat. "That sounds…"

She never finished the thought and gave herself up to the passion she trusted him to bring her while keeping her safe in his arms and in his heart. Whatever he demanded, she wanted, then wanted more, until all that existed were the two of them and white hot, absolute pleasure.

Duncan worried about pushing her too close to the edge of her comfort zone, but she was so open, so willing to go where he wanted to take her, he couldn't stop. Not without paying a price all his own. His dick throbbed painfully, the need to fill her and feel the clench of her body surrounding him with her heat had him breathing as hard as her.

He sat on the bed, then moved her over him so she was facing away from him. On her knees, she straddled his legs with her back arched and her bottom lifted high in the air; she was parted for him, open for his pleasure as well as hers. He slipped his fingers inside her and her nails dug into his calves as she emitted a low, rough sound reminiscent of a primal growl. He'd pushed her, made her wild with need, but tonight he pushed her further, harder and wanted more. He wanted all of her.

He stroked her, slow, then increased the tempo and pressure until the sound of her breathing changed, indicating she was close to falling apart. Without mercy, he slowed down, never letting her go too far or allowing her to cool, holding her close enough to the edge where she couldn't quite reach it.

She widened her stance, demanding more, then dug her nails into him when he refused. He held her hips and lay back against the mattress, bringing her with him. With one hand on her bottom and the other pressing open her folds, he tongued her swollen bud, teasing then pressing against the throbbing pulse.

"Oh, oh," she whimpered, and her legs began to tremble. She reached, but he pulled her back, slowly lapping her, sliding his tongue over every part of her until her whimpers became pleas of frustration.

Her hand slipped around his cock, followed by the heat of her mouth over the head. He nearly exploded. "Not yet, baby," he said and rolled her onto her back.

"Why are you doing this to me?"

He leaned over her. "Doing what? Loving you?"

"Making me so hot," she cried. "Too hot."

She reached for him, but he moved down the bed and parted her legs. "Tell me what you want?"

"I don't care." She threw her arms over her head and turned her face to the side. Her breasts rose and fell with the rapid pace of her breathing.

"Do you want this?" He dipped his head and tasted her. Her hips bucked. "Yes," she said, her voice strained.

"Or this?" he asked, holding up the flesh-toned dildo.

"You promised me," she whispered on a strangled cry. Her hips moved, rocked and he wasn't even touching her. Her feminine flesh glistened, her need flowing from her and he knew she'd never be more ready or so completely mindless.

He slowly drew the dildo down her folds and she released a hiss of breath, her hips lifting, searching. He answered the demand of her body, sliding the toy inside, then withdrawing it with the same agonizing slowness.

"Duncan," she cried out, her voice hoarse.

He entered her again, the thrusts slow and easy, her hips lifting higher, demanding more. He was mesmerized by her, by the way her sheath tightened around the shaft as she pulled it deeper inside. He stilled, letting her stroke the toy with the give and take of her body, riding closer to the orgasm he held just out of her reach. She set her own pace and her cries grew louder, more insistent, rocking her hips higher and faster as she drew the dildo deeply inside.

She was so hot and wet, and he had to taste her one last time before made her completely his. Still holding the toy for her pleasure, he dipped his head and lapped at her. The rise and fall of her hips grew frenzied, her body frantically demanding release.

Unable to hold himself back much longer, he withdrew the toy and moved over her. She cried out in frustration because he'd changed the pace on her again, then sighed as he buried himself inside her to the hilt.

She rose up off the bed, and rammed her fingers into his hair, grabbing a fistful. "Now." She sank her teeth into his bottom lip, then looked at him with such raw, naked emotion, he wondered if he'd pushed her too far. "Now," she demanded again between hard pants of breath. "Damn you, now."

He took her there as swiftly as possible, the microthin thread of control beginning to fray as he saw the beauty of her flying apart beneath him. When her back arched off the bed, and her eyes widened with wonder, he fulfilled his promise to her. The sound of his name tearing from her lips filled his ears seconds before he joined her.

17

HOPE TEMPLETON reminded Sunny of an Eliza Doolittle wrapped in a steel magnolia. She lacked the innate sophistication of Margo Wilder, didn't have the advanced educational benefits of Joy Tweed, but there was just something open and honest about the twenty-six-year-old widow of Darrin Templeton that Sunny found amazingly refreshing.

Hope hadn't grown up under the influence of wealth and privilege, but was a small-town southern girl from Petal, Mississippi. After high school she'd taken a secretarial course, then moved as far away from her country roots as possible and landed a job as a secretary in Darrin Templeton's prestigious Chicago law firm. Within eighteen months, Tempie, as Hope called her late husband, had divorced his wife of twenty years and married his young, pretty secretary with her pouty pink lips and voluptuous body.

Because she lacked higher education and spoke with a heavy accent, Sunny suspected most people mistook Hope for ignorant white trash trying to better herself by marrying a rich man. Within five minutes, Sunny knew that Hope was a sweet, down-to-earth woman with down-home values whose only mistake was falling deeply in love with a married man, who'd done her best to fit into a world that would never fully accept her as anything more than the trophy wife of an older man.

Sunny covered her butt this time by making her unit chief, Clint Burrows, as well as Reece Klabo, aware of the tip she'd received from Duncan. Burrows hadn't been happy when she'd asked if Duncan could sit in on the interview with the vic. Yes, she and her team would've been in Chicago thanks to Ned's incredible find, but without Duncan's tip, it may have taken weeks before they'd learned about Hope Templeton. The Chicago P.D. was so backlogged, the incident report Hope filed hadn't been entered in their computer system two weeks after the theft. In Sunny's opinion, Duncan had earned the right to accompany her to Hope's interview.

Burrows started spouting Bureau regulations, but Klabo had shut him down and gave her the green light. She figured he was more accustomed to bending the occasional rule based on the urgency of the cases his unit handled.

After spending most of the morning at the Chicago field office and arranging for Ned and Georgia to oversee a search of the suite used by the Seducer at the Drake Hotel, Sunny and Duncan had driven out to the palatial home of the late Darrin Templeton. The home itself wasn't all that different from the grand estate of Margo Wilder or any of the other victims, but rather than stately, the Templeton home was just that—a home. They sat in the kitchen, where Hope had personally served them sweet tea—just like her mama used to make—and attempted to stuff them full of homemade cakes and pastries she'd baked herself.

Sunny and Duncan were seated across from each other while Hope sat at the head of the oak kitchen table. Sunny recorded the session and was already on her second tape.

"Hope, are you certain you'd never seen Peter Seville before the bar association dinner?"

Hope sniffed. "The thieving bastard, you mean. Did I mention he drugged me?"

"Yes, you did mention it."

"I should've listened to my housekeeper. She didn't like him. That's why we went to a hotel to…you know."

Yes, Sunny did know, but couldn't assume facts. She needed Hope to be as specific as possible and to answer the questions to the best of her recollection. "Why did you go to the hotel?"

"You know." Hope cast a nervous glance in Duncan's direction. "Did the deed," she said, looking back at Sunny. "Got it on. Had sex."

"I realize how uncomfortable this is for you, Hope, but it would be helpful to our investigation if you could provide me with the details of your liaisons with Mr. Seville."

"Oh, my," Hope's big blue eyes widened. "You really have to know all that?"

"I understand the sensitive nature of what I'm asking of you, however the smallest detail can sometimes be what leads us to the suspect's arrest."

"I don't care what you do to the son of a bitch, I just want my Harry back."

"That would be the Harry Winston wreath Mr. Seville removed for your neck while you were sleeping sometime between Friday night and Sunday morning?" Sunny clarified.

"He drugged me and stole it," Hope said sharply. She looked at Duncan. "You can get Harry for me, can't you?"

"That's why I'm here, Hope."

Sunny didn't miss how Duncan's own lazy Texas drawl had become more pronounced. Whether it was Hope's Mississippi accent bringing it out or he was using it to charm the young widow into giving them the information they sought, she couldn't be certain. She highly suspected the latter.

"But to find Harry for you, Sunny needs your help. Okay?"

If the man said pretty please, she was going to have to resort to violence. A swift kick under the table should do it.

Hope nodded and adjusted the straps of her bright yellow sundress. "I can do that. It's embarrassing, but for Harry, it'll be worth it."

"You told the Chicago police that following the bar association dinner, Mr. Seville accompanied you home," Sunny prompted Hope.

"He said he knew Tempie when they had a big case together years back. I remembered the name, because I used to be Tempie's secretary and all, so I thought he'd be okay." Her darker blond eyebrows pulled together in a frown as she looked at Sunny. "I've never been the kind to bring home strange men, if you know what I'm sayin'. It just isn't smart. But I sorta knew him, and he was talkin' about Tempie, I felt real lonely all of a sudden."

"What happened after Mr. Seville accompanied you home?"

"We had some wine, er, some sherry. Talked a bit, about Tempie mostly. We didn't do it then, but we did fool around a little, but he got embarrassed and left. Oh, and he asked me to supper the next night."

Sunny reached for the glass of tea. "What do you mean by 'he got embarrassed'?"

"Well," Hope said, and blushed. "When we were foolin' around, it went kinda far. But he was such a good kisser, I couldn't help myself. If he's good with the lips, he knows how to move the hips, you know what I'm sayin'?"

Did she ever.

Duncan coughed and tried to hide his smile. Sunny thought real hard about that swift kick. "Yes, I know what you mean," she said to Hope.

"That's just a little thing we girls used to say back home. Anyway, I...I..." Hope's soft round cheeks turned a deep shade of pink and she fanned herself with her hand. "Do you really have to know all this?"

"Yes, I do," Sunny told her. "I'm sorry. I know it's hard—"

"No," Hope said suddenly. "That's just it. It wasn't."

Sunny frowned and ignored Duncan's second cough. "Excuse me?"

"I felt him up, and it wasn't hard," Hope said in a low voice. "That's why he got embarrassed. He was a real gentleman about it, like it was his fault, sayin' he was sorry for takin' advantage of me, because I was missin' Tempie."

Shock rumbled through Sunny. The Seducer couldn't get it up? "He couldn't sustain an erection?"

Hope slowly shook her head.

Sunny cleared her throat. "When did you see Mr. Seville again?"

"The next day. Friday night," Hope said. "I met him at The Drake for supper. He made reservations at the French restaurant, but I started thinkin' that maybe fresh oysters would help him, you know, with his little problem. I told him I didn't like French food, and we had supper at the Cape Cod Room. If you're gonna be in town long, you should go. Best seafood in Chicago."

"What did you discuss at dinner?"

"Me, mostly. Growin' up in Mississippi, stuff like that. He didn't mention Tempie once. I thought that was why he couldn't...you know...the night before, so I was okay with it. After supper he said he would be honored if I would accompany him to his room."

"You stated earlier that you went to the hotel with Mr.

Seville because your housekeeper didn't like him," Sunny said.

"When he was here, Stella gave him the evil eye." The way Hope said evil eye, rushed together, made it sound like one word. "She doesn't really have an evil eye. Not like my grandma on my daddy's side, but Stella likes to think she does. But I think that's why he didn't want to come here."

"What happened once you reached his room?"

"Peter ordered champagne from room service, we started foolin' around again, drank some more champagne and fooled around some more. That's all I remember until I woke up around three o'clock Sunday morning. The doctor said the pills Peter put in my champagne act different for different people, that's why I slept so long. Rema-something."

"Remeron?" Duncan clarified.

"That's right," Hope said. "Remeron."

"It's an anti-depressant," he said to Sunny. "Sometimes it's used to treat sleeping disorders."

Hope made a little huffing noise. "You won't get any argument from me."

The widow may have been taken in by the Seducer, but Sunny found her attitude toward him admirable. No wistful sighs, no weepy statements and no denial. A testament to Hope's upbringing. What she lacked in sophistication and breeding, she more than made up for in street smarts and common sense.

"Do you have any recollection of having actual intercourse with him?" Sunny asked. She thought about Margo Wilder calling Justin Abbott a master of foreplay. Was that all that had occurred?

"Oh no," Hope shook her head. "We never did it that way."

"You're certain?" Sunny asked. "When you woke up

Sunday morning, there was no evidence that he might have taken advantage of you while you were unconscious?"

"No," Hope said. "Nothin'. He has his little problem. I think it's sad. He is real good about pleasin' a woman, even if he is kinda finicky about it."

Sunny sat back in the chair. "What do you mean, finicky?"

"He never touched me...down there. Not with his hands."

Sunny thought about Margo's statement again and how the suspect had seduced her with warm oil and paintbrushes, using her body as a canvas. Alicia Dearborn had mentioned a similar interlude involving a mink stole and a vibrator, and then there was the wine bottle involved in Maddie Bryson's seduction. Even Celine Garfield had spoken of an erotic encounter involving a pearl necklace. Sunny would have to check the statements to be absolutely sure, but she couldn't help wondering if the UNSUB's masterful seductions consisted only of his mastery at foreplay as Margo had suggested.

"Did Peter happen to use any props when you were together?" Sunny asked her.

Hope turned scarlet. "A shower massage," she said in a hushed tone. "And he liked to watch."

Duncan's foot brushed Sunny's under the table. She shot him a warning glance. He sat quietly, giving her a look of pure innocence when she knew better. She could kick him, anyway, just because she knew exactly what he was thinking. "Hope, thank you, I know this has been difficult." No way was she saying hard in front of this woman again. "You have been extremely helpful." More than she knew, because the profile that had been evading Sunny began to form in her mind.

"If you could do one more thing for me, I'd like to arrange to have one of our sketch artists visit you," she said to Hope as she began to gather her things. "Would tomorrow morning be convenient for you? It'd help us out if we had a better idea of what the suspect looks like."

"I can show you what he looks like."

Sunny's hand stilled over the opening of her briefcase, her tape recorder slipping from her fingers. "You have a photograph of him?"

Hope nodded and stood. "Tempie had a security camera put in after 9-11. It has sound and everything."

Hope led them from the kitchen to another room toward the front of the sprawling home with comfortable sofas and chairs arranged around a big-screen television set. Hope opened a massive cabinet and pulled a black video cassette case from the shelf. "Do you want to see it now or take it with you?" she asked.

"Can we view it now?" Duncan asked.

"Make yourself at home," Hope said and handed him the video and the remote control.

Sunny was nearly beside herself at a chance to finally get a real look at the UNSUB. Hope Templeton was quickly becoming one of her favorite people.

"There," Hope said suddenly. "That's him. That's Peter."

The camera had been set up so that anyone who came to the front door would be easily identified. Duncan paused the tape, and other than a few fuzzy white lines, the clarity was good enough to provide them with a perfect full-frontal shot.

Sunny stared at the image of the UNSUB. He wasn't a bad-looking guy. It was difficult to tell from the video, but he looked to be around five-nine or ten, with sandy-brown hair. He didn't have what she thought of as the bored, useless look of an attorney, but if Hope sat with a sketch artist, she suspected that was how the composite would look.

"When was this taken?" Duncan asked. Like Sunny, he stared hard at the image on the screen.

"Thursday night. He's leaving here. There's another shot earlier, but you have to rewind some more."

"How old would you say Seville is?" he asked Hope, his attention glued to the screen.

The sharpness of his tone drew Sunny's attention and she looked at him curiously. Tension emanated from him and he seemed much paler than usual.

"Not as old as Tempie," Hope said. "'Bout forty, forty-two. Sometimes I thought maybe younger, you know the way the light would hit him, but then it'd be gone. Oh, he says somethin' in French here."

Duncan turned up the volume.

"Je t'ai sous la peau."

A chill chased down Sunny's spine at the sound of the UNSUB's voice. There was a smoothness to it, an almost disembodied quality that gave her a case of the creeps.

"Sounds pretty, doesn't it? Do you know what it means?" Hope asked them.

Without tearing his eyes from the screen, Duncan said, "I've got you under my skin."

Sunny stared at him. An eerie chill slide down her spine. He'd used the same tonal quality as the UNSUB and it spooked her.

"I'll need to take this with us," Sunny said.

"Keep it as long as you need it," Hope said. "You sure I can't get some macaroons to take with you. I baked them fresh just this mornin'."

Sunny's cell phone rang. "No, thanks," she said, reaching into her briefcase for her cell. The Caller ID indicated the call was from Georgia. "Would you excuse me?" she said and moved toward the back of the room. "Mac, here."

"Ned's gloating," Georgia said, but she didn't sound miffed, just excited. "You better get over to the Drake before I shove him down an empty elevator shaft."

"He found something."

"What do you think?" Georgia laughed suddenly. "Mac, we got him. Forty-eight hours tops, and this piece of scum will be in our hands. We're almost certain he's in New Orleans, provided we're not too late."

"I'm on my way. Oh, hey," she said before Georgia could hang up. "I got visual aids."

She slipped the phone back into her briefcase just as Hope and Duncan were walking toward her. "Hope," Sunny said, "I want to thank you again. I'll be in touch soon."

Five minutes later they were heading down the long, winding drive in the rental car. Duncan hadn't said a word since he'd translated that phrase for Hope.

"I like her," Sunny said. "She's still been victimized, but she's not like the others, is she? It might be a little late, but at least she can see him for what he really is."

"Where to?" he asked once they reached the street as if he hadn't heard a word she said.

"The Drake Hotel." She watched him closely, trying to read him, but he was completely stoic, shutting her out and she wanted to know why. "Georgia called. They found something."

Without a single comment, he accelerated and drove silently to the hotel. Thirty minutes later he pulled up to the entrance of The Drake.

"I need to get back," he said in an abrupt tone.

"That's fine. I'll catch up with you later." She unbuckled her seat belt. Something was up and she wanted answers. His reaction to the Seducer nagged her, and she could only wonder at his noncommunicative behavior.

He turned to look at her, but she had the impression it wasn't her he saw. "I need to get back to the coast," he said. "Right away."

An odd combination of disappointment and wariness filled her. "I have a feeling I'll be flying down to New Orleans tonight or tomorrow, anyway. I could be gone a few days."

He nodded, but said nothing. Wherever he was, it wasn't in the car with her.

"Duncan?" She laid her hand on his arm. "Did you even hear what I just said?"

He looked at her as if he had just woken from some dream and didn't quite know where he was, or if he was seeing her for the first time since viewing the videotape. "I'm sorry, babe," he said, sounding a little more like the Duncan she knew. "I was thinking about something I need to take care of."

"Are you all right?"

He leaned toward her and gave her a quick kiss. "Don't worry about me. You have a bad guy to bring down."

If Georgia and Ned hadn't been waiting for her, she would've questioned him further. With her briefcase in hand, she slid from the car, looking over her shoulder as he drove off.

"Watch your back," she whispered, then entered the hotel.

18

GEORGIA'S FORTY-EIGHT-HOUR prediction had been off by a couple of days, but Sunny was no less relieved now that Glen Specht—and his laundry list of assumed names—was finally in their custody. It would take months before they realized the full extent of Specht's damage. In addition to the nine victims they knew about, she'd gotten another fifteen names from Specht during her last interrogation session, and those were just the ones he could recall off the top of his head. It'd only taken her a day and half to wear him down, and another two to obtain the details of his confession.

Georgia and Ned had been in Specht's hotel room at the Drake with the crime scene investigation team when Ned had been standing in the right place at the right moment. He'd caught a glimpse of silver that had fallen behind the bedroom dresser, and from there, everything began to click into place, like the tumblers of a combination lock.

The notebook Ned had found provided them with a detailing of another of Specht's aliases, Farley Madison, as well as the intended mark, an Elizabeth Southern, the recently widowed wife of Richard Southern, a New Orleans neurosurgeon. Specht extensively studied the backgrounds of each of his marks, ran asset checks and full background checks all with the use of a computer, using libraries and

Internet cafés across the country. He had an eye for detail that even Sunny could appreciate.

There had also been a notation of two additional aliases and potential marks, as well as intended locations. They'd recognized the Jefferson Wright alias immediately from the bank information Ned had uncovered, but the Parker Atascadero alias had been news.

They'd had no idea if Elizabeth Southern was indeed Specht's next mark or one he'd planned for a future scam, but they'd operated as if she were his next victim, rather than taking the long shot at the San Diego or Phoenix locations noted for Wright and Atascadero, respectively. The three of them had been on a flight to New Orleans later that night.

On the off chance Specht showed up in San Diego or Phoenix, she'd put agents on surveillance of the possible, intended victims. Then with the assistance of local federal agents, the New Orleans Police Department and Elizabeth Southern, they'd set the wheels in motion. Not wanting to tip off Specht and have him disappear if he was in the area, they waited for him to approach Southern.

After three days of surveillance and no sign of Specht in New Orleans, San Diego or Phoenix, Sunny's patience had worn thin. The final break in the case came early Monday afternoon when she received a call from a detective in the N.O.P.D. not associated with the investigation. He'd received an anonymous tip on Specht's whereabouts.

They'd moved out and surrounded a run-down shack in the Bayou roughly fifty miles outside of New Orleans. The arrest of Glen Specht had been anticlimactic when their suspect had surrendered peacefully.

She hadn't had much hope of uncovering DNA in the suite in Chicago after so much time had passed, and Ned's stumbling across Specht's notes nearly two weeks after the fact had been a miraculous gift, as had the anonymous tip, but Sunny didn't much care. Specht might be a nonviolent offender and nowhere near the type of monster she'd be dealing with in the coming months now that Klabo had informed her she'd be coming to work for him once she wrapped up SEDSCAM, but in her opinion, Specht was a monster nonetheless.

One monster down. In the end, that's all that mattered.

She and Georgia stood outside the New Orleans P.D. interrogation room watching Ned through the one-way glass as he questioned Specht. Her end of the interrogation was complete, but Ned needed to clarify as much as possible so the information could aid the FBI in preventing electronic crime.

They were scheduled for a flight back to D.C. in four hours. After eight long days in Louisiana, Sunny was more than ready to go home. She wanted to see Duncan so badly she ached.

Georgia took a sip of coffee from her cup, winced and set it on a nearby table. "Hard to believe he's only twenty-six years old," she said with an inclination of her head in Specht's direction. "Looking at him now, I still don't see how he passed for someone in his forties."

"We see what we want to see," Sunny said. "He's a chameleon, Georgia, with an ability to become what will appeal the most to his victims. It's the same principle any good deep-cover agent would use."

Georgia gave her a sympathetic glance. "And he learned this skill from one of our own. Doesn't the irony blow your mind?"

More than her mind had been blown. Her cage had been rattled when she'd been interviewing Specht and piecing his background together. She wasn't proud that she'd faltered during the interrogation, but she'd promptly called a halt to the questioning. No way was she letting a piece of scum like Specht into her head.

She'd realized early on while speaking with Specht that he was indeed unbalanced as Duncan had suggested the night they'd been discussing his last undercover assignment. She hadn't realized how close his prediction of unhinged had been until she'd worn Specht down and he started confessing. Whenever he spoke of his victims, his personality underwent a dramatic change. In discussing Celine Garfield, he became Ian Banyon. When Sunny had questioned him about Margo Wilder, she'd literally been introduced to Justin Abbott, and Marcus Wood, the animal rights activist, had appeared when she'd steered the interrogation to the Tansey Middleton incident.

If that hadn't been enough to keep her on her toes, Sunny had been blindsided when gathering background information from Specht. As he talked about the grandmother he'd visited as a boy, he became that young boy again. But it was the subject of his father that had caused her to call a halt to the interview. Before her eyes, Glen Specht had assumed the personality of the man he viewed in his unbalanced, weak mind as the one responsible for the deaths of the two men he'd admired most—his father and the man he'd assumed had been a gifted confidence man.

Duncan.

She had never realized how close she'd been to profiling Specht the night she and Duncan had discussed his final assignment for the Bureau. More irony, she thought. Not once had Duncan mentioned Specht's name, but for a guy who continued to beat himself up over a poor judgment call, he wasn't quite the rebel rule-breaker he believed. In keeping the identity of the people he'd been investigating at the time to himself, he'd done exactly what he'd been trained to do.

Unable to look at Specht, she turned away from the window and rested her backside against the dull, greenish-gray wall. She might never fully understand the depths of Specht's many psychoses, but he certainly made for an interesting case study. Although a physical examination would eventually confirm her suspicions, she'd been mildly surprised to learn Specht claimed he wasn't impotent as she'd initially believed following her interview with Hope Templeton. According to him, he never engaged in intercourse or became aroused by his victims because he didn't see them as sexual objects. He used sex against them because he claimed a woman's need to feel admired sexually made her weak. To him, he was simply capitalizing on a weakness to gain what he wanted from them.

"What did Duncan say when you told him?" Georgia asked her suddenly.

Sunny tucked her hands inside the front pockets of her black slacks. "I haven't talked to him."

She hadn't known what to say to him, or if she should even tell him about the details she'd uncovered surrounding Specht's personality. For that matter, she wasn't sure how she was supposed to feel. A part of her wasn't too happy with him for not identifying Specht once they'd seen the video at Hope's. The other part of her, the one that loved him, continued to take precedence. She worried about him, plain and simple.

Having his past slam into him so unexpectedly had to have had an effect on him. Specht had been the kid he'd trained, the one who had shot him, and was ultimately responsible for the end of his career with the FBI. But what had her even more concerned was the guilt he must be feeling because Specht had been one of the few who'd gotten away. Far from obtuse, surely Duncan realized he may have been the catalyst for Specht's lucrative career as the Seducer. She knew how difficult the what-ifs were to live with and overcome, and Duncan was hardly a shining example to the contrary.

Georgia made an exasperated sound. "Are you trying to torture the guy? He has to know by now that we've got Specht in custody. The press has been crawling around this place all week."

"He has my cell number," Sunny said, wondering why he hadn't called her. But then, she hadn't called him, either.

"He's probably giving you time to cool off because he didn't ID Specht when he had the chance."

A smile touched Sunny's lips. "Trust me, Georgia, Duncan is *not* the cooling-off type." Not in the way her friend was thinking, she was sure. "He owes me an explanation about the ID, but I'm just as guilty. How am I supposed to tell him about all this?"

"You know, I would've thought you'd be ready to tear him a new one. You're getting soft, Mac."

She shrugged because it was easier than admitting Georgia was right. "He has a few things to answer to, but…" She checked the hallway to be sure they were alone and kept her voice low. "I'm not a fool, Georgia. I have a lot to be thankful for, too."

"He doesn't deserve all the credit," Georgia reminded her.

"I know, but he's the reason we're here now instead of weeks or maybe months from now. If he hadn't given us the tip on Templeton, who knows how much time would've passed before she showed up on our radar, if at all. Yes, Ned does deserve a lot of credit for leading us to Chicago. And his finding Specht's notes brought us to New Orleans, but without Templeton's video, we wouldn't have known who we were looking for and that gave us a huge advantage."

"Okay, fine. I hear what you're saying," Georgia admitted. "If this twisted ticket had spotted us during our stakeout, he would've known we were on to him and disappeared."

"You can bet he wouldn't have gone on to San Diego or Phoenix then, either," Sunny added. "We would have been back to square one."

"Which was turning into a big fat zero." Georgia took another drink of the cold coffee in her mug and cringed. "God, that's nasty. What are these guys weaned on down here? Kerosene?"

"Swamp water," Sunny told her, then let out a weighty sigh. "The three of us worked hard for this. We did a good job, Georgia, we got him. Isn't that what's important?"

Georgia shrugged. "Look, Mac. I know Duncan is the real deal as far as you're concerned, and that's fine, but maybe your judgment isn't as clear as it should be. We would've eventually made the connection to Templeton once we tracked the info to the Chicago P.D. report." A half smile tilted her lips. "And as much as it *pains* me to admit this, a lot of the credit belongs to Ned."

'I know it does. To both of you," Sunny said, and straightened. "Klabo called me last night at the hotel. The job is mine as soon as we wrap up SEDSCAM."

Happiness filled Georgia's eyes. "Ah, Mac, that's great news. I'm going to miss having you around all time, though."

"You won't have to," she said, unable to contain the smile threatening to erupt. "I told Klabo I wanted you and Ned to come with me. Ned's already agreed."

"The little weasel never said a word," Georgia said, looking through the glass at Ned.

"What about you?" Sunny pressed. She'd had a long discussion with Klabo last night and while she wasn't about to turn down the chance to finally get her hands on her own brass ring, she'd hedged her bets and let him think Georgia and Ned were part of the deal. She wasn't sure she'd fooled him, but he'd promised to put the paperwork through just the same.

"I analyze data, Mac, not psychos."

Sunny cleared her throat. "You do know the *A* in NCAVC stands for analysis, right?"

"With my runaway theories, I'd be bounced down to file clerk the first week."

"You'd have to go through ISU training, but we do make a good team. At least consider it, okay?"

Georgia reached for the mug, but apparently thought better of it and crossed her arms instead. "Have you seen the studs who teach all those classes we'll have to take?" A lascivious grin widened her mouth. "That's enough consideration for me. Count me in."

Twenty minutes later, Ned finally emerged from the interrogation room. "There goes one scary guy," Ned said shaking his head as the three of them watched a subdued Specht being led away by a uniformed cop.

Sunny couldn't agree more, and said a silent prayer of thanks that the Seducer had finally been captured.

LATE FRIDAY AFTERNOON, Duncan leaned against the file cabinet behind Lucy's cubicle where she could see him actually reading her weekly status memo. He reviewed the open and closed file count with a sense of pride. For the second week in a row, Colin had kicked his tail in recoveries.

He noted Marissa had brought in two new insurance clients this week, and landed one of D.C.'s largest law firms, which would result in more straight investigative work. A quick glance at the balance sheet showed the agency was in better shape financially than it'd been almost a month ago, but after the decision he'd made, he knew it'd be a while before they were steadily operating in the black.

He glanced around the wall of the cubicle at the sound of Jeri's voice. His new administrative assistant pleasantly greeted a visitor in the lobby then let out a sharp, "Hey!"

He stood and his heart slammed sharply into his ribs as Sunny stalked past Jeri and headed straight for his office. For the past eight days, he'd been teetering between dread and longing, he couldn't begin to guess which emotion currently held the top position. She didn't look angry, just determined and anxious—no doubt to serve his nuts on a platter because he hadn't identified Specht. He'd been on the verge of telling her, too, until she'd announced she was flying to New Orleans. If he'd told her about his hunch, he didn't doubt for a second she would've taken off after him; and worrying that he was going to try to capture Specht on his own.

"Hey! You can't go in there!" Jeri went after Sunny and grabbed a handful of Sunny's blazer when they reached the midway point in the corridor near his office. "You're not allowed back here."

Sunny whipped out her ID. "Special Agent MacGregor," she snapped at the girl. "FBI. And I suggest you get your hands off me."

"But you can't go in there," Jeri wailed, blocking Sunny's path.

"Where is he?" Sunny demanded.

She wasn't being fair taking her frustration out on Jeri when she was ticked off at him. He tossed the report aside and left the cubicle.

Relief crossed Jeri's face when he approached.

"Duncan," Sunny insisted when Jeri didn't answer. "Where is he?"

"It's all right, Jeri," he said.

Sunny spun around at the sound of his voice. The tension of the last eight days drained out of him at the relief in her eyes when she finally saw him. She rushed toward him and plastered herself against him, wrapping her arms tightly around his waist as if she were holding on for dear life. He hung on to her just as tightly.

"You look like hell, Fibbie," Lucy's brusque voice came from somewhere behind him.

"It's been a long week," Sunny said, her words muffled against his shirt.

"A hell of a long week," he said.

"I'll say," Lucy complained. "If your attitude doesn't improve, you're going to end up with a strike on your hands every time Fibbie goes out of town."

Sunny tipped her head back to look at him. "Have you been a grouch?"

"That's not the word we've been using," Lucy said, then stormed off in a huff, taking Jeri with her.

Duncan led Sunny into his office and closed the door, then hauled her up against him to kiss her so soundly she couldn't possibly mistake how much he wanted her. Her arms slipped around his neck, and her mouth went soft and hot beneath his.

Reluctantly, he ended the kiss, but refused to loosen his hold on her. Whatever remnants of dread he'd been harboring, vanished when he caught a glimpse of longing in her gaze. "Missed me, did you?" he teased her.

She smiled, slow and easy. "Maybe a little."

"I could tell." he said dryly. He drew in a deep breath. "Does this mean I stand a chance of getting laid again?"

She pulled her arms from around his neck and stepped away from him. "We'll have to see." She leveled him with a stern look. "You'll increase your chances if you tell me why you didn't ID Specht when we were at Hope's."

His dread returned. "Maybe you should sit down," he suggested.

Skepticism crossed her features and it took her a moment longer than he was comfortable with waiting for her to occupy chair behind his desk. "Would you feel more comfortable if I surrendered my weapon?"

If her lips hadn't twitched, he might've taken her seriously. He moved to sit on the edge of the desk in front of her. "I was going to tell you," he said in his defense, "but when you said you were flying down to New Orleans, I made the decision not to say anything until I could confirm my suspicions."

She leaned back in the chair and crossed her legs. "An ID would've helped. You didn't know what we had, I could've been chasing more shadows."

"I had a hunch and I played it. I was right," he said unapologetically. "Specht's off the streets. That's what you wanted."

Her eyes widened. "So you *were* the anonymous tip we received."

He shook his head. "It wasn't me."

"We got him," she said, changing the subject. "He didn't have any of the stolen property on him. And he wouldn't give it up during the confession, either. I'm sorry, Duncan. I tried. Georgia tried. If we do get a line on the goods, I'll do what I can to be sure you get it all back."

He shrugged. "I know you will." She looked at him suspiciously. "What aren't you telling me?"

He smiled at her, but remained tight-lipped. She claimed

to be a whiz at solving puzzles, so he waited for her to figure it out on her own.

"You are aware of the penalty for perjury," she reminded him.

"That only applies in court, and I'm not under oath."

"My court, my rules." She gave him a tolerant look. "What are you hiding? I've had a really crappy day. My flight was delayed, the traffic horrendous, and if you haven't noticed, I'm not in a very good mood."

He reached for her and she came willingly. "That's because you need to get laid," he said, nuzzling the tender spot between her shoulder and neck.

"Oh, God, do I ever." She let out a sigh and sagged against him. "You have no idea how lonely a hotel room can be in the middle of the night. Eight *long* nights."

"Quiet, too, I bet."

"Shhh." She giggled "Someone might hear you."

"The twenty-third floor probably heard you."

He loved her so much it hurt, deep in his chest. He'd been miserable the time they were apart, but he blamed most of his misery on his fear for her safety and the uncertainty of her reaction when she found out he could've identified Specht. He'd breathed a whole lot easier once he'd heard she'd had Specht in custody.

"So why were you in such a hurry to get back to D.C.?" she asked, pulling back to look at him.

"Since I'm no longer at risk of having to sleep alone again tonight, I didn't come back home. I went to Hoboken."

She smacked her hand on his thigh. The pieces finally fell into place for her as she suddenly realized who was responsible for the anonymous tip. "Specht's grandmother!"

"I bet they call you Sunny because you're so bright."

"As the morning sun," she smiled at him. "How'd you finally convince her to turn in her own grandson?"

"Finally? Hey, it took time to find her," he said dryly. "She was my hunch, and before you ask, I didn't tell you because I didn't want you following me thinking I was going after Specht myself. He used to talk about her, so when I heard that line he'd said to Hope, everything clicked."

Sunny frowned. "I've got you under my skin?"

"*Je t'ai sous le peau,*" he said. "Sinatra recorded it in the sixties."

She rolled her eyes. "And Frankie was from Hoboken, New Jersey. Bet it's not a stretch that ol' blue eyes is *Grandmere's* favorite singer."

"Aveline Glennuad is Specht's maternal grandmother. I don't know what happened to Specht's mother, and I don't think even the grandmother knows for certain. Specht's old man would send his son to the grandmother for visits." He shrugged. "No one really knows why, maybe guilt. But she's the gentler influence you were talking about when you profiled him."

"Well, Georgia is going to be thrilled when she finds out she was right. She kept insisting Specht was from New York, but she couldn't prove it." She let out a sigh and her hold on him tightened. "You know what? I don't want to talk, think or hear about this case another second." She wiggled closer, and smiled when her hip brushed against the ridge of his penis. "Oooh, take me home now and we can talk about the first thing that comes up. I…"

She frowned suddenly. "Wait a minute. How did you know we didn't find any of the stolen goods on Specht?"

He chuckled and reached behind him for a piece of paper. "I was wondering when you'd figure that out. And to think I called you bright."

"I'm tired, I have an excuse." She pulled her arms from around his neck and took the paper from him. "What is this?"

"Your evidence." He set his hands on her waist. "That's the address of a storage facility in New Jersey. Specht was sending his take to his grandmother. I don't know if she had any idea of the value or not. That's something you'll to figure out."

Moisture instantly brightened her gaze. "Duncan, you can't do this," she said, her voice suddenly tight. "Your fees? That's a lot of money."

"Worried about your future?" He said the words teasingly, but God help him, he was dead serious.

"No." She glared at him. "Yours."

He tugged her to him and wrapped his arms around her. "I don't see much difference. Do you?"

A smiled brushed her mouth. "Not really," she answered, sounding a tad smug. "Eventually."

He wasn't thrilled with the disclaimer, but if that was all she was willing to commit to at the moment, so be it. Not that he was too worried. She never had been able to resist him for long.

"Without the stolen property, you'll have a tougher time getting a conviction. I'll still collect my fees, it'll just take longer while the Bureau catalogs the evidence," he finished with a shrug. The way he saw it, everybody won. The clients saved a bundle, the claimants' stolen property would eventually be returned to them, he'd collect his fee and Sunny would have the evidence necessary to keep Specht behind bars for a lot of years.

She tucked the note in her blazer. The smile faded from her lips as she pulled a black velvet box from her pocket and handed it to him.

Curious, he plucked the box from her trembling hand and opened it. "A key chain?"

She nodded and reached back into her pocket. "I thought it'd come in handy—" she slowly opened her hand "—for these."

One by one, he took a key from her hand and silently placed each key to her condo, mailbox and Jeep on the key ring. He knew what her decision meant, and understood the trust she placed in him. His heart squeezed in his chest.

"When I was in New Orleans and we had Specht, I realized my defining moment hadn't really occurred all those years ago," she said. "It hadn't even happened until Chicago, with you. I figured I might need a little help unlocking those doors you were talking about every once in a while, so you should have your own set of keys."

"Thank you. It's exactly what I've been wanting," he said, before kissing her tenderly. He would move heaven and earth to keep her safe, and would love her just as fiercely for as long as she'd let him. Forever sounded like a good place to start.

He gently set her away from him. "Now don't get too excited." He slid open the bottom drawer of his desk and grinned at her. "I picked you up a little welcome-home present."

Her eyes widened as she stared down at the package wrapped in pink-and-white-striped paper with a fat matching bow. "Uh-oh," she said, pulling the box from the drawer. Wariness filled her gaze. "I should probably be nervous, shouldn't I?"

"You trust me, don't you?"

His question had the desired effect. Color tinged her cheeks. "Yes," she said, but she didn't sound all that convincing.

"Go ahead. Open it."

She caught her bottom lip caught between her teeth. With a great deal of apprehension, she slowly peeled away the bright paper. "Oh, my," she whispered, tentatively fingering the top-of-the-line shower massage. "I think we need to go home." She lifted her gaze to his. "Now." A sinful smile slowly curved her lips. "You know what I'm sayin'?"

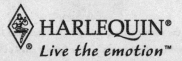

HARLEQUIN® *Blaze*™

HARLEQUIN® *Temptation*®

Single in South Beach

Nightlife on the Strip just got a little hotter!

Join author Joanne Rock as she takes you back to Miami Beach and its hottest singles' playground. Club Paradise has staked its claim in the decadent South Beach nightlife and the women in charge are determined to keep the sexy resort on top. So what will they do with the hot men who show up at the club?

GIRL GONE WILD
Harlequin Blaze #135
May 2004

DATE WITH A DIVA
Harlequin Blaze #139
June 2004

HER FINAL FLING
Harlequin Temptation #983
July 2004

Don't miss the continuation of this red-hot series from Joanne Rock!

Look for these books at your favorite retail outlet.

www.eHarlequin.com   HBSSB2

HARLEQUIN®

Temptation®

It's hot...and it's out of control!

HEAT

The days might be getting cooler... but the nights are hotter than ever!

Don't miss these bold, ultra-sexy books!

#988 HOT & BOTHERED
by KATE HOFFMANN
August 2004

#991 WICKEDLY HOT
by LESLIE KELLY
September 2004

#995 SEDUCE ME
by JILL SHALVIS
October 2004

#999 WE'VE GOT TONIGHT
by JACQUIE D'ALESSANDRO
November 2004

Don't miss this thrilling foursome!

www.eHarlequin.com

HTITF

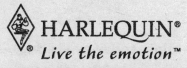

HARLEQUIN®
Temptation.

**When the spirits are willing...
Anything can happen!**

Welcome to the Inn at Maiden Falls, Colorado. Once a
brothel in the 1800s, the inn is now a successful honeymoon
resort. Only, little does anybody guess that all that marital
bliss comes with a little supernatural persuasion....

Don't miss this fantastic new miniseries. Watch for:

#977 SWEET TALKIN' GUY by Colleen Collins
June 2004

#981 CAN'T BUY ME LOVE by Heather MacAllister
July 2004

#985 IT'S IN HIS KISS by Julie Kistler
August 2004

THE SPIRITS
ARE WILLING

Available wherever Harlequin books are sold.

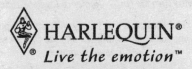

HARLEQUIN®
Live the emotion™

www.eHarlequin.com

HTTSAW